THOUGHTWALL CAFÉ

Espresso in the Third Season of Life

Cameron Miller

To Michael— Keep submitting!

Published by Unsolicited Press.

Unsolicited Press is small press based in Portland, Oregon. More information can be learned at www.unsolicitedpress.com

Printed in the United States of America.

Attention schools and businesses: for discounted copies on large orders, please contact the publisher directly.

ISBN: 978-1-947021-99-0

Dedicated with the joy of loving James, Sarah, Abram, and Anne, and bringing their friends to gather around our table. To Katy for all of that and everything else.

Contents

Tableology

Table 54 – Harrison Jordan

Table 12 – Bernie Weinberg

Table 27 – Google and Enid

Table 81 – Harrison Jordan

Table 86 – Hobart Wilson

Table 14 – Wilma Nester

Table 84 – Harrison Jordan

Table 74 – Cressida

(On the floor behind) Table 91 – Cressida

Black Couch Number 2 – Cressida

Chapter One

Thoughtwalls

A life, a death, and more than one love were born in this café on a single day.

Any café is a universe unto itself, a constellation of never-touching planets and stars, intersecting objects that land with fierce impact or disappear unnoticed in the atmosphere, all of it surrounding each person as they come and go. Even in the humblest café, incidents of life and death abound, love and friendship, too, but at *the spot,* even the mold spores on the floor come and go with greater frequency than most. Few have the eyes to see it, but daily slivers of light are given birth in litters across the darkened space between the lives of café regulars and strangers. This story reveals the universe of unseen relationships and serendipity in ordinary moments, and the never-ending rave inside the mind.

Table *54 – seats four comfortably, plywood top arranged with brio train pieces covered with clear fiberglass resin, and sanded to a smooth finish.*

Harrison Jordan, a young man with two last names, liked plain bagels toasted with butter and spread with green olive cream cheese. He didn't know why he liked them and his catlike mind gingerly pawed the question as he sat, otherwise listlessly, waiting at The Caffeination Journey on Brindle Street for a friend who was half an hour late.

Was it something from childhood, he wondered to himself. Was taste born of circumstance, constructed with the slow deliberateness of experience as genetic code is across generations, or was taste something more whimsical like wind shifting the direction of grass?

No question was too small for Harrison's thoughts because he found endless joy balancing on even a small idea of little consequence, wobbling to balance himself the way he did when descending a steep plunge on the concrete skateboard track at Solar Field. Whereas most of Harrison's friends had gone to state universities and earned cookie-cutter degrees that prepared them for a single profession, Harrison traveled beyond the bounds of distance and comfort to attend a prestigious private school in upstate New York. He minored in philosophy of religion, which had given him the habit of ogling every little thing and pondering even single-syllable words. It made Harrison happy, although his lack of training for any one profession left him working at the cash register of an independent bookstore.

What did not make Harrison happy was when he hit a *thoughtwall.* That's what he called it when, push and shove as he might, his thoughts wouldn't move any deeper into an idea. It was especially frustrating when he could not discern the reason for an idea, the why underneath the why. Lately he felt himself becoming unraveled because of hitting a thoughtwall about values. He could always trace the origins of a particular value, as in the cultural history of any particular morality. But why did he have *his* values, and what made them the right values? It was a thought worm that had taken up residence in his brain, writhing and curling its way through tunnels of agitation.

Why did he believe in human rights, for instance? Sure, it was better for him if the society where he lived respected and protected privacy and free speech. Was self-interest the only reason to wave that banner, though? Was there something deeper and broader than self-interest? If not, then it was just his self-interest pitted against someone else's. This had become a thoughtwall he could not break through. Was something true and valuable just because he believed, valued, or declared it? Was there an authority out there somewhere that was beyond others, a higher power he could point to and invest in?

"Don't fall into your latte," Cressida whispered into his ear from behind, up close where she was able to walk without notice. Harrison jumped a little, then smiled.

Cressida, whose name had been Ruth when they were in high school, was tall and thin and wore only purple and black. Lately, she even had a thin streak of purple in her short black hair, at the back so that it could only be seen up close from behind. It was just a hint.

"You're late."

"No, I'm not. I am within my usual forty-five minutes, so, in fact, I am early."

Harrison knew that within the logic of Cressida-world, she made perfect sense. He also had assumed she would be at least a half hour later than the time they agreed on, so he wasn't annoyed.

"How's your mom?"

Cressida's face dripped downward. Suddenly, even her cheeks seemed to sag and her half-moon eyes turned upside down to became quarter-moon squints holding back tears.

"Not good. I mean, she's Mom, so she's good; you know what I mean. But they had a conference with the doctors this afternoon and she agreed to call off further treatments. Now they're talking hospice. Oh God." She buried her head in folded arms on the table.

Harrison wasn't sure what to do. He wasn't used to Cressida crying, though if the situation were reversed he would be crying a lot harder than she was now. The only two emotions Cressida had ever offered Harrison were anger and lust. *Is lust an emotio*n? His mind darted to the thought but pulled back to the moment. What he wanted to do, felt like he should do, was pull her over to his chest and let her cry there. But he wasn't sure she would accept the offer. It wasn't that tears would create a scene at The Caffeination Journey because the coffee culture atmosphere was one in which indifference was a studied art. It was one of those socially neutral spots that is at one and the same time hip and normal, where people in business attire sip frou-frou coffee drinks at little round tables in close proximity to hipsters flopping on couches while communicating on their phones as they also talk to other floppers next to or on top of them. No one called the café by its actual name either. The Caffeination Journey was always referred to as *the spot*. Cressida snuffling into a slump at the table drew no stares.

Finally, Harrison slid his chair toward Cressida, the sound of wood crying against wood blanketed by a jazz saxophone wailing from the invisible sound system. He leaned over from his chair and scooped her into his arms as she folded into them willingly. Even after she stopped crying, she stayed there, buried in the dark for a long time. Harrison's back started to burn from the awkward position he was in but he sacrificed the pain. *Why do we sacrifice comfort or even safety for others*? He had begun to drill into this thought when Cressida stirred. She sat up and he leaned back into his chair.

"It's so fucking wrong. Who do you know that is a better, kinder person than my mom? She fucking doesn't deserve this. And neither do I! Isn't it enough that my dad freakin' disappears into the night, never to be heard from again, and my mom works her ass off and we move from one shithole to another? The last five years have been great. She finally got a job that pays something, where she can be creative and respected, and we are settled into a cozy, safe house big enough for two. Five years, that's all we get? Who the fuck wrote this script?"

Harrison didn't know what to say. Who did write that script?

He suddenly felt incredibly guilty that his mom and dad were still married, that he had brothers and sisters he liked and cared about, and that they lived in a house that nearly anyone would love to live in. But Cressida, through no fault of her own, pulled the short straw and had known insecurity, violence, sorrow, and loneliness. When her mom died that would be it - there would be no other family she knew of.

Nobody. Connected to nobody in the whole wide world. *Who the fuck did write that script?*

Harrison started to say something, wanted to say something, but nothing came out of his mouth. He sat there looking at Cressida's cheeks glistening with tears and streaked with black makeup. She looked at him, searching for something he might say, but received the silence as a nod to reality.

In fact, Harrison realized, there was nothing *to* say. *Be there*, he thought to himself. That was all he could do. The idea behind the thought began to filter through him like water leveling down through sand. When bad things happen that are beyond anyone's control, the only thing we have to give is our presence. *Simply be there*, he stuttered on the thought.

Cressida leaned into him again, burying her eyes from the world and from his powerlessness. They sat there without talking, intermittently leaning into one another and sitting up to sip thick espresso that had turned cold.

The Spot – nickname for The Caffeination Journey: the most popular café in the city.

The spot was not a cozy place, except that somehow it was.

It was a large empty shell with fully exposed and brightly painted pipes, vents, and ductwork spidering all around the space. It was the first floor of a corner building near center city, harbored by a narrow one-way brick street without parking. The three stories above the café were newly fashioned studio and one-bedroom apartments, but the only division within *the spot* was for kitchen and bathrooms. The coffee bar was a large oval island situated in the exact middle of the vast cavern. There were two windowless walls, the longest a brick-painted mural of an urban streetscape, and the other dark blue. One windowed wall looked out onto the narrow street shaded by the next building hovering close by. The other windowed wall leaked in more light and motion from a broad, four-lane commercial thoroughfare.

Three corners of *the spot* featured a mismatched gathering of assorted used furniture, including large antique-like couches and chairs upholstered with garish fabric. Mingled among them, without a pleasing intention, was more contemporary, overstuffed, well-worn leather furniture. Scattered willy-nilly to fill the room around the oval bar were tables of various size and shape, attended by chairs that rarely matched. The highly glossed dark wooden floor and unadorned walls would have created a loud, echoing chamber if not for strips of broad and darkly colored fabric billowing from the ceiling. The effect of such a cavernous space, populated by the dozens of living room pieces and scads of chairs around at least a hundred tables, all under a roof of sinuous fabric and exposed veins of electric current and forced air, was that of a warm womb. The chaos of the outside commercial energy had little effect inside *the spot*, wrapped as it was by the quiet brick corridor from where all entered and exited.

Adding to these features an almost constant population of people sitting alone and in groups, murmuring or studiously pecking away at laptops and tablets, *the spot* offered a strange and unique combination of anonymity and familiarity. Whether by design or happy serendipity, the local owners had created a near perfect café.

Table 54 – *three hairpin café chairs with black padding, one ladder-back chair with a woven straw seat.*

"Hey, will you come with me to see my mom?"

"Right now?"

"Yeah."

"Isn't it kind of late? I mean, your mom must get really tired, right?"

"Yeah, but the effect of the medication is restlessness. She sleeps and is then up, wide-awake at strange hours. I'm pretty sure she'll be awake, and you know what, she loves you. It would be a nice distraction."

"Uh, sure, okay. Let's go."

Harrison loved Cressida's mom, whom he called Mimi while everyone else called her Mrs. Fruith (an unfortunate pairing with Ruth, which is why Cressida changed her name). He dreaded seeing her now, and knew in his gut he would have even less to say than he had been able to offer Cressida. *Present, just be present,* he said, assuring himself.

710 North Dill Street – *gray asphalt siding shingles with new vinyl replacement windows, some with black vinyl shutters.*

Walking to Cressida's house, a tidy saltbox home on a shabby one -block side street that dead ended at a railroad track embankment, Cressida slipped her soft hand into his. The initial infusion of groin gases was immediately followed by the buzz-killing images of the end of their romantic relationship on Valentine's Day seven years earlier. That was the day he discovered Cressida had been sleeping with 'Jerk' Chamberlain. It turned out everyone had known but him, even his sisters. But then, everyone had warned Harrison not to go out with Cressida. It was common knowledge that she was never faithful to anyone she dated, and yet, instead of being called a slut, there was a kind of quiet acknowledgment she couldn't help it. It was like not expecting too much from the Special Education kids in gym class; she had been incapable of saying 'no' to anyone who showed her the least bit of positive attention.

'Jerk' Chamberlain was all about using people, and when he loudly dumped Cressida during lunch in the high school cafeteria and announced her STD, Harrison's heart thawed toward her so that they became friends again. Now, they were better friends than they had been a couple, and he grieved in advance for the day they might lose their friendship. He shook his head, shooing the thoughts and memories away. Cressida looked up at him momentarily and knew he was exorcising bats from his brain. She smiled.

Mimi was lying on the couch laughing at Jimmy Kimmel. She had on a fake leopard-skin nightgown made out of T-shirt material and big ugly carpet slippers. In spite of what she wore, and the fact that she was dying, Harrison embarrassed himself by thinking how attractive Mimi looked. Younger than any of his friend' parents, it was sometimes whispered back in high school days by the other moms that Mimi must have been a teenager when Cressida was born. Nothing about her said *dying* and Harrison found it confusing.

"Oh, Harrison, come give me a hug and kiss." Mimi sat up and leaned toward him with open arms.

"Hi Mimi," Harrison said in a high prissy voice, and then hugged her with dramatic flair.

"Oh, stop it," she chuckled with mock severity, "you're so straight, you can't even act gay."

"Hi, honey," she said to Cressida as her daughter opened the refrigerator and took out two beers and the Bison's Onion Dip while tossing a bag of Doritos at Harrison.

"I told him," Cressida grimaced.

Harrison felt like he had just been stripped naked. He sat down next to Mimi but could not look her in the eyes. Mimi reached over and took his hand.

"Oh honey, it's okay. Look at me."

Harrison lifted his eyes and peeked for a split second, then looked down again. Mimi put her hand softly on his cheek and he felt its warmth through his scraggly new beard. Slowly, gently, she guided his gaze upward by lifting his face from his chin.

"Harry, honey, I want you to be able to be here without feeling like you're going to catch the cancer yourself so we can be like we've always been. Cressida needs you to help her, even though she probably wouldn't tell you that, and I need you to be here for her. Okay?"

"Okay."

"I'm not feeling too bad tonight and the hospice people said that when the time comes, they will give me some good drugs so that I don't feel pain. So, I don't want you to feel sorry for me or treat me like I'm dying." At this Mimi hooted. "Even though I am dying. I can't believe it. I am dying. Wow, I guess it hasn't really hit me yet."

"Mom, we're not going to have 'Come to Jesus' talks and shit, are we?"

"Watch your language, and I think it is a little late for Jesus, don't you?"

Harrison stuttered on that thought. *Was it ever too early for Jesus?* Harrison knew very little about Jesus except for the baby in Crèche scenes, a few jokes, and the gross Sacred Heart of Jesus statues at his friend's Catholic School. In high school, before his college comparative religion classes, he had postulated that maybe Jesus, Buddha, and Krishna were incarnations of the same deity, only no one knew it. Moses and Mohammed could be agents of another, angrier god, he surmised. Finding out in college that they were each really different made it much more complicated than he had imagined.

"Do you know Jesus, Mimi?" Harrison squinted.

"Hmm, not the way those really religious people do, Harry. I was raised Methodist and always liked the Jesus stories but never met that Christ figure they were always talking about. Even now at my church, I like the stories more than the prayers and creeds that talk about Jesus. You know, it's funny, I never doubted God. Never. Ever since I was a little girl, I knew there was a God, and still do. It helps, especially now, I can tell you."

"Mom, you never told me that. How do you know there's a God?"

"I'm not sure I can tell you, darlin'. I just feel it. Once, a long time ago, I think maybe I was touched by God and after that, I went from believing to knowing."

"Whoa, you were touched by God?" Cressida was taken aback. "You never told me that! Are you kidding?"

Harrison bit his lip, wanting to ask her about it, but afraid to.

"No, honey, it's not the kind of thing you talk about much, now is it?" Mimi seemed to be drifting a little, as if remembering the moment. "It was near the time your father left. He had slapped me around again, this time with you watching, from your crib in the corner. All I could think about was you, sweetie. Even as the pain streaked across my face, all I could think about was how you shouldn't have to see your mother being hurt by your father."

Now Harrison stiffened. He wasn't sure he should be hearing this, and he was positive he didn't *want* to be hearing it. He could see in Cressida's face the hues of black and blue emanating anger and fear. She was at once a child looking up in innocence and a streetwise young woman scarred by cynicism. Mimi, on the other hand, sitting next to him and still holding his hand, seemed to be basking in a warmth and light that no one else in the room got to enjoy. She was looking up and out to another dimension, even though she was talking to her daughter there in the room. Harrison seemed to be the conduit, her touch turning him into a medium through which a strange communication was taking place.

"That was the lowest night of my life. After I tucked you in and sang to you, and you fell asleep, I sat on the floor of your room, leaning against your bed in the dark. I was so low, I couldn't cry. I was numb, frozen inside to everything except you, sweetie. You were the one thing I could feel in my life - the only thing. But that night, I realized if he wanted to hurt you, I was powerless to stop him, and that when he hurt me, he was already hurting you. I sat there in the dark, bruised and with cuts stinging against the air. That's when I was touched."

Harrison had been looking down at his feet but now he looked back at Mimi, expecting her to say more. She didn't. He looked over at Cressida, who was staring down at the floor before she looked up to see what was next. But there was only silence. Neither of them wanted to poke the shroud of memory around Mimi, so they waited. The only thing Harrison could hear was the clock from another room ticking relentlessly against the silence. Then, he heard a car alarm in the distance. Then, it was the clock again against the silence.

"I just felt held, that's all. It was as if I was being held by love itself. Plunged into a deep warm pool and totally submerged - that's what it was like. 'Loved' is the only way I can explain it. I was just completely and totally loved like I had never been loved before. When you feel loved like that, everything else becomes crystal clear. I knew what to do and I knew that it would all turn out okay. And look, it did."

Mimi turned her face toward her daughter and smiled the most beautiful smile Harrison had ever seen. It was just a story and these were just two people he had known forever, and yet he had been taken up into a moment that turned them each into something else. Time had stood still, and the world around them had disappeared, and they didn't even know what was happening until it was over. Suddenly, it was over, and they were there in the house again in the blue light of a muted television, with Jimmy Kimmel mouthing unheard humor.

Walking back to *the spot* after midnight, Harrison wondered about what had just happened. Was it his imagination or had they all been scooped up, for just an instant, in the love Mimi was describing? Did it really happen? It was a thoughtwall, one he didn't even mind because he was just a little afraid of where such thoughts lead. *I wonder if that's what being truly present feels like*, he pondered as he walked into the café and stood for a moment by the door to see if he recognized anyone there. Nope, he was alone.

Chapter Two

Melanerpes formicivorus

Table 12 – round table big enough for three, rod iron pedestal with plywood surface painted barn red, names and hearts scratched into it.

Bernie Weinberg stared at a springtime bug on its back trying to right itself. Top heavy, the ugly little thing's legs bicycled relentlessly without successfully changing its situation. Bernie recognized the bug but didn't know what kind it was, so he Googled it.

He was watching the demise of a Brown Marmorated Stink Bug. Since Bernie, along with everyone else in his family, had no sense of smell, he was not vulnerable to the odor Stink Bugs emit when threatened. That scent was now surely passing beneath his nose.

When Bernie looked back from laptop to the Stink Bug, it had somehow gotten right with the world and was ambling on the table toward him. Bernie looked left and right, then with his middle finger and thumb flicked the little sucker to kingdom come. The bug went flying and disappeared into the shadowy distance of *the spot*. He regretted it immediately, if for no other reason than Bernie had had company for a moment.

Bernie Weinberg was a *spot* regular, there in his place every morning from 7:30 to 9:00 AM, and then again from 5:30 to 7:00 PM. In between, he was a Ph.D. student in Ornithology, now working on his thesis that penetrated the question of whether or not woodpeckers get headaches. Hammering their beaks into trees as fast as twenty times a second, up to twelve thousand times each day, the question naturally arose in Bernie's mind about headaches. When he discussed his work with the family members he could get to listen, Bernie would curl his lips into a sideways grin and say, "Of course, woodpeckers turn out to have pretty small brains."

Bernie had a very big brain, so big he was great at research and reading arcane histories, but his emotional intelligence lagged far behind all his academic cranial activity. In fact, Bernie had no true friends because he was so socially awkward that he would be silent in moments calling for him to speak and a chatterbox when listening would be appropriate. His personality was so top-heavy with thinking and reason, like the Stink Bug weighed down by its shell, that Bernie's emotions churned in a froth of constant anxiety, making it difficult for him to decide upon even mundane choices. Consequently, he had been writing his dissertation for four and half years and was running out of time for its completion.

Bernie's dissertation was, thankfully, nearly ready to defend. He had finished the research and writing, and presented it for preliminary approval up the ladder of academic hierarchy (whose minions outnumbered angels dancing on the head of a pin). All he needed to do was make the suggested corrections and edits before scheduling his final defense. He had been hovering over this place in the process for twelve months, paralyzed by undulating waves of anxiety and depression.

The spot was his only true place of comfort, if that was what it could be called. It was his daily exercise in the muted hope that he would meet someone, especially a woman. Like a hapless fisherman waiting for a fish to come along and nibble the worm that would pull the bobber and trigger the jerk of his response, Bernie sat at the same table at the same times each day, hoping a woman would introduce herself. He was ready if one did. He had run the scenario over in his mind a thousand times, exactly what his response would be to any one of a dozen sentences she might say to introduce herself. Oh, Bernie was so ready.

The inside of Bernie's mind was truly amazing. Bernie's thoughts were a brilliant kaleidoscope of crisscrossing patterns bubbling into new shapes and wonderful colors. His face may have been as plain as an Indiana interstate, and his stooped and lumpy body more penguin than stallion, but what went on inside his mind would have created gasps of awe if only someone could witness it.

Bernie thought a lot about purpose and meaning.

Was there any purpose or meaning, or was life, and his life in particular, simply a one-lane road disappearing into the horizon that necessarily met an eventual dead end? At one and the same time, such a thought caused Bernie's mind to sparkle with intense curiosity and a surprising anticipation for being able to discover an answer, while also gnawing the lining of his stomach, reminding him of the dark echoing aloneness that formed the chamber of his lower regions. That was Bernie: a density of astronomical incendiaries flickering brilliance in the dome of his heaven, and a subterranean lake, bubbling hot mud, festering with unseen creatures living without light at the bottom of a shaft leading from his head to his bowels.

Recently, he had been laying bricks one at a time along a lane of thought that seemed to be taking him someplace. In the midst of cruelties being inflicted on people around the world, his research on woodpeckers could seem an obscene waste of time. When genocidal madness bloodied the soil in faraway places like Syria and South Sudan, and marginalized people were shot by police during simple traffic violations, what possible value could there be in asking if woodpeckers get headaches? That question and such comparisons were deadening, and enough to make anyone doing research in a world begging for action to throw up their work and walk away, repenting with remorse.

But Bernie had the same feature to his thinking that Google Maps had, allowing the zooming in and out for greater perspective. He could back away one step at a time, taking snapshots of each perspective and adding them frame by frame to the equation he was configuring. Up close, the murderous violence and pervasive degradation swamping human beings made everything else in the picture seem small and insignificant. But back away and one by one, the small, insignificant activities began to add up and come into focus.

Plato's quip that, "science is nothing but perception," echoed in Bernie's thoughts. He kept a list of accidental discoveries that changed the world like penicillin, microwave ovens, and Velcro. His handwritten list was up to ninety-three and still growing as he stumbled upon discoveries great and small that added up to life-changing and world-enhancing human resources.

Bernie knew that his dissertation on woodpeckers might not change the world, but it might, in combination with other information from other Bernies around the world, one day save people or birds from pain, danger, or even death. He knew that no scientist could count on the work of his or her lab or small field activity to make a singular difference, but he knew that if none of them were doing their work, each in their own little world of ideas and study, that human beings would never move forward. If there was ever going to be a solution to violence, it was going to come from the Bernies of the world trying to figure it out one small piece at a time rather than armed victory and coercion by warriors and governments.

When Bernie could remember that every great, world-changing idea grew up from the detritus of thousands of other ideas, all forming the loam in which every idea, great and small, is rooted, he felt energized and excited about his work. He didn't have to measure himself against John Audubon or Louis Fuertes because he knew that his work was just as important in the universe of ideas.

All of this was going through Bernie's mind when a voice intruded, "Are you Bernie Weinberg?"

The protective glaze surrounding Bernie shattered into a million pieces, and he was sure the crash was so loud everyone in *the spot* would be glaring at him. His eyes went immediately to the other tables and cluster of couches and chairs instead of to the voice coming from just above him. Then, he realized he should be looking to the voice, which he did.

Standing just above his right shoulder was a woman. In her hand, she had a steaming mug and on the opposite shoulder, a canvas computer bag. He looked at her, forgetting he was supposed to respond. Instead of words automatically leaving his mouth, the image of the stranger sent a flood of data to his brain which he processed instead of speaking: *don't know her, she spoke to me, her face is pretty, I like the colors she is wearing, what's in the mug, she has a computer bag that looks like mine, those are nice glasses, I hope when I flicked that Stink Bug it didn't hit her...*

"Are you Bernie Weinberg?" she repeated.

"Uh, what, yeah, yes, I'm Bernie."

Somehow, in all the scenarios he had practiced in his thoughts, no fantasy woman had ever asked if he was Bernie Weinberg. He didn't have a ready answer and had to think about it.

"I am Wilma Nester, one of the new Ph.D. candidates in Ornithology. Professor Lister suggested I talk to you about *Melanerpes formicivorus*, the Acorn Woodpecker. I heard your lecture in his class and have wanted to introduce myself. But honestly, I felt a little shy about it. I hope you don't mind. I mean, I hope I am not intruding."

Bernie was not prepared for this and panic took up residence in his stomach, sending jamming signals to his thoughts. He was all twisted and tied and his stymied thoughts left a vacuous and dry mouth. He stared up at her.

Wilma's thick red hair touched her shoulders, then curled slightly. Her glasses were stylish, a thin strip of solid blue frame in a modern angular shape from ear to lens that then disappeared around the lenses. Her eyes were large and round, and he could see they were hazel green, which he knew was actually a shade of blue when it comes to eyes. Wilma's neck was thin and elegant, pulling his gaze downward to the open v of her blouse revealing slight cleavage.

Suddenly, Bernie realized he hadn't answered her and didn't know how long of a pause he had left with her question dangling in it.

"Uh, yes, I'm Bernie. Oh, I already said that. I mean, no, you're not intruding. I was just flicking, I mean, no, I was just sitting here. No, I mean, please, do you want to sit down?"

Wilma chuckled slightly and smiled. She seemed totally at ease, while Bernie was a bundle of conflicting signals in a race for supremacy. She placed her coffee on the small round table and Bernie realized he needed to move his computer to make room for her. He flipped it closed and placed it on another nearby table as Wilma took off her bag and coat, slipping the coat over the back of the chair. Bernie could feel himself staring at Wilma, mostly in disbelief.

She talked about her program and hopes for her research and asked Bernie about his. Her relaxed posture and easy conversation began to put Bernie at ease, too, and he found himself listening to her every word and mostly able to respond to her many questions. Suddenly, Bernie realized it was 9:22 AM and, though he had nowhere he had to be, his instinct was to jump up and make a dash toward his routine, which had already been bent. He resisted. He listened and smiled, and smiled and smiled. Bernie felt himself to be happy.

It was Wilma that finally had to go, and before she did, she wondered out loud if he would like to have dinner with her that night. Bernie almost sang that he would and they made arrangements before she left. He watched her exit *the spot* through the glass doors out onto the narrow brick street and followed her progress through the windowed wall until she disappeared.

What just happened had changed Bernie's world. It was a fantasy that had replayed in his thoughts for years, but he assumed it would never actually happen. This was a small variable in the mass of countless days and events in Bernie's life that changed everything, just like the accidental discoveries of science that sprang up to change the world. He heard himself wondering if Wilma had an unobserved connection to some previous experience and event in his life, or was she a free-floating radical randomly entering his routine, a spontaneous incident exploding previous possibilities and creating new ones.

Unconnected to Bernie and Wilma in any observable way, and beyond Bernie's attention at the moment, Harrison Jordan entered the spot. Out of Bernie's purview, Harrison had just helped Wilma up from the sidewalk, where she had tripped over a protruding brick. Like all days, the cocktail of unplanned randomness with anticipated events to come would change lives and lay bare the common lie of comfort people tell themselves, that "everything happens for a reason."

Chapter Three

Spinning Dancer

The Tunnel – *hallway to the bathrooms, with galley doors that lead to the kitchen at the far end.*

Harrison Jordan needed to piss in the worst way. He leaned against the wall, holding in the pressure building up from his bloated bladder. Harrison bounced slightly as he leaned on the wall opposite the bathroom, staring at the GI Joe doll dressed in fatigues affixed to the door, indicating the Men's Room. He looked over at the WNBA Barbie on the Women's Room and wondered if anyone was inside. What difference would it make if he used that one?

Harrison looked both ways down the dark narrow hall commonly referred to by *the spot* regulars as "the tunnel," because the ceiling and walls were painted black. Finally, he knocked on Barbie's door, gingerly tried the knob, opened the forgiving door, and peeked inside. Then, he moved fast. In deference to his invasion of their space, he unbuckled his pants and sat down instead of lifting the lid to pee. The relief was immediate and he drained himself for several minutes, to the point that he couldn't believe how full he had been.

As Harrison sat there, he noted the difference in how clean this bathroom was compared to the Men's Room. There was a large, nearly life-size 1960s era poster of a puppy pulling down the swimsuit of a giggling young girl, revealing her tan lines. Next to it was a Rosie the Riveter poster. On the opposite wall, a smiling Amelia Earhart giving the thumbs up hung next to a particularly hostile-looking Margaret Thatcher walking with Ronald Reagan. No crumpled paper towels had missed the trash can, no urine splattered on the floor or wall, no pink strings of liquid soap crisscrossing the sink. None of the standard chaos of a Men's Room was evident.

The sound of the brass knob twisting from the outside jerked Harrison back to the present. He stood up, zipped and buckled, flushed, and washed his hands. He was careful not to splash water around and to get the paper towel fully inside the trashcan. Harrison Jordan felt the watchful eyes of his mother's and grandmother's peers glaring from the walls.

When he opened the door and passed by a middle-aged woman in a business suit, she glowered at him. Harrison flashed an Alfred E. Newman grin and peace sign. At the very same moment, the Men's Room door opened and Bernie Weinberg nearly ran straight into Harrison, but Harrison was agile and swerved to miss Bernie. Bernie jumped, Harrison nodded, and the two passed wordlessly.

The Bar – *a long, oval fishbowl in which baristas make hot and cold drinks and retrieve baked items from glass cases atop the bar.*

The problem Harry stuttered over and over again was hope, and how to tell the difference between hope and wishful thinking. This was Harry's most recent thoughtwall. Climb as he might, he never reached the top to look over.

Harrison Jordan's great uncle walked the Edmund Pettis Bridge in 1965. He had aunts and uncles bloodied in Chicago in 1968 and tear-gassed in Washington in 1970. His mom and dad were active at the tail end of the Anti-War movement and protested Reagan's nuclear arms buildup and Central American policies. They were always quick to debate the latest controversy. He wondered if maybe that was part of his problem.

Harrison was beginning to think that the Baby Boomers were the ones who had mistaken wishful thinking for hope, and because of it, all of them were now cynical. His generation was pessimistic, but not cynical. They could see the dark clouds hanging over the horizon but wanted to do something about it. The Boomers had given up, were retiring in droves, and now pulling the covers up and going to sleep. *Thanks a lot.*

"Harry! Harry!"

He turned away from the barista from whom he had just ordered a cappuccino to see who was giddily calling his name.

"Harry Jordan!"

It was Miss Landrace, Harry's high school Latin teacher. He wanted to slide down beneath the bar, but instead stood his ground with an ever-reddening face. Who would have thought Miss Landrace ever stepped foot inside *the spot*?

Miss Landrace approached Harrison with the force of a vortex, placed a hand on each of his cheeks, and pulled them with force down to her five-foot level for a loud smooch. Harrison nearly gagged at the sickeningly sweet smell of her perfume and scent of make-up powder caked on her rose cheeks. He restrained himself from the urge to jerk away and instead submitted to her affection.

"Harry, Harry, Harry, my best student ever! How are you, Harrison? I can't believe it has been so long – how long has it been Harry? Five, six years since you graduated?

"Seven."

"Seven! Oh my goodness, seven years. Bless your heart, Harrison. How are your sisters, all of them such good students?" It was a question she never paused for Harrison to answer. "And your mother and father, how are they? I haven't seen them in several years, either. It is so amazing how you can see people every day for years and years and years and then suddenly, not again for years. It is just a very strange world, isn't it, Harrison? Well, I should think you are nearly in charge of it by now!" With that, Miss Landrace cackled. Without pausing, she looked at the barista and ordered a tall mint mocha with extra whipped cream and extra milk. Then, seamlessly, she was back at Harrison. "Harry, let's sit down and catch up. This is such a wonderful surprise."

Harrison was already exhausted and the encounter had only lasted a full forty-five seconds. The thought of sitting down with Miss Landrace, and enduring still more of it, flushed every light and lyrical emotion from Harrison, leaving only the darkest, most despairing feelings to fill the chambers of his heart.

Miss Landrace grabbed his elbow and pulled him to a small round table, the very one he had occupied after the After-Prom party his junior year in high school when his best friend's date, Erin Laptricz, groped his crotch. The image of Erin's hand roving around his junk while sitting down with Miss Landrace was a Harry Potter *Dementor* that sucked the life right out of him.

"Harrison, you couldn't have known this, but we just buried my daddy."

Two competing thoughts jolted Harrison, that Miss Landrace's father had only just died, and that she called him "daddy."

"I'm so sorry, Miss Landrace. How old was he?"

"Daddy was eighty-seven. Well really, he was almost eighty-seven, but he passed just two weeks shy of his birthday. Oh Harry, I miss him so." She began to cry, and as she did, she squeezed Harrison's hand tightly.

Harrison sat ramrod straight, his hand a limp detachment from his stiff arm. He was frozen by an attack of emotions and thoughts from all directions. Later, as he thought about the moment, he would be relieved that a little compassion leaked through the overlapping sensations of embarrassment, repulsion, entrapment, deer-in-the-headlights, and resentment.

Harrison Jordan darted a look at Miss Landrace's face. It was round, framed by several chins below and thin, colorless hair frozen in unnatural shapes by unseen chemicals above. It was an hairstyle that reminded him of textured icing on a cake. The poor woman had scores of moles and skin tags peeking out of crevices in her chins, eyelids, tucks at the base of her nose, and even on her ears.

Why he had felt scorn for her in high school rather than compassion, he could now not imagine.

"Harry, he was just too young and vital to leave us. I don't know what I'm going to do now that he's gone. Such a deep, dark void." Then, she sobbed some more, intermittently sipping her mint mocha.

Harrison quickly calculated. His own parents had been thirty-seven when he was born, so eighty-seven minus thirty-seven was fifty. *Miss Landrace was only fifty*? Along with all his friends in high school, he had thought Miss Landrace was ancient back then but she had been younger than Mimi was now! *What? How was that even possible*? He peeked again at her face. There were not the wrinkles he saw around the eyes of old people like his grandparents, and her neck didn't have those goose-skin ripples oldsters get either. *Eighty-seven is young and vital*? It was a delayed thought.

Harrison was still rigidly locked in place but now, in addition to the buckshot thoughts peppering his brain about Miss Landrace, he started to look around *the spot*. The guy he had almost run into at the bathrooms was leaning into a conversation with the woman he helped up off the street the day before. Cressida was lounging on an overstuffed chair, one leg flung over its bulbous leather arm and the other crossed, with her bare foot pulled close to her face where she picked at it. There was a line at the coffee bar with loud banter between some of the customers and their baristas as other patrons either slumped patiently or rocked back and forth, counting seconds. Miss Landrace was talking about her father as if he was someone Harry had known well, interrupted only by the blowing of her nose, sniffling, and sipping.

"Daddy helped in the killing of Oscar Romero and he was so proud of how he had helped to stop the dominos from falling down there."

The words gonged in his brain, jarring him awake from the mental stupor of calculating minutia and endlessly tracking the movements around him.

"What? He killed who?"

"Well, Daddy didn't actually shoot the archbishop himself, but he worked with the group that did, just one of the ones he trained when he was down there."

"Who? What? I missed something, Miss Landrace, I'm sorry. Who did your dad kill and why was he wherever he was?"

"Oh Harrison, you didn't listen very well in class either. How you ever got all A's, I'll never know. I was telling you that Daddy was in the CIA and he was involved in helping Reagan stop the communists in Central America. It was a very dangerous time for this country, you know, and thank God for President Reagan. Cuba was playing dominos down there, hoping to tip every country over into the Russian column. But my daddy and Ronald Reagan stopped them! I don't know everything he did, of course, but I know he was in Nicaragua and El Salvador. He told me that he helped train the squads of freedom-lovers fighting the communists; one of them was a team that finally had to target that communist bishop, Óscar Romero. They warned him over and over; they even asked the pope for help. But the bishop wouldn't stop agitating for the communists and he even had priests fighting with them – shooting guns! Well, they shot him. Shot him in the heart while he was saying Mass. That showed 'em."

Harrison realized his mouth was hanging open. Miss Landrace just kept talking with pride about her father's life work, which involved training assassins in other countries. She glowed as she unfolded wistful descriptions of the heroic efforts of her CIA father and his mythic President, both of whom saved the world from Communism. *OMG. Miss Landrace, our high school Latin teacher, is a fascist.*

Harrison finally unlocked from Miss Landrace, who had finished her mint mocha and so was more amenable to closure. He nearly ran to the table on the other side of *the spot* where Google and his girlfriend, Enid, were sitting.

Table 27 – *large, round patio table for eight right in the middle of the spot, frosted glass top with center hole for missing umbrella, unremarkable metal frame painted light gray.*

Google was the nickname they had given Carl Prichard because he read Wikipedia all day, every day, and was a non-stop river of factoids and misinformation. They got to know one another as suitemates freshman year of college when Google became obsessed with reading online dictionaries while everyone around him got stoned.

"Google, who the hell is Oscar Romero?"

"He was the archbishop of San Salvador from 1977 to 1980 when he was assassinated by a right-wing death squad because he implored Catholics serving in the armed forces not to follow orders when told to kill civilians. He also organized an effort to find out what happened to the thousands of civilians that disappeared, not to mention attribute guilt for numerous massacres. Now, even though he was betrayed, and some say condemned, by Cardinal Benedict, when John Paul II was pope, he was on the way to being made a saint."

"My high school Latin teacher was just bragging to me that her dad worked for the CIA and helped kill Romero!"

"Lovely. Where'd you go to school, Opus Dei High? Do you know how many people the United States has killed in undeclared wars since World War II? Guess."

"It's gotta be a least a million," Harrison answered.

"Two million," Enid said nonchalantly without looking up from her phone, on which she was browsing pornographic sites with the word "thumb" in the search line, just for the heck of it.

"Try twenty-five million, give or take five."

"No!" Harrison was incredulous.

"Shit." Enid was almost alarmed.

"No shit," Google droned as he offered a list of 'victim' nations: "Afghanistan, Angola, Argentina, Bangladesh, Bolivia, Brazil, Cambodia, Chad, Chile, China (900,000 during the Korean war), Colombia, Cuba, Congo, Dominican Republic, East Timor, El Salvador (we gave six billion dollars to their murderous campaign), Grenada (Reagan actually invaded a little Caribbean island), Guatemala, Haiti (yep, we invaded Haiti!), Honduras, Indonesia, Iran, Iraq (200,000 in Bush the First's war and 650,000 in the Bush-Obama war), Laos, Nepal, Nicaragua, Panama, Paraguay, Philippines, Sudan, Vietnam, and some people would say we had a lot to do with what happened in Yugoslavia as well."

"But we don't get the blame for all of those killings. I mean, there were other bad guys involved in all of those, right?" Harrison was certain Google was exaggerating.

"Where are the 'good guys'? That's debatable, but those are the numbers of people killed in 'our' undeclared wars since World War II. Even if it is off by ten percent, we're still talking millions and millions."

"That is so depressing." Harrison suddenly felt heavy all over.

He watched as Google picked his navel and smelled it. It was a disgusting habit he did with some regularity, on occasion tasting whatever he retrieved. Harrison shuddered at the sight and walked away.

Tables 81 and 86 – *81 is small round wooden table for three painted lime green all over, 86 a 1960's oval dinette table for six with wood grain natural finish and an extensive quote from Che Guevara carved meticulously in the middle.*

Haphazardly, he made his way from the coffee bar, where he ordered a Redeye, then retreated to *the darkness.* The darkness was in the northwest corner of *the spot,* where a black light glowed purplish instead of the normal lighting, and where a swath of fabric hung particularly low from the ceiling joists, giving it a tented feel.

He slumped into a chair at a small round table, leaned on one arm with his chin on the palm of his hand, and held the hot paper cup in the other. Harrison Jordan was hiding from himself as much as anyone else, wanting to leave his body now that it was so heavy with the accumulated weight of the world's carnage.

"You look like you have a flat tire."

The voice came from behind him. Harrison knew there was only one table wedged further into the darkness than his. He didn't turn around until he connected the familiar sound of the voice with a face.

"Hey, Peedad. A tire with a hole in it."

Harrison had gone to high school with Hobart Wilson, known to one and all as Peedad. Hobart was three years older than Harrison, so Harry knew his younger brothers and sister much better. Now, Peedad was a United Church of Christ minister, working his first job out of seminary at Mimi's church. But Peedad was still a stoner and that confused his peers - none of whom were church people.

"*Whatsamatter,*" Peedad slurred.

"Oh, man, sometimes there is just so much shit in the world, you know? It just feels like things are so terrible and we're never going to get out from under them or be able to make anything better. You know what I mean?"

"Yeah, like a week without sun and it rains every day, and you go to bed thinking that if you wake up in the morning and it's cloudy again, you're just going to stay in bed all freaking day."

"Uh-huh, something like that," Harrison nodded.

"I don't know how to keep that feeling from happening, especially when the news cycle is pounding us with one catastrophe after another. But I know how to fix it."

Harrison cocked his head and looked at Peedad's face shrouded in shadow. He was pretty sure Peedad was about to give him some minister-type advice, and he wasn't at all sure how he felt about it. In fact, he looked hard at Peedad and was flooded with memories of Peedad's oboe-sized bong and the parties they had enjoyed at Becky Robbins's house the year her divorced mom had to work nights at the hospital. Even though Hobart Wilson was three years older and had a master's degree, Harrison wasn't so sure that life had bestowed upon him any extra wisdom or knowledge.

"The dancer trick is what I use," Peedad chirped, "and ganja of course." He looked sheepishly at Harry and continued, "You know how a dancer gets up on her toes and twirls? I heard that if they don't train their eyes on a single stationary point beyond them, they will lose their balance. So, that's what I do when I'm leaking air; I focus on something positive or hopeful, or even some small thing I can actually accomplish. Does that make any sense?"

Harrison had to think about that for a moment. He envisioned a ballerina spinning on her toes and keeping her eyes fixed on an exit sign backstage. He knew that was the trick for not getting seasick, too, keeping your eyes focused on the horizon. He stared out at Cressida, lounging across the room with an air of innocence about her. He smiled and chuckled. Of all things to focus on, Cressida was probably the least likely to help him keep his balance.

"Yeah, that makes sense," he muttered to Peedad, but his thoughts had split into two parallel tracks, which sometimes happened.

On one rail, he was thinking about keeping a focus on things he had control over, even while caring generally about all the other stuff going on around him. The question was what to focus on and if, like Peedad, he would ever find any work that defined him. Did he even want work that defined him?

On the other rail, his thoughts were traveling down the road of Peedad being a minister, his having just received some pretty smart advice from a stoner who does the God thing, and how far they both now seemed from Miss Deutro's biology class in high school when Harry was a freshman and Peedad was Miss Deutro's "senior helper."

Suddenly, Harrison's job at Slow Roasted Books and living above his parent's garage felt like a Nike sneaker two sizes too small.

Chapter Four

Fresh Baked Bread

Table 14 – *rectangular table seating four with large wood inlay of yin-yang symbol in black and white at the center and a cup-holder hole at each corner.*

As long as she could remember, Wilma thought nerdy was sexy, and when it came to sexiness, she thought Bernie was the nerdiest. They had had five dates in two weeks, and even though she initiated four of them, what bothered her was his pattern of lateness. Wilma knew she could be a little obsessive about being on time, but something seemed weird to her about Bernie's tardiness because he otherwise appeared to be courteous. If he didn't get there in three minutes, it would be a new record for lateness: forty-five minutes.

It was a slow time of day at *the spot*, the in-between hour when most people were having dinner or taking advantage of Happy Hour to get some free bar food while paying too much for a Three Floyds Zombie Dust beer on tap. That long-legged chick with the little purple stripe at the back of her head was lounging on the chair as she always did at *the spot*, but otherwise Wilma didn't recognize the half-dozen patrons scattered at tables throughout the café. She marveled at how the eccentric cavern of a coffee shop had become home already.

Where is he? Wilma started to fidget. How had she gotten so smitten so fast? Was Bernie just a fix for the loneliness and anxiety of being new in the department, a bridge to help ease the transition from college to grad school? Her head hinted that might be the case, but her gut bubbled with the goo of something much different. She hated feeling like this – jumbled and exposed. The last few nights, she had dreams about suddenly finding herself in public not fully dressed, one in which she saw herself in a public mirror with gum, feathers, and all kinds of lint in her hair. *He was supposed to be here forty-eight minutes ago*!

Just then, Bernie walked into *the spot*, slightly bumping a table on his left while surveying the scene in search of Wilma. She stood up and he made a beeline for her table, tripping on a chair.

"Oh Wilma, I'm so sorry, I lost track of time." He was visibly jittery and more awkward than usual. If she weren't so furious, Wilma would have found it endearing. "I was working on my citations and footnotes because they got all screwed up somehow when I re-paginated." This was the best excuse he could think of, even though he had been trying to come up with something better the whole way over.

"Oh, it's okay Bernie," she lied. "I was just enjoying a latte and the opportunity to take it easy." The anger seething from each syllable would have been discernible to most people, but Bernie was not only stuck in his head and unable to read such emotions even in the light of day, he was also stuck in self-orbit and not even looking.

"We still have time to grab something to eat before Trivaphobia starts at Merlin's. You wanna snort some chili dogs from Fuzzy Barney's?" he asked as he leaned forward to give Wilma a little hug.

"Smells like you already started. You been drinking?"

"Oh, sorry, I forgot to brush my teeth. Yeah, I had a beer while I was working this afternoon. It was gross, though, almost skunk."

"I'd fall asleep if I had a beer in the afternoon, but then again, I'm a cheap date when it comes to booze, aren't I?"

"Yeah, I've never known anyone who can nurse a drink as long as you can. I don't get it, but hey, whatever." Bernie reached for the door and opened it for Wilma as they exited *the spot*.

GI Joe's – *men's bathroom featuring cement floor painted black, one toilet, one urinal, dirty white sink, blue and gray tile wainscot with beige painted drywall above.*

From his field of vision framed by the window, the scene appeared serene. Under a cloudless pale blue sky, the dark cobalt lake wiggled with current as it moved toward the mouth of a river. Manicured lawns interrupted by occasional birch, spruce, and oblong islands of landscaped features offered the impression of sweetly domesticated safety. But lurking just outside the purview of the window was danger. The looming mountain forested in wildness was home to bear, lynx, and timber rattlers. Fishers, coy wolves, and badgers ventured secretly within proximity of the nestled houses each night while falcon, osprey, eagle, and the Great Horned Owl attacked from overhead, snatching at will what they desired. A small pug sat at the end of its owner's driveway without any premonition it was about to be eaten.

That is what Hopi imagined as he stared at the picture that hung crookedly on the wall opposite the toilet in the Men's Room at *the spot*. He had time to kill waiting for the bowel crawl to produce a winner.

He could hear people waiting in the hall to take his place in the sanctuary for human waste, but for now it was his porcelain throne. Finally, there was movement afoot as slowly the tight, dry mash composed of breakfast's spinach omelet mixed with lunch's pork and black bean burrito and nachos, all dehydrated by at least six cups of coffee, was given birth into the clear water of the bleach white basin.

Hopi got his nickname from the frequent claim he was "two-sixteenths Hopi blood," which, he also asserted, made him "spiritual." He was also born into the wrong generation. At odds with his peers, he listened exclusively to music his parents had listened to in their youth. He had earphones in right then, listening to a mix that featured Boz Skaggs, Laura Nyro, and most of the Terrapin Station album. Boz Skaggs was singing "Look What You've Done To Me" as Hopi flushed the toilet with the satisfaction of a job well done, washed his hands twice with water and once with hand sanitizer before leaving "Joe's Room", where he was greeted by the next person standing in the tunnel who wore a twisted sense of urgency on his face.

Black Leather Couch Number 2 – *northwest corner furniture cluster, overstuffed wrinkled leather in perfect condition.*

"Hey Cress," Hopi said to Cressida as he sidled up next to her on the couch, "who you giving face to these days?"

"Fuck you. Get off my couch, jerk."

"No, I didn't mean it like that," Hopi said with remorse in his voice. "I meant that I heard you were hanging with someone but I don't know who it is."

"Nope. No one. Single, for over a year."

"She likes it better that way," Harrison said from behind Hopi. Hopi looked up to see Harry, Google, and Enid walking towards them, each with a drink in one hand and food in the other. "Here," Harrison handed Cressida a white plate with a steaming cinnamon roll, corn-yellow butter dripping down the sides.

"Oh man, that looks good," Hopi sniffed the air to catch the aroma.

"Someday, I'll have fresh bread and cinnamon rolls every morning." Google pronounced as if it were an oracle from on high.

"How do you figure?" Hopi asked as the rest of the group rolled their eyes in anticipation of a familiar announcement.

"My wife will bake bread every day. That's my prerequisite for marriage. I don't care what she looks like, how smart or dumb she is, or whether she can make a bed, so long as she bakes bread every day and I wake up to that aroma. 'How about a cinnamon bun today', I'll ask and it will happen. That's marriage, bra, the only kind I will hang for."

Google said it as if a well-rehearsed plank in a political platform, and with the confidence that it was truer than the sun. He closed his eyes to better imagine how it would be.

"My dad had a friend," Enid said drolly, her words dry as an Arizona gulch. "He married a woman because she fulfilled his three absolute standards: exquisite tits, keep a clean house, and make a righteous sausage lasagna. He dated scores of women. Tits were the beacons announcing potential candidates because he could kind of get a read up front as to how they would look when uncovered. While he waited to see them naked, if it took a few dates, he could sometimes determine how clean her apartment was if she didn't have too many roommates. The lasagna was always third in order of discernment because it took more than a few dates for women to be willing to cook for him on request."

"But lo and behold, after searching for a couple of years, the woman of his dreams appeared out of nowhere, and in one delicious evening revealed her perfectly round, supple breasts with nipples like he'd only seen in magazines (this was before the internet), uncovered at her pristine apartment where, after sex, she fed him sausage lasagna as good as his grandmother made. He proposed on the spot."

"My dad says they married within a few short months. He was happy at first, enjoying the three-legged stool of his desires kept in perfect balance. Then, they had children and a dog. The house was no longer pristine. Toys, chaos, and dog hair touched every floor, ceiling, and corner of the house. His perfect wife who had kept everything so very clean seemed unconcerned, caring more for nurturing the children and dog than for keeping the house in that then unattainable condition."

"Then, his wife got breast cancer and eventually, she had a double mastectomy. While he was grateful that she survived the cancer and seemed to be well beyond the five-year mark, the loss of her perfect breasts secretly agitated him even more than the unfavorable condition of his home."

"Then, the unthinkable happened. She stopped making the lasagna. Not only was she working outside the home now, the cancer had made her more health conscious and she cooked differently than when they married. He needed to lower his cholesterol and she wanted to lose weight, so carbohydrates were seldom seen at the dinner table anymore, replaced by a multiplicity of fresh vegetables."

"My dad said that his friend slid into a serious depression. His whole reason for loving her and getting married had vanished. He was surrounded by a chaos that had eroded the soil of perfect routine, replaced by disorder and fresh vegetables. His mood grew darker and darker. His wife, unaware that she was the source of his downer, urged him to go to the doctor. He did, and his doctor prescribed hydrocodone for the pain lodged in his lower back and the darkness that had taken over his mind. Before long, he was addicted to the opiates and descended into a deeper depression as he battled the crashing surf of emotional turmoil followed by long periods of numbness."

"Eventually, racked by the loss of his wife's perfection, tormented by imprisonment to opiates his doctor would no longer prescribe, and failing at his efforts toward recovery, the man stuffed a rag in the tailpipe of his car. He rolled up the windows, locked the doors, and turned on the ignition. He sat there in a very clean car in which nothing was out of order, listening to music of his own choice, and remembering how it was when he and his wife were first married. They found him the next morning, the car still running, his face black and bloated twice its size from carbon monoxide. He died remembering a time when he was happy. The end."

The gaggle surrounding the black couch was seared by a prolonged silence, their eyes darting back and forth at each other, brows furrowed, each one searching for something to say. Finally, Google complained, "What kind of a story is that Enid? Such a downer."

"That guy was a selfish prick," Cressida muttered.

"Too bad he couldn't get some help," Harrison frowned.

"How else could it have ended for a guy who only saw other people as an extension of his own needs?" Hopi ventured as everyone looked at him with a dawning recognition.

"Yeah, like a guy who will only marry someone that bakes bread for him every day." Enid unrolled it like the flypaper it was.

Enid was not a big talker, so her telling a story at length was a surprise, but a story with such a deep stinger silenced the group. Google, normally irrepressible, now looked away in silence as others picked at their food and sipped drinks. t*he spot* was crowded, and the din held them in a canopy of voices while they sat in the discomfort of Enid's double-barreled story.

Hopi broke the silence. In total denial of the morose atmosphere, he popped up like a prairie dog and chirped, "Hey, you guys want to take the trolley down to the harbor? There's supposed to be a bonfire tonight. It's something about a pre-Oktoberfest celebration, and they're serving only beer from city microbreweries."

An excited and relieved enthusiasm bubbled up immediately, except from Google and Enid, who went along in silence.

As Google, Enid, Harrison, Cressida, and Hopi went out one side of the door, Bernie and Wilma entered the other. Harrison nodded at Wilma, who he recognized from helping up off the street one day. She smiled back.

"I want a Flower Shake Tea," Wilma told Bernie, who responded that he was hankering for a whip-less mint mocha.

Dinner and Trivaphobia had moved Wilma's angst and resentment to the background and they were lovebirds once again. Wilma hung on Bernie's arm as they waited for their coffee drinks, both of her lithe arms embracing one of his long gangly arms, all three hands entangled at the bottom and a manic stroking of thumbs and fingers in worm-like rapture.

When Bernie looked at Wilma, he saw a woman wrapped in a soft glow - Photoshop effect. She was the cheerleader in high school that never gave him the time of day and mocked him to her friends. Yet here she was, holding his hands and leaning so close; the warmth of her skin penetrated through the sleeve of her blouse and raised the hair on his flesh uncovered by the short sleeve of his Hawaiian shirt. She was so eager to love him and he didn't know how to trust it. *What's wrong with her?* He found himself questioning her judgment or motives since no one outside his family had ever lavished him with such affection.

But here she was, in the flesh. And Bernie had seen all her flesh. They slept together on their third date, an explosion of exquisite intensity and awkward newness, for Bernie anyway. Once his attention leaked beyond the sensation of his face actually kissing hers, their tongues excitedly licking taste and texture inside one another's mouths, he became aware of his hands roaming aimlessly over her back and then tentatively feeling the slight ripple of ribs below her armpits. Then, with one hand, she moved his hand over her left breast and he felt a jolt of white light electrocute the inside of his body as it traveled from his toes to his ears and shot outward from his groin to the tip of his hardened antennae. Defibrillation continued through the thrill of her graceful two-armed motion to remove her blouse and seamlessly open the cups of her bra from a clasp at the center as he, fully clothed but prone beneath her, watched two breasts surge outward. He gasped, remembering it while standing in line for his mint mocha. There were moments nearly every day, sometimes looking at her and sometimes just remembering, when he continued to gasp. Bernie found it difficult to believe that this was real, that it was happening, that it would last.

Wilma was so happy. She loved everything about Bernie. His rat's nest of curly hair springing outward in an unkempt mess made her giggle. *How could he even try to make something of it?* she thought. It disabused her of any inkling to 'fix' it. *It's that nose I love most*, she twittered to herself. It was big and crooked and wonderful and perfect on his long bony face. She almost laughed out loud at the thought of how he would age; his nose would seem even bigger as an old man with hair thinning and face shrinking around it. She loved his skinny, shapeless body and the way he walked haphazardly, like a dreidel winding down. All of it was because his brain is so big that it outweighed the rest of him by double, maybe not in actual weight, but in the power-ratio of mind to body. *Mmmmm, a big brain like that is sexy, sexy, sexy*, she smiled to herself.

On their third date, it was something about listening to him discuss the bone structure of *Melanerpes formicivorus* that caused her stomach to flutter. *They can slam a tree with their beak at a thousand times the force of gravity*, he had told her, *while humans can only survive a g-force of forty-six times that of gravity*! He explained this with great wide-eyed excitement and went on to describe in detail the thickness of the woodpecker's neck muscles and how those muscles also act as shock absorbers to diffuse each wallop. *Then*, he added with unique Bernie astonishment made of one-part awe and one-part incredulity, *they have a third inner eyelid that keeps their eyeballs from bursting out*! That was when she couldn't restrain herself anymore and the excitement that had lightly moistened her underwear exploded into a kiss.

Still, his lateness bothered her. The undulating tummy bubbles of remembering that third date percolated below, but caution flashed in her head even while leaning against him as she waited for her Flower Shake Tea. She couldn't put a finger on it, but something wasn't quite right about Bernie's various excuses for his expanding bad habit. He was never late for the sections he taught or the tests he administered. Everyone in the department loved Bernie and respected his mind and his research, and yet everyone was worried about whether he would finish his dissertation in time. There was something unseen, she could feel it, and the feeling made her anxious.

Chapter Five

Ruthie

710 N. Dill – *sidewalk to the house cracked in several places and crumbled completely at its joint with the city sidewalk.*

Mimi never told Cressida the full story of her father's disappearance. The clock ticking inside her body provoked memories and agitated secrets, and it had become a worse plague than the suds of invisible cancer bubbling in her organs.

She wanted to go upstairs and lie down with Cressida as she slept, just like when Ruthie was a little girl, and feel again that dark loneliness of a single parent lightened by the love within she held for her daughter. But Mimi could no more ascend the stairs than climb a ladder to the roof in waders full of water. Some nights, it was all she could do to get to the bathroom, so she lay there awake on her improvised bed in the dining room, picturing little Ruthie sleeping in a loose fetal position and sucking her thumb. She had had to cut holes in Ruthie's sleepers when she was a little girl because her feet got too hot, and even now Mimi could imagine her street-smart daughter who had changed her name asleep under a sheet with her toes sticking out.

Just then, she heard the refrigerator door open and the clink of a bottle.

"Ruthie...I mean, Cressy?"

"Hey mom," Cressida said dryly, rolling it out of her mouth with a lazy rhythm.

"What's the matter, honey?"

"Can't sleep. You?"

"Not much."

Then, Cressida entered the room with a bottle of beer in one hand and a lighted cigarette in the other. The light from the kitchen shone behind her and accentuated the long thinness of her silhouette.

"You're so beautiful, but I wish you wouldn't smoke. It gives you wrinkles, you know, besides cancer and heart disease."

"Yeah, not smoking was good for you, huh?" Cressida chuckled at the bitter irony. "I know, Mom, I'm gonna quit, but right now, it's just a little tough. I don't mean to whine or anything; it's just that everything is a struggle right now and I don't need to inflict the heebie-jeebies on myself, too."

"I'm sorry, honey, I know my sickness is hard on you."

"Oh please, Mom, don't be apologizing for having cancer! This is not your fault, and it's not my fault either. It's goddamn God's fault if you ask me."

"Ruthie, God didn't do this to me, us. You don't believe that, really, do you?"

"I don't know what I believe, Mom. I don't even know if I believe in God anymore. What's God ever done for us, anyway? Everything we have is because you clawed your way up a steep ladder all by yourself with me hanging on your neck. You did it, Mom. You." She started to sob.

The two women put their arms around each other and cried until Cressida dropped her cigarette and yelled "Shit!" as it burnt a small hole in the sheet. They laughed and rearranged themselves, and then Cressida put down her beer, squashed her cigarette in an ashtray, and lay down next to her mom, spoons.

"I used to lie down next to you like this when you were a little girl, already asleep."

"I know, Mom, I wasn't always asleep."

"Really? You remember?"

"Yeah, it was the best."

They were quiet. The small light from the kitchen mixed with the very dark of the dining room melded to a shadowy yellow in between. Mimi smiled as the words of an old trope whispered to her, "even a small candle enlightens the deepest darkness."

Mimi smelled the bitterness of beer and the staleness of smoke on Ruthie's breath from behind her. It didn't matter.

"What will you do, Ruthie?"

"You mean after?"

"Well not just after, but I mean what do you *want* to do?"

"You mean, 'what do I want to be when I grow up?"

"I guess so."

"I'm gonna finish my goddamn bachelor's degree. I have three semesters left. Then I'm gonna get an MSW and find a job working with kids who've been beat on and neglcted. I'm going to be a social worker, Mom. That's what I'm going to do when I grow up."

"Oh, honey, you will be so good at that, so very good at that."

"Thanks, Mom."

After more quiet in the darkened room, Mimi added, "That will be hard work. Sad work. Really important work, but sad."

"Yeah, life is sad, Mom. That's what I decided: life is sad enough as it is without people who heap more sadness on top of it with their meanness, and who add some brutality 'just cause.' So, if I'm going to be sad, I might as well do something to help other people who are even sadder than me."

Another lull rested over them.

"That's kind of a sad point of view, sweetie. I always tried to be upbeat with you; even when things were very tough I tried to bring some light and happiness into the room so you wouldn't be afraid. I guess I didn't get that done as well as I might have, huh?"

"Oh, Mom, you're not responsible for everything in the whole world. You're just my mom. You couldn't make me one way or another, you know. Besides, just cause I know there is a lot of sadness in the world doesn't make me depressed or something. I'm just not in denial about the way things are and what people have to deal with, what I have to deal with. You taught me not to expect life to be fair and that there are more important things than being rich or famous, like family, even if ours is really, really, really small."

They both laughed. Mimi thought about her daughter and the loneliness of an only child with no extended family anywhere in the world. Then, she thought about the family Cressida didn't know she had and panic blew a cold breath into her heart.

"Ruthie," Mimi started but was interrupted.

"Mom, you can call me Ruth if you want, but you know that's not my name anymore, right?"

"Right. Sorry, honey. Cressy, have you thought about talking to Hobart? It might help you with, well you know, my being sick and when the end comes."

"Peedad? Mom, he's still a stoner and besides, what's he know that I don't know? We were in school together. That'd be like going to an OBGYN you went to high school with and really, who's gonna do that?"

"He's helped me. I very much look forward to Hobart's visits, much more than Rev. Miller's, who I'm afraid has his head too far into the business of running the church and taking care of that huge building."

"Peedad's been visiting you?"

"Honey, don't call him that; he is grown up like you are, Cressida. He deserves to be called by an adult name. And yes, he has been here every week and I think would come every day if I asked him to."

"Huh, who knew?" Cressida was speechless for a moment. "What do you guys talk about?"

"Oh, sometimes just small talk and sometimes big things. Dying has a way of narrowing your focus. Suddenly, the things that really matter become clearer than they used to, and the less important things just kind of fall away. We often wander into the big things that matter."

"Like what?"

"Like forgiveness, healing...death...hope, you."

"Me! You talk about me with *Peedad*?"

"Hobart. Well, not so much about you as about me, and what I want to make sure I talk about with you before, before...I die."

"Mom, you don't need 'HO-bart' to help you talk to *me*. I can't believe you talk to him about us."

"Would you feel better if I was talking to a social worker or counselor?"

"Yeah, I guess so. Yeah, I would."

"But that's just a prejudice, honey. You think a social worker or counselor has more training or knowledge than a minister?"

"No, I guess not, I mean, actually, I don't know. I have no idea what kind of training or knowledge they have. Aren't they just like, you know, Bible readers or something?" Cressida burst into laughter at the thought of a stoner Bible reader. "Really, what the hell does HO-bart do other than hang out at *the spot* and wear dresses for church? Is that like drag or something, when they get those robes on? Church drag?" Cressida laughed ruefully until she felt her mother go limp and she knew her feelings had been hurt. "I'm sorry. Okay, I'll admit I don't know anything about ministers and church, and I have no idea about his training, knowledge, or anything."

"I wish...I wish I could have given you faith. I wish you could know what I know, but I don't know how to even tell you. Hobart knows, and I've told him, and he is helping me to find some way to tell you what I need you to know – about your father and what happened when you were very young, and how we survived terrible times. It is such a dark night to re-enter, but I have to, and somehow, I have to bring you into it so you'll know the rest of it."

"Mom, what are you talking about?" Cressida sat up both frightened and impatient.

Visibly shaken, Mimi curled up even more and pulled the sheet over her shoulder as if to get warm. A long, bristled silence followed, in which Cressida wanted to urge her mother to talk, but didn't. Leaning on her elbow and looking down at her mom's shadowed face, Cressida wanted her mom to tell her what she had told Peedad, Hobart, and that she, her own daughter, should be able to know.

Silence followed silence, in which Cressida's restless mind churned while Mimi's breathing became slow, then silent. When she was certain her mom was sound asleep, Cressida got up slowly, and, with her bottle of beer and cigarettes, slid into the big red chair in the living room.

What could her mom have told Hobart Wilson that she couldn't tell her own daughter? Was it about the night her father disappeared? It peaked her curiosity, but also agitated her that a stoner minister nearly her own age knew something about her personal history that she didn't know. What do ministers know, anyway? What do they actually do? The more she thought about Hobart Wilson, the deeper down her resentment burned.

When Mimi awoke, sunshine was streaming in the windows and the aroma of bacon and coffee brought a reflexive grin to her face. "Are you making me breakfast?" she asked with an obvious thrill in her voice.

"Why the big surprise? It's not like I don't make you breakfast several mornings a week."

"But bacon and eggs are different than cereal or an English muffin" she smiled from her bed while trying to brush the night out of her hair. "Did you sleep down here all night?"

"No, I hung out for a little while after you fell asleep, drowned in my computer and went to bed. I've got to meet Harrison at *the spot* in about an hour, so are you okay for me to leave?"

"Of course honey, I'm not incompetent yet. Moving slow, to be sure, but I can still look after myself. Don't worry, but I do want you to be here at four when the people from Hospice come. Okay?"

"Of course, Mom, I wouldn't miss that."

Cressida served her mom breakfast in bed then went upstairs to shower. She wiped away a swath of steam from the full-length mirror on the back of the door and looked at her naked self looking back. It was a game she had been playing for months now, an exercise, really, an act of will. When she started, Cressida could hardly stand to see herself naked in the mirror. Her right breast was larger and shaped differently than her left one. Her nipples were too long. She had an outie instead of an innie. Her ribs to her waist to her hips were a straight line, but even so, she had a slight pouch in front while her butt sagged a little in back. When dressed just right, she could feel as hot as people often said she was, but with the steam wiped away from the mirror, the woman looking back filled her with a grim shame.

She had begun willing herself to look. It was an exercise in self-acceptance, she hoped. But so far, even after several months, there had not been any meaningful reconciliation.

Today, she would wear a sheer blue bralette underneath a cobalt blue T-shirt dress. Cressida knew that nipples showing through made Harrison Jordan a crazy man, and it gave her pleasure to excite Harry. Besides, the vibrant blue of her dress looked great with her dark hair and the thick black cat-eye lines she gave herself around the eyes. If she wore her soft leather stilettos with straps up the calves, it would be over the top for a morning coffee date, so she just wore sandals. She also had in mind to talk with that *minister* Hobart Wilson, who would always be Peedad to her.

Chapter Six

Confession

Table 86 – *"At the risk of seeming ridiculous, let me say that the true revolutionary is guided by a great feeling of love." Che quote etched with a jackknife at the center of the table.*

Hobart Sherwood Wilson, the Reverend, was anxious about his pot habit. He knew it was a habit, and he knew it in spite of what 'everyone knows' about pot not being addictive. Hobart smoked every day, and if he didn't, his anxiety level rose to an intolerable fibrillation. Pot was the background of his life, the stage on which he acted and without it, he would be...Hobart was afraid to know.

He had been smoking pot since seventh grade and on a daily basis since midway through high school. Occasionally, he would get drunk or play around with more intense drugs, but marijuana was his go-to for self-medication. It was great. He loved it. Hobart loved everything about it except the nagging suspicion that underneath every toke, there was an enormous landfill of buried fears, sores, and wounds. He was afraid that one day, it would just blow. His head would separate from his neck with a ragged tear of the skin, blood spurting out in rhythmic jets to the beat of his heart, and his face, frozen in wide-eyed surprise, would become a rocket racing across the sky. Then, *blam!* His stomach would blow and, out through the gory hole of meaty tissue, a pressurized stream of shit would discolor the world all around with a stench evoking universal gags and retching.

In the meantime, he was cool.

A mellow little edge during the day and a deep cushion of smooth when evening came. "All shall be well," as the mystic Dame Julian of Norwich had written, "and all manner of thing shall be well." Thank you, Jesus.

Cressida is smoking hot today, Hobart was thinking as he watched her enter *the spot* alongside Harrison Jordan. He retreated into writing his sermon about Jesus's friend Peter, who liked fishing a lot more than church.

From his perch in the darkened corner, Hobart could survey about eighty percent of *the spot,* which was why he liked that seat. He wished it wasn't quite so darkened and blue from the black light, but he cared more about the perspective than the light. Was it his imagination or did Cressida keep looking at him? He tried not to notice, but whether it was his imagination or not, the squirrel was loose again in his stomach.

Now it looked like she was walking toward him. She was! She was walking in an almost straight line in and around tables directly toward him.

"What did my mother tell you?" she demanded to know from Hobart.

"Huh, whaaa? Hi, Cressida, would you like to sit down?"

Hobart's squirrel was doing the crazy dance in his stomach while the reasoned, adult, minister's voice in his head tried to gain control of the class. Belatedly, he thought to stand up and pull a chair out in a mannerly gesture. Cressida wasn't having it.

"You've been talking to my mom. I want to know what she told you."

Cressida was not thinking, and she hadn't even meant to be standing where she was standing or saying the things she was saying at that moment. But she couldn't help it. She was drunk from a cocktail of grief and fear and something else she couldn't put her finger on, even in a clearer state of mind.

Hobart hemmed and hawed within himself about whether standing or sitting was the better gesture, and unbeknownst to him, he was crouching in between. He cleared his voice and finally sat down, which he thought showed greater willingness to be vulnerable and flexible."Yes, your mom is amazing. I love talking with her," he smiled up at Cressida.

"She said she told you something about my dad, the night he disappeared, and I want to know what it is. You have no right to come into my house and talk with my mom, and..." she began to cry. Cressida had not had a blow-out cry in years, but suddenly, without warning, she was flooding *the spot* with a spectacular torrent of tears and embarrassingly loud sobs. Her feet were momentarily frozen to the sticky wooden floor in front of Hobart's table. She wanted to run, she wanted to collapse in a heap, she wanted to cover her face, she wanted to sink into his arms, she wanted to escape and did as soon as she found the release to her feet. Cressida ran toward the tunnel, knocking tables along the way, and, in a rare instant within the cavernous and oblique café, drew all attention to a single person. In the hallway, she ran head on into Bernie, who was coming out of the bathroom. They both fell backward and onto the floor from the impact.

"What the fuck?" Bernie muttered with bewildered agitation as he struggled to realize what had just happened. While he was searching for understanding, Cressida was already up and disappeared into the bathroom. Bernie shook his head, and as he pushed himself up from all fours limbs, he saw a single sandal left in the hall. *I'm not looking for that Cinderella,* Bernie thought to himself.

Meanwhile, back in the dark corner, Hobart sat rattled and stunned. Harrison Jordan ran to see what was wrong, and not far behind, but ambling more than running, Google and Enid approached.

"What happened, Peedad? What's going on?" Harrison's face was contorted.

"I don't know, honestly. I mean, I just, she wanted to know something about Mimi, but we didn't really have a chance to talk when she kind of just exploded with tears. I'm sure, knowing Cressida, she is embarrassed, but clearly, those tears have been building."

"Gosh, I didn't know you knew Cressida so well," Harry's voice dripped with sarcasm.

"Well, okay, I don't know Cressida *so well,* but you know, we were all in school together, weren't we? And we all think we know one another, don't we?" Hobart returned snide for sarcasm. Then, added with a softer voice, "I just never saw Cressida cry like that."

"Yeah, well, her mom is dying so I guess she has an excuse."

Harrison's bitterness had not abated. He turned and went toward the tunnel, passing without a word between Google and Enid, who stopped in their tracks and looked quizzically at Hobart, whom they did not know.

"You'll have to ask him," Hobart smiled and went back to the sermon.

The Tunnel – *wall sconces with flame-shaped fifteen-watt bulbs line both sides of the block box hallway.*

Harry waited in the hall across from the women's bathroom playing on his phone. He leaned against the wall, but after about five minutes, slid down and sat with his back against the wall and legs folded. Harry scrolled through his Facebook page for anything interesting and found nothing to keep his attention. He tweeted, "the floor is not the spot to sit at *the spot,* covered as it is, with spots and spots of ick"

The phone glowed in the darkened hall and its light was tinted by the colors of what he saw in the monitor. This caused Harry to think that everything he saw, he was seeing through the lens of his phone. Not literally, of course, but he tried to imagine anything he looked at that he did not see through a lens tinted by previous experiences or assumptions given to him by others. The thought startled him. Everything he looked at in his phone was from someone else's eyes, and their eyes were giving him a view of what they wanted him to see. Then, he looked up and around from where he was sitting. He looked down toward the darkest end of the hall where doors exited into unknown regions of *the spot* where people worked. Then, he looked back toward the other end where the hallway opened into the cavern of tables and chairs. Bluish-gray light flowed toward him from that direction and it formed halos around the silhouette at the tables. His view was severely limited by the hallway-size lens.

What if this was all he knew of the world? What if the only thing he could ever know was what he saw from this angle in this spot at *the spot? But that is all I could know*, he thought to himself. *Wherever we are, we are that limited all the time*, he reasoned. *But we think we see everything, and we imagine we see everything as it is.* He muttered this to himself, almost out loud. *But we don't.* He answered his own thought. *Everything is filtered through the limits of our own perspective. How can I open my perspective so it's a wide-angle lens?* That was his last thought before he was distracted by the sound of the lock on the women's bathroom clicking.

Harrison stood up quickly. Cressida's face was red and streaked, and her eyes locked onto his when she saw him standing there. It was immediately clear to Harrison that he was supposed to put his arm around her and take her out of there. He did. They walked briskly through the maze of disordered tables and chairs to the exit onto the brick street. They left largely unnoticed, as the elastic anonymity of the café had quickly returned into place.

Table 86 – *six wooden captain's chairs without padding that do not match the table surround the dinette.*

Hobart studied them. He noted Harry's arm around her shoulder and Cressida's slight slump forward. Loneliness stabbed at him, once, then twice, and a third time.

"Peter simply disappeared, it says." he typed it without looking down. "Peter left with his wife, and then we don't hear anything else about him. That's it. 'He left with his wife. There is a legend that Peter was crucified upside down in Rome, but no one really knows what happened to Peter – or his wife. All we really know is that soon after a meeting of the church in Jerusalem, one of the first for that earliest generation of followers that survived Jesus and were organizing it in a way they thought Jesus might have approved of, there was a massive argument. Jesus's brother James took over, and Peter left afterward with his wife. It doesn't say where he went; he just left. I bet he went back to fishing and said to himself, 'enough of this.'" Hobart stopped fingering his keyboard.

Hobart liked the idea of fishing more than he liked fishing. Hobart liked the idea of church more than he liked church. Hobart liked preaching, though. Even so, he felt awkward about it because he knew ninety-nine percent of the people in his church were older than him and didn't think they had anything to learn from him. Hobart thought that, too, sometimes, but he could also get puffed up. He had a Master's degree, after all. He had done the work, and he had studied Greek and Hebrew, and poured over arcane passages that had nothing to do with anything anymore, just so he could say he had read them. But he didn't know about being married, and he didn't know about having kids, and he didn't know about being ill. There was a ton of life the people looking up at him in the pulpit knew about that he didn't, and that kept him humble – almost.

Suddenly, Hobart just wanted to talk with Cressida. That was the only thing he wanted to do. In lieu of that, he thought about going to see Mimi, but maybe he shouldn't until after he had a chance to talk with Cressida again. But what could he say to Cressida? She would probably just yell at him again.

He could not tell her anything about what Mimi had told him. He could not tell anyone. It was the first confession he had ever heard and he wasn't allowed to tell a single soul. In fact, according to the rules of Confession, once a Penitent has confessed and been absolved, neither Confessor nor Penitent can ever discuss it again. Because the sin was absolved, left as a mineral in the bedrock of history, never to be ruminated over again, it was a dead subject that could not be mentioned. There was absolutely nothing that Hobart could tell Cressida about the conversation he had had with her mother, and that caused an ache in his stomach.

Strange, he thought, that some emotions can cause ache while other feelings burn. Then, there were still others emotions that were downright tremulous, and some that were swaddling.

Taste has salt, sour, bitter, and sweet. He conjured them with his eyes closed and chin resting between his hands. But emotions, he reckoned, sing or stroke the lining of tissues inside the body. *Cressida is salty and sweet.* The thought surprised him and he left it as soon as it appeared. Mimi was his concern, not her daughter. Not only was Mimi's his first Confession, she was his first true pastoral relationship.

No one else had embraced Hobart as a minister, or for that matter, as an adult. He was either "that kid who grew up around here," "the guy I went to school with," or "that nice young man learning how to be a minister." But Mimi had accepted him as both an adult and a minister. Hobart knew it was just Mimi's nature to accept people, so it was nothing he could feel proud about, but it still felt good, even though it was also shadowed by death.

Hobart felt like a fraud half of the time with Mimi, because truth be told, he wasn't sure he was an adult yet. And a minister? He wondered if he would ever feel like one of those. But Mimi's embrace of who he was trying to be made it real for him. Mimi's acceptance was a warm towel on the face of his every anxiety, and he loved to be with her, even if she was dying. She made him feel successful as a minister, mature as an adult, and sometimes, he even felt as if returning to his hometown to begin his career wasn't a mistake after all.

Lake Park – *small grassy knoll overlooking the lake with scattered benches at the edge on a concrete pad lining a massive break wall of Volkswagen Beetle size boulders.*

Cressida was livid and scared. What had her mom told HO-bart Wilson, and why him?

After the funeral, she was going to leave town. For good! No one around here knew her. They took her for a fool and a slut. *You can never escape high school,* she thought to herself. *They should tell you that in eighth grade,* she concluded.

Harrison was a love, but he would be gone one day. She knew their friendship had a limit and she was good with it. Cressida was nothing if not adaptable. The lesson of dinosaurs and other extinct creatures that couldn't adapt to changing environments had not been lost on her. Dinosaurs had been an obsession of hers as a child, and as much as she cherished knowing all their names and being able to tell adults which ones lived in which epoch, she had always been captivated by their disappearance. That led to concept the of extinction generally, which was filled with a child's attraction-repulsion to death. How could it be that an entire species disappeared into rock? Just gone. The Dodo Bird, too. Extinction fascinated Cressida, and she took from it the lesson of adaptability and embraced it with as much passion as she felt for all things she cared about.

It was getting to be time for her to adapt to a new life, and to a new home. She would have done it anyway, even if her mom hadn't gotten sick. She could feel the pull of childhood's gravity on her ankles, and being around so many people that knew her 'back when' kept her from flying. Cressida was a creature that needed to fly.

Cressida and Harrison sat quietly on the bench like an old couple who know each other's thoughts without speaking them. It was a favorite of theirs, the third bench on the eastern side of Lake Park facing the water. Gulls screeched and picked at the garbage on concrete as happily as the dead fish floating on the surface of the lake. Cormorants dive-bombed the water with an angry splash and came up elsewhere a few minutes later. Most of the people migrated to the western side of the park where the concessions were, leaving the eastern side for large groups of hipsters playing hacky sack, or the adventurous ones learning to rope walk or juggle. It was also where the homeless slept during the day when it was warm and sunny.

That afternoon was a stunning, early autumn day; the sun still felt like summer but the leaves were just beginning to hint at the coming change. The blue of the sky went deep into the water.

Cressida gave Harrison props for being able to just be together without talking. She didn't want to talk. Her thoughts were too jumbled and complicated and she didn't want to say something stupid or something she would would regret later.

"What's the deal with you and Peedad?" Harrison finally broke the silence. Silence was Cressida's response. "Okay, just thought I'd ask."

"He's talking to my mom," she said it so quietly he had to tilt his ear toward her to hear. "HO-bart is being Mom's minister, and she's talking to him about stuff she's never talked to me about, and it pisses me off. She told him something about the night my dad disappeared, and I wanted him to tell me what it was."

"He can't do that," Harrison objected.

"I know he can't," she snapped. "Still, it pisses me off."

"Hmmm, now I see why he said that," Harrison said to himself more than to Cressida.

"Said what?"

"Well, after you ran into the bathroom, I didn't know what had happened and was worried about you. So, I asked him what happened. I may have been a little snippy because, after all, it was Peedad. And he got snotty back, and then he said something about how we all *think* we know each other just because we went to high school together – but he said it like it was one of those obvious 'truths' that are false."

It was quiet again. Then, Harrison asked Cressida, "Why do you think we all find it so annoying that Peedad is back here, and that he's a minister?"

Cressida turned to look at Harrison as if he were crazy for asking such a stupid question. "Really?"

"Really what?"

"The dude's a total stoner, has been since junior high. All through high school, he sat in the back of the class, hovered around the edges of the crowd, didn't really participate in anything, and then he comes back as a *minister*? God? Really? And he's still a stoner! What the fuck does Peedad know about God shit and, I mean, really, who do you know that goes to church anyway?"

"Yeah, I guess that's right. The whole stoner thing is weird next to the religion thing, and it doesn't make any sense. Because it's *Peedad,* it makes even less sense. Sometimes, things we don't understand piss us off."

"What are you trying to say, that I'm pissed off about Peedad and my mom because I don't understand it? Fuck you."

"No, I didn't mean anything about you. I was just saying that maybe that's why Peedad being a minister is so annoying, because it agitates us that we we don't understand. *You're* the one that leaped to another conclusion."

Cressida steamed, jumped up, and started walking fast along the lake. Harrison took a deep breath and followed her.

"Cressida, come on, slow down."

"Fuck you, fuck you, fuck you! I don't need you to analyze me, goddamn it!" she yelled over her shoulder without slowing down. Then, she stopped and turned. Harrison stopped immediately and kept six feet between them. "I understand stupid stoner Peedad; it's my mom that doesn't and it makes me want to scream." Off she went again.

Harrison let her go and walked at his normal pace, knowing that when her sails were full like that, there was no point in trying to ride with her. And anyway, she didn't really need him now. No matter what anyone thought about Cressida, she could take care of herself and had been for a very long time.

Chapter Seven

Shit Happens...for a Reason

Table 27 – *high back patio chairs with woven plastic webbing tightly bound to metallic frames matching the patio table.*

Google is a very strange dude, Harrison thought to himself as he leaned on the table with his chin cupped in his hands, his elbows the pillars holding the weight of his head and thoughts. What was he to make of his friend who read endlessly, topic after topic, on Wikipedia? Google's goal was to be the first person to read the entire online encyclopedia, never mind that it was a Sisyphean task because Wikipedia was endlessly edited. But there he sat, day in and day out, reading with Enid by his side.

Google was six feet six inches tall when he stood, and shaped like a peanut. He had bulbous shoulders that slid downhill toward a thinner waist, though he had a little spare tire that rimmed his belt, and after that, he ballooned outward again at the hips and ass. His rear end flared with an enormous spread, which meant he had to buy pants that were too baggy at the waist and usually, given his height, too short at the ankle.

Google also spoke Bro, sort of. While never tested for it, Google was likely on the very high functioning end of the autism spectrum and so his Bro dialect was slightly stilted and without the flow-someness of a real Bro. But, as in all Brospeak, Bronouns replaced pronouns, vagueness was better than being specific, and the subject of a sentence becomes a barject - which meant that partying or clubbing was the universal metaphor.

"This chick's hanging at the place with the red sign for green, soaring on fumes 'til her daddy takes her home," would be one way for Google to say, "Enid is at Walgreen's buying some perfume and waiting for me to pick her up."

It took Harrison Jordan most of their first semester as suitemates to decipher Google's lexicon, but now he translated freely as Google speaks. He had, on occasion, also interpreted Google to the world around him.

Then again, Google could easily slip into normal conversation without warning, and seemingly without cause. At that moment, he was wandering in and out of Brospeak.

"Woodpecker man is harshing down the paper thing but getting no traction. He is running out of time."

"Dude, what are you talking about?" Harrison asked in mock disbelief.

"The Bernie-man is ticking down on his party-time and there ain't no afterparty with that gig."

"Whoa, wait a minute," now Harrison was truly lost. "Who is Bernie-man and what is his party gig?"

"He's talking about Bernie Weinberg, the woodpecker guy from the college," Enid translated. "He's been working on his Ph.D. dissertation for almost eight years, and if he doesn't get it finished in the next few weeks, he will run out of time."

"Ouch. Don't know him, but having invested all that time and coming up short would be a disaster, wouldn't it?" Harrison said with earnest compassion.

"Dude would be ouching, alright, in a rave without a partner and trampled by the crowd."

"He's got the Nester, so maybe he wouldn't be alone. But then I wonder if she would stick with him if he does bottom out. She's working on her doctorate in bird stuff so that would be weird." Enid's voice was as dry as a creek bed at the height of summer, matter-of-fact as it always was.

"Nester?" Harrison asked, "Wilma Nester?"

"That chick has stars," Google said with widening eyes.

"I know her," Harrison quipped, "sort of. I mean, I met her, but I don't know her. You're right, she is hot."

Just then, Bernie and Wilma walked through the glass doors and stopped, looking for where they would put their briefcases and sling bags down. Enid and Google waved, and they waved back. The odd couple picked out a square table and set their bags down, got out their computers, hung jackets over chairs, and generally made a nest for themselves to settle into. Then, they went to the oval coffee island and ordered drinks.

On their way back, mugs filled with dark, steaming liquid in hand, they stopped by to greet Google and Enid.

"Hey, the Google, how you hanging?" Bernie said lightly.

"Hi guys," Wilma chirped.

"The Bern and Nester, what's going on?"

"Hi," said Enid.

"Hey," Harrison nodded to Wilma.

"Hi, how are you Harrison?" she smiled.

"Sun's shining, I'm good!" Harrison grinned.

"Hi, I'm Bernie," he said to Harrison.

"Hey, Harrison Jordan."

"Well, see you guys, it's crunch time for us right now," Bernie said with a grim look on his face. A chorus of "hey ho's" and "see ya's" arose as Bernie and Wilma headed for their table and Google and Enid went back to reading. Harrison found himself watching Wilma.

Was it the way she dressed or just her? he wondered. It wasn't the kind of clothes she wore, he wasn't even sure what her style would be called. But she was always adorned in the perfect combination of colors. It was her colors that were always just right in combination but also with her dark red hair and slightly olive skin.

What is the source of attraction? Harry wanted to know. They say women are more attracted to a man's face than men to a woman's face, but Harrison was always drawn first to a woman's face even before he noticed anything else about her. Wilma's face was long without being too thin, and her eyes large round jewels of liquid light. Sometimes, she wore glasses that were also perfect, like those she was wearing then: electric blue frames that made the green in her eyes shine brilliantly. Harrison could feel a watermill churning in his stomach, down low near his pelvis.

"Did you know that in spring, woodpeckers find the loudest thing they can to beat on as a way to call for a mate?" Google said without looking up from the Wikipedia page he was reading on his tablet. "If you hear Woody banging loud on a gutter in April, he's rocking a love song, offering drinks and a red one to any date that'll listen."

"You helping Bernie with his dissertation?" Harrison wanted to know.

"Na, just reading the matrix, bra, keeping an eye out for a glitch."

"So, Enid, what's a woman look for in a man?" Harrison was an earnest puppy looking for a treat.

Enid looked up slowly from her iPad-mini, rolled her eyeballs slowly to the corner of her eyes where she might have been able to peek at Google from the edge of her peripheral vision, then, more slowly looked at Harrison with a stare so blank she could have been in a coma. Enid was so droll, it could take a week for the humor of one of her comments to catch up with you.

"I am not qualified to answer that question." Somehow, the words escaped without her rubber-band-thin lips moving and her half-closed eyes never leaving the stare she had cast his way. "Clearly, I did not look before I leapt."

"Where did you leap, boo?" Google asked without looking up from his screen, and Enid's eyes slowly rolled as her lips cracked the border of her cheek with a subtle leftward lean as if to say, "See what I mean."

"Well, where did you meet Google, you know, like where did you start hanging out?"

"In the dark," she smirked. "It was Occupy Wall Street and it got cold and someone pointed me to a tent where I could get warm. I unzipped it and got inside where he was sleeping. After a little bit, he thought I was someone else and put his hand up my shirt. It was warm, and honestly, I kind of liked the way he touched me, so I didn't say anything." Enid chuckled ever so slightly, "Then, he started feeling around for more than was there. He sat straight up, fumbled for his phone, and turned the flashlight on. 'Hi,' I said, with him looking down at me. 'Hey boo,' he said, squiggling his face up, wondering if we had ever met before. Then, we fucked and that was it."

"Whoa, that is the most unromantic story I have ever heard in my life," Harrison slumped dramatically in his chair.

"No accidents, Bra. Everything for a reason in the Earth-zone." Google declared without ever looking away from the screen.

"That's bullshit, you know," Harrison shot back.

Google lowered his glasses and looked down his nose in a scholarly way toward Harrison as Enid looked up with slightly perceptible lines of surprise on her face.

"Don't harsh the mellow, dude. Like, it's just an expression."

"Yeah, but don't you get sick of that superstitious bullshit? I mean, like, people say it so much, they must believe it's true when it isn't."

"No man, 'everything happens for a reason' is like, well, a gap-filler. But maybe it's true, you never know."

"Yeah, we know, everything doesn't happen for a reason. There is randomness, that's a fact. Shit happens and sometimes, there is no reason for it other than shit happens."

"Whoa dude, that's dark night of the soul stuff right there. You gotta be careful, 'cause the universe brings you what you ask for, man."

"See, now, that's bullshit too. You don't really believe that, Google. Do you really think that if you ask the 'universe' for something, it will come your way? What's the universe, a giant algorithm searching our desires in order to give us a cupcake and happy ending? Come on."

Enid looked at Google, then at Harrison, then with another owlish pivot of the head, she looked back to Google. She stared at Google, her big eyes magnified even larger by her glasses.

"No man, like that's just what people say, 'you get what you ask for, and you see what you're looking for.' I guess I think that if we want certain stuff, we have to put it out there for the universe to know we want it, and then maybe we will get it someday."

"Oh, like Christmas? You hint to your mom and dad what you hope you'll get for Christmas and then anticipate unwrapping it under the tree? There's a cosmic mommy and daddy out there, is there?"

"No, man, you make it sound stupid when you say it that way but it's not so weird. I mean, shit does happen and sometimes, it's good shit and sometimes, it's bad shit, and sometimes, the shit happens for a reason. That's all."

Google sounded unusually hesitant for a fact-reading machine. They had strayed into unfamiliar territory, far away from the factoids of Wikipedia and onto the soft moor of speculation where Harrison had the upper hand.

"This is the problem," Harrison complained. "People say shit like that and they don't really mean it, not literally anyway. But then scratch the surface and they do. 'Everything happens for a reason' fills the gaps in our ignorance, but it fills them with shit. It's like God. For centuries, religious people used God as the answer for all the things they didn't know or understand but, as science has answered more and more questions, God has gotten smaller and smaller. It matters what we think, Google, because what we think shapes what we do and how we act."

"Harry-man, how you know everything doesn't happen for a reason?"

"Oh, I dunno, maybe I can't imagine a good reason that Cressida's mom is dying of cancer while Dick Cheney isn't?"

"We don't know everything, man, I mean, maybe Dick Cheney is suffering righteous woe right now and the longer he lives, the more he suffers. And maybe Mimi is being saved from a fate worse than death. What about that? We don't know."

"Really? You're making shit up now. What is the reason that the three of us get to be hanging out, drinking four dollar drinks at *the spot*, enjoying the day and each other in a nice safe place, while millions – millions – are starving, getting raped, and murdered in South Sudan, Syria, Yemen, and Nigeria? Is there a reason we've been saved in order to enjoy a cappuccino?"

"Man, you're so harsh. No one knows the answer to that 'why.' It's just a lot better to think things happen for a reason than swim with eels in the dark waters you're talking about, dude."

"See, that's what I'm talking about! You're just filling the gap because you don't like the way ignorance feels. I say it's better to live with brutal honesty about our ignorance than it is to pretend and live in make-believe. When we wrap ourselves in 'pretend', we stop looking and we miss seeing stuff when it happens. Better to be awake and alert to truth coming our way than blinded by a cocoon."

"Sheesh." Google looked at Harrison with rare speechlessness.

"The Harry has a point," Enid said as if reading a recipe out loud. "We're together because of an accident more than a reason. I probably went in the wrong tent, you thought I was someone else, and we found each other by random happenstance – not for a reason."

"You too?" Google complained. "Maybe we were meant to be, what about that? Maybe that was how the universe was bringing us together and it couldn't find any other way? What about that?"

Enid looked at Harrison to see which of them was going to answer first. Harrison piped up, "I see, God created 'Occupy Wall Street' to bring the two of you together?"

"No, man, not like that," Google whined, "it wasn't *God* and 'Occupy' didn't happen for us, but it was the source of chaos that brought order to our world. It was meant to be, that's all."

"What about the bread? I don't bake bread." Enid stepped on Google like a bug.

"There's still time to learn," he said, raising one eyebrow and smiling.

"G-man," Harrison steadied his gaze at Google but softened his posture and voice at the same time, "what's the reason you became bipolar and someone like, I dunno, like Bernie Weinberg or even me, didn't? Why you, man, you are one of the 'greats' and yet here you are, living on SSI? What's the reason for that, man?"

Enid's face suddenly softened into an expression of deep concern, and she moved her hand slowly across several inches of space to touch Google's hand on the table with just her pinky and the outside fleshy edge of here hand.

"Let's see, what's the reason I get an SSI check every month and you work at that shithole bookstore? God loves me more?" Google said it without a smile, without a bro-brogue, and with shark eyes leveled at Harrison's. "Fuck you, Harry, you'd kill your mother to win an argument."

"No wait, I didn't mean anything bad, Carl, I'm just saying, if there's a reason for everything, what is the reason for suffering and shit happening that's not fair? Why can't random shit just be random instead of making up an order and explanation that doesn't really exist?"

Google and Enid were looking at him with daggers surrounded by frozen silence. They said nothing. Suddenly, there was an impenetrable see-through wall between his side of the table and theirs, and Harrison knew it wasn't coming down any time soon. He had unintentionally pressed the wrong button with Google before, and there was no use trying to dial it back.

"More coffee," Harrison mumbled as he kicked his chair back and headed for the bar. "I'm sorry man, I didn't mean to hurt you," he turned back to say before walking on.

Tables 84 and 86 – *84 small, round rod iron bar height patio table with two matching rod iron swivel chairs, additional graffiti carved into 86 reads, "I love you, Raiza."*

It was just that kind of a day, bone on bone without cartilage, and things hurt. Harrison had finished a short shift at the bookstore and returned to *the spot* to see who was still there, but none of his posse was anywhere to be seen. The café was crowded with the after-work crowd slumping into the evening. Harrison was also slumping a couple tables away from Hobart in the dark corner, thinking about how people create a fluffy mental nest for themselves and use it to explain away pain and pretend all the dangers that lurked around them were actually far away.

While he was still pondering how fragile people can become when their nest is challenged, his attention was drawn to the entrance when Wilma burst through the double glass door, with Bernie in hot pursuit making excuses for something. Harry couldn't actually hear what was going on from across the vast expanse of *the spot,* but he could see that Wilma was pissed off and Bernie, riddled with anxiety, was desperately trying to reel her back.

Harrison was uncomfortable with the spike of excitement he felt at the prospect of a fracture between two people he hardly knew. His feelings were ugly and cruel, and having just hurt one of his best friends, these sinister urges caused him more than a little remorse. Even so, the angel of his better nature was unable to suppress the darker one.

Harrison slid, in a single liquid motion, over two tables and lithely insinuated himself into a chair at Hobart's table. Hobart looked up from his computer with a bluish glow on this face.

"Peedad, I mean, Hobart," Harrison began.

"Thank you." Hobart inserted.

"I pissed off my friend, Google, er, Carl is his real name, and I'm trying to figure out what it was I did." Harrison explained in detail the conversation they were having and how he had meant to take It to a more personal level so that Google could see how 'everything happens for a reason' didn't really make sense, and that it wasn't something people who saidy it really believe anyway. Harrison wanted Hobart's opinion about why that conversation turned out so crinkly.

"Because you challenged his reality. If you want to agitate someone, poke at the frame they have constructed to explain the world and their own life. And by the way, if it is someone with a mental health problem already, challenging their sense of reality will produce an especially intense reaction."

"But peeling back the layers of the onion is what it's all about! If we can't do that, then what's the point of being able to think?"

"That is your frame. What if I were to say to you that everything we need to know in order to have a good life is found in the Bible?"

"Oh man, you're not one of those, are you?"

"No, but what if I was? How would you feel about it?"

"Yeah, okay, I would get agitated real quick."

"Exactly, because it challenges your reality. That is what you just did to Google, and because he is bipolar and on SSI, when he would rather be living the life he had once imagined for himself, you pushing him like that just to prove your point was actually pretty brutal."

"But people shouldn't walk around shrouded in fantasy, either. 'Friends don't let friends be blind.' Right?"

"Well, you can push someone into a pool fully dressed when they don't want to swim, or you can walk in the rain together and both get wet. Which is more collegial? Even though you think someone needs to interpret life differently because what they believe is clearly fictitious, that doesn't mean they need to change - or that it is a good time for them go down that road. It takes both courage and support to dismantle a worldview, and having it ripped away from you is just plain traumatic."

Harrison was quiet for a while. He sat there, leaning back on two legs of the chair with his fingers laced behind his head as he thought about what Hobart had said. Hobart went back to pecking at his keyboard. The two of them occupied the same space without talking and it suddenly struck Harry how easy it was to sit in silence with Hobart. It was actually easy not to talk. He mused that such moments of peaceful quiet required a special comfort level between two people and that made Harrison wonder how that comfort came to be with Hobart – *Peedad* after all.

Table 12 and 14 – *napkins and matchbooks wedged under 12's pedestal feet do not solve its lopsidedness; someone has booby-trapped the salt shaker lid on 14 to fall off when used.*

Wilma and Bernie were sitting two tables apart. Wilma's back was to Bernie and Bernie was leaning face down into his folded arms. Wilma was shaken and didn't know what to do.

Bernie's tendency to be tardy had devolved into absence. For the fourth time, he hadn't shown up for a date or meeting they were supposed to have, and Wilma was not used to being neglected. She had been frozen between worry about Bernie and self-pity for the hurt and inconvenience it caused her. Now, she was just angry.

"I'm soooo sorry," Bernie whined across the distance. "I'll never screw up again, I promise."

Wilma had heard it too many times already and didn't feel it deserved a response.

"Come on, Wilma, give me another chance, it's just been so stressful, I'm not usually like this," It was more whining followed by more silence.

Whatever he said or pleaded landed in an ice-cold pit between her heart and stomach. She wasn't going to fall for it anymore because she now believed that something was terribly wrong with Bernie, but he wasn't telling her what. At the bottom of the pit, she still had the warmth of concern for him, but she wasn't going to allow him to take her on this rollercoaster again unless he opened up about what was really going on.

Wilma stood up and turned toward the door. "Don't follow me anymore," she said, looking down at him through fierce green eyes. Off she walked, briskly and erect.

"See ya," Harrison said to Hobart as he nonchalantly followed Wilma out the door, keeping a respectable distance so that no one would have noticed.

Bernie collapsed again with his face on the table. Hobart watched from his corner and wondered if he should offer Bernie an ear even though he didn't know the man. He decided not to and went back to working on a sermon.

Chapter Eight

Dark Hole

Bernie's Apartment – *studio above a convenience store near the university, one bare light bulb without a lampshade burning over the kitchen sink.*

Bernie knew he was in a bad way. He had not done more than change a word or two of grammar on his dissertation in over a month. He had exactly three weeks until the Thanksgiving break to schedule his defense before the end of the year, and in the meantime, he had to address a significant controversy in his research data. It was an arcane debate about his woodpecker's incredibly long tongue, which some creationist had begun erroneously touting as an example of something that could not have been an adaptation over time and so an argument against Natural Selection. Bernie had all the information he needed but he could not make himself write it.

Bernie could hardly make himself do anything anymore. He had been drinking too much – for a long time. He was good at hiding it. He drank alone at night, and if he weren't going to be by himself, he would drink for hours before he met Wilma or his Department colleagues. If he was heading into a social situation where alcohol would be served, he made sure to have several drinks before he got there, guzzle his first drink when he arrived, and then slowly nurse one throughout the night so as not to arouse suspicion.

Dating Wilma had made things more difficult because he saw her in the evenings, and that meant he needed to drink earlier before they were together. Too often, though, he drank himself to sleep and didn't wake up until after he was supposed to meet her. But, he comforted himself, falling asleep only started happening after he began taking Vicodin. If he stopped with the pills, then he could minimize the hazard, he told himself. Still, he didn't stop with the pills. Just the opposite. Bernie began taking just one little five-milligram pill, but had worked his way up to two forty-milligram yellow ones. Some days, he felt like a puddle on the floor and wanted nothing more than to remain melted at home. Other days, his guts felt so tightly strung that even taking a step made him quiver from chin to his toes. Sometimes, he ducked at movements he spied from the corner of his eye that turned out to be his imagination. At other times, he thought he heard strangers whisper about him. He chocked it up to dissertation stress and knew that as soon as he was awarded his Ph.D., all this silliness and agony would be behind him.

The truth was that Bernie had been crawling down this narrowing tunnel for some time, and now, the scent of moist soil and exposed roots spiraled closer and closer to his face. He was afraid to keep going and yet, he could not stop.

Harrison's Apartment – *above the garage behind a suburban ranch on an acre and a half of wooded and mown lawn, behind the tall fence surrounding the pool house.*

Wilma stifled a giggle knowing that at such moments, even the slightest titter could convey unintended humiliation.

She had never seen pubic hair shaved before. Harrison had carefully removed all vestiges of hair within six inches of his genitals in an oval pattern, the shape of an eye, but the rest of his body was covered by a fairway of fluff. She stifled another giggle when his uncircumcised penis rose on cue as she unhooked her bra and released her ample breasts into the cool air. Harry's penis hardened forward and angled severely to the left. It was as if it was pointing to someone behind her, and that struck Wilma as comical even as the waves in her tummy moved her to want to wrap her fingers around it. Harrison was quite large, and the thought of him entering her sent a shot of fear mixed with excitement through her body.

Harrison's exposed penis hardened in the cold room as Wilma undressed her breasts. They were a pinkish-tan color, a pleasing complement with the color of her hair. Two dark nipples puckered at him in the chill as he felt locked between two competing urges, to gaze on her beauty and to consume her. A slight moment of stillness held between them, Harry fully naked and Wilma with only a thong remaining, and then the explosion.

Harrison's garage loft was a large studio strewn with clothes, trash, and food debris, but neither Wilma or Harrison were aware of anything but each other. The frenzied tonguing, groping, and restless touching formed a four-armed, two-headed body entwined. They dove as a mass upon the unmade bed where they sucked and licked and ate each other with voracious hunger. After fifteen minutes of eternity, it was over, both cumming at precisely the same moment. Wilma exhaled a slight squeal of delight and Harrison smiled proudly as they both relaxed into one another.

What will Bernie say? Wilma shuddered to herself. *Fuck Bernie*, another voice within her barked. She was so angry with Bernie for standing her up time and again, but she also knew in her heart, she was really just deeply disappointed in him. She was worried about Bernie, also. Something wasn't right, yet she couldn't figure out what, because Bernie was both clever and closed off. He was keeping something from her and all she could see was the behavior it spawned, which had been driving her away. Bernie, and Bernie's problems, raced through her thoughts as she felt the weight of Harrison's head press upon her chest and heard his breathing became slow and snuffled.

In the fading light, Wilma looked around Harrison's apartment for the first time. It could have been nice. It was only one large room with the kitchen stretching across one of the short walls, an island sink and counter with black leather bar-height stools. At the other end was the door to the bathroom and a tiny alcove where the exit led to outdoor wooden stairs descending to the driveway. The rest of the room was large enough for a couch and TV/gaming station near the kitchen, along with the double bed at the bathroom end. Harrison was a pig. She suddenly became aware that the sheets looked like they had not been washed in months, and it made her want to shower. She looked at the open bathroom door and was sickened at the thought of what grew in the shower. She liked Harry, quite a lot, she thought to herself, but this would never do. *He'll have to change.*

710 N. Dill – *magenta door with two brass bolt locks and a lion's head brass knocker.*

Hobart knocked quietly at first, but after no one answered, he flapped the brass knocker hard against the strike plate. He heard footsteps falling in rapid succession as they arrived on the other side of the door.

When it opened, his stomach jumped as Ruth, Cressida, stood like a wall in front of him.

"What do *you* want?

"Hi, nice to see you, too. I'm here to visit your mom."

Cressida was already frowning, but now, she grimaced. Hobart caught himself smiling at her scowling face and instinctively wiped it away, knowing nothing made a frown angrier than a smile.

"Ruth?" He paused.

"Cressida." She frowned.

"Sorry. Cress...Cressy?"

Bigger frown.

"Cressida, I'm not sure why you don't want me visiting your mom, but we have great conversations together. You're welcome to join us, really, I think it would be good if you did."

"Fat chance."

"You know, your mom needs more than you. Since she is able to go out less and less, she needs to have other people in her life. You can't be everything for her, even though you are everything to her."

Cressida turned her back to him and walked into the house, leaving the door open. Hobart tentatively poked his head inside to see where she had gone and decided it was okay to enter. He closed the door behind him, took off his shoes, and left them on the entrance rug. The cool of the floor bled through his socks as he walked toward the dining room where Mimi's hospital bed was now the focal point.

"Hey, Mimi," Hobart smiled broadly as he walked in. Light streamed in from windows lining the opposite walls and warmed Mimi, who was sitting up reading.

"Oh, Hobart, thank you for coming," she smiled back. "You know, Hobart, you can come on Monday, Wednesday, Thursday, or Friday, too."

Hobart blushed as he realized it was obvious she was on his Tuesday rotation of visits. *Note to self*, Hobart thought, *change up the routine*. "I don't want you to get sick of me."

"Seriously, could you come more often, if just for a little while?"

Mimi's voice was plaintive and serious at the same time. Even if he didn't want to visit her more often, he could not have said no to that voice. But he was happy to see her more, and Cressida, too. A caustic wind of guilt blew in and scorched his heart as he realized his complicated feelings about Cressida were mingled with his professional duty to Mimi, who herself had become a relationship far deeper than the rigid boundaries he was supposed to keep with parishioners.

Some people were more pleasant to visit than others. The irony of this situation was new to Hobart. There was no denying he felt more enjoyment visiting someone like Mimi, even though she was dying, than someone like old widowed Mrs. Pinster who might live forever. Pinster was a widow of forty years who regaled Hobart with the same crowded litany of complaints on every visit as he drank tea in her eighty-four-degree living room, squeezed into uncomfortable antique furniture, and desperately fought the urge to fall asleep. Mimi, however, was dying, but rarely had a complaint. Instead, they talked about life.

"Hobart, could we have Communion today?"

"Where two or three are gathered together..." Hobart smiled.

"Oh, what a good idea. Ruthie? Ruthie, can you come in for a moment?"

Cressida appeared at the doorway between the kitchen and dining room, a skeptical and worried look creasing her eyebrows and slanting her lips.

"Honey, we're going to have Communion. Can you get us a small glass of wine and a Ritz cracker – is a cracker okay?"

"Sure," Hobart assured.

"And you know, Ruthie, Communion is better if there are three than two. Will you sit here with me?" She patted the bed and smiled up at her daughter.

Cressida's eyes widened. Something other than anger appeared on her face, a slight tinge of pink that revealed the surprising presence of embarrassment.

Hobart recognized it immediately, even though he would never have imagined Cressida capable of it when it came to religion. It was the unmistakable, telltale sign of guilt.

Ministers had to get used to evoking the stale voice of parental guilt in people who had long since stopped going to church or caring about things religious. Waiting in a grocery checkout line, someone would explain, unsolicited, why they hadn't been coming to church lately. On an airplane, a passenger seated next to him, upon discovering he was a minister, would suddenly unveil all the reasons they stopped going to church as if he cared or his judgment mattered. Hobart saw that same glimmer of guilt flash across Cressida's face and it truly surprised him, even gnawed at him like a rat inside, because it was not what he wanted to represent to Cressida.

Cressida turned and disappeared into the kitchen without speaking, followed by sounds of cabinets opening and closing and glass clinking. Mimi looked at Hobart as if to say, *I think she's going to join us.*

"How are you feeling?" Hobart broke the pause.

"Up and down," she replied flatly.

"Any of it you want to talk about?" Hobart asked with studied nonchalance.

"You're too young to have the experience yet, but when you get older, suddenly something you used to do all the time changes. Maybe the time it used to take you to run a five-kilometer race suddenly becomes much harder or even unachievable. Or maybe you can't jump as high or run as fast on the court as you used to. You greet those moment at first with surprise, then agitation, and probably anger. Some people simply refuse to accept it and they go crazy trying to overcome the limitation. But sooner or later, the limitation wins and you accept it. Hopefully, you make peace with it. But dying is kind of different."

Mimi paused, looking past Hobart to the window outside. A chickadee alighted on the windowsill and was pecking gently at something unseen on the other side of the glass. She smiled and continued.

"Here's an example. A woman will hit menopause and feel grief that she can no longer have babies, even though she didn't want any more. But she gets over it because she knows there is more life ahead. Then, your body starts doing weird and crazy things, making you hurt here and feel lame there, gain weight you never had before or joints swell up - whatever. It is the fact that something is happening to you beyond your control that makes it so aggravating and depressing. But still, you look for what is coming because there is always something to look forward to. You keep looking ahead because you know that even though life will be different because your body or circumstances have changed, there will still be life. But when you're dying, there is no looking ahead. Now there is a wall, an end."

Suddenly, both Mimi and Hobart became aware that Cressida was standing in the threshold again, this time holding the elements for Communion. She had been listening and her face was changed, softened, even curious.

"Sit down, honey, here next to me."

Cressida put the saucer and glass on the television tray and climbed up on the hospital bed to sit at her mom's feet. She looked at her mom and at the bread and wine, but not Hobart.

"Is that scary?" Hobart asked Mimi.

"Not mostly. Sometimes. It's scary in the way that not knowing is always scary but it's more, I don't know, interesting maybe? It's funny. I am not worried about God. Ever since the night Derik 'disappeared,' I have trusted God. Isn't that funny? Even when I felt like God was far away, I still trusted God. Why do you think that is, Hobart?"

"Hmmm, I'm not sure. I suppose it is like love. Maybe you don't know exactly what love feels like, but you know instinctively when you love someone – even when you are angry as heck with him or her. The anger doesn't take away the love, at least not unless or until the anger is left to fester and poison the love. But when you have had an experience of *God*, it stays with you. You question it off and on, of course, but it can take on the shape and feel of bedrock – always there."

Cressida could feel a chunk of something melting inside. As she listened to her mom and Hobart talk, there was a shift like one season melding into the next.

"Did you hear that story about Mother Teresa?" Mimi asked Hobart.

"Yeah, unsettling and at the same time, affirming."

"What?" Cressida heard the word appear out of her mouth before she knew she was saying it.

"It seems," Hobart answered as if there were never any enmity between them, "that Mother Teresa had some kind of mystical experience with God, on a train as I recall, but I might be making that up. Whatever the experience, it convinced her that God wanted her to serve the poorest of the poor, and so she did, for the rest of her life. She went into the worst, cruelest neighborhoods of Kolkatta, India, and eventually created a worldwide ministry of care and service among the poor. When she died and her diaries were read, it was revealed that she had sought the voice of God throughout her life, including some very dark times. But she heard nothing, only that initial mystical experience that had remained with her over decades. While she wrestled with God for not being more forthcoming, she never gave up on God and never abandoned that first and long-ago revelation."

Hobart's voice was gilded with silver as he told the story. He trailed off into a peaceful quiet that rested between the three of them for several moments.

"Well, why don't we share Communion?" Hobart almost whispered into the silence.

For the first time, he noticed what Cressida had brought to them. She had used a clear glass goblet with a bluish hue and a saucer of matching glass. A dark, fruity wine filled a quarter of the glass while a small, white party napkin had been placed between the saucer and a piece of thick, grainy, whole-wheat bread from which she had cut the crust, so that it formed a perfect circle the size of a traditional host wafer. What struck Hobart was the care with which it had been prepared, another surprise from Cressida.

"Before I say the words of blessing, let's have a moment of prayer in which to offer our prayers silently or aloud. Is that okay?" He looked at Mimi, who smiled in affirmation, and then quickly looked at Cressida, whose eyes darted toward his before they both looked away.

The silence of prayer followed. At first, it was stiff and grinding for Cressida. She was an introvert, so silence didn't bother her - it was not knowing what was expected that she found jarring. Public praying was always like that. What was she supposed to say? Was she supposed to say something or could she say nothing? What if she wanted to say, *Fuck you, God?*

"Protect my Ruthie," Mimi prayed in a low, gentle voice. "Bring her the joy you brought me through her. And in the time we have left, may it go gently for us."

Cressida was crying. No noise, just a flow of tears thoroughly wetting her cheeks. Hobart marveled at the ability to cry without noise, something he longed to be able to do. He could feel himself holding back his own tears.

"Be gracious to us, O God," he said in his own voice but with the slight formality of a professional prayer. "Bring your healing presence among us, that we might know the power of your love."

There was another silence, and Cressida felt as if they were waiting for her to say something. They would wait a long time for that. She sat there holding her mom's hand and bowing her head to hide her tears.

Hobart stood up. He faced Mimi and Cressida on the other side of the television tray, picked up the saucer, and said, "On the night he died, surrounded by his friends, just as we are here at this table, Jesus took bread. He held it up and said to them, 'Take, eat, this is my body which is given for you. Eat this in remembrance of me, and live your life with me in it.'"

Hobart set the saucer down and picked up the small goblet of wine. He raised it toward the ceiling and said, "After supper, Jesus took the cup of wine and blessed it. Then He said to His friends, 'Drink this, all of you, in remembrance of me.'"

Hobart set the wine glass down, then extended a hand toward Mimi and, more hesitatingly than he intended, to

Cressida. Mimi took his hand immediately. Cressida saw her mom take Hobart's hand as if this were a routine part of the process, and then her eyes darted toward her side to see if he was going to try to grab her hand. Hobart did reach for her hand, placing it gently underneath her fingers, palm up so that she was in control.

"Could we please say the words Jesus taught us?"

"Our Father, who art in heaven, hallowed be thy name," and Mimi enjoined her voice with his. Cressida found herself automatically mouthing the words off and on out loud without even meaning to.

"Thy kingdom come, thy will be done, on earth as it is in heaven. Give us this day, our daily bread, and forgive us our trespasses as we forgive those who trespass against us. Lead us not into temptation and deliver us from evil. For thine is the kingdom, and the power, and the glory, now and forever. Amen."

Hobart broke the round of wheat bread into three pieces. Mimi held out her hands, palms up, and he placed a piece in her hands. "The body of Christ," he said as he gave her the bread.

Hesitantly, always hesitantly as if reaching to stroke a skittish horse, Hobart extended his hand with a piece of bread toward Cressida. She stuck out one hand and took it with her fingers. He raised the third piece of bread to his own mouth and all three of them ate.

Then, he took the cup of wine and handed it to Mimi. She took a sip. Hobart wiped the lip of the glass with the party napkin, then handed it to Cressida, who took a deep sip and handed it back. He did not wipe the glass before holding it to his lips without drinking. Then, he placed the wine back on the table, covering it with the napkin.

"Let us pray," he concluded. "Eternal God, please accept this, our act of praise and thanksgiving for all you have given. Bless, preserve, and keep us in your love. Heal us with your presence, and allow us to be your presence to those with whom we live and work and play. In Christ's name, we pray. Amen."

"Amen," Mimi agreed.

There was a pause, and then Cressida stood up and reached for the glass and saucer. Mimi reached out and touched her arm, "Thank you, honey."

"You're welcome," Cressida responded in a hoarse whisper.

At the sound of clinking and tap water, Mimi looked at Hobart and said, "I noticed you didn't drink the wine."

"Wow, that was astute. I'm going to have to be more careful around you or you'll know all my secrets."

"It was just different for you, that's all. I didn't mean to embarrass you. I'm sorry."

"Oh, no, it's okay."

Hobart felt caught in the act. He looked around for something to busy himself with, but there was nothing but him and Mimi and the sound of Cressida in the kitchen.

"Actually, okay, I am a little embarrassed, but it's something I'm going to have to get used to so I might as well get used to it with you, 'cause I know you care about me. If I can't trust you, who can I trust?" Hobart chuckled insincerely and sighed deeply, going on.

"So, I started going to AA."

The sound of broken glass in the kitchen made them both jump, and Hobart suddenly realized he had told Cressida at the same time he was telling Mimi. He hadn't intended to tell anyone, but certainly not Cressida. He wanted to jump out of his skin at the thought of one of his peers knowing, especially her.

"Oh, Hobart, that is wonderful." Mimi reached out to hug him, and Hobart leaned in somewhat stiffly to receive it. "I can't tell you how happy I am for you, and for everyone else in your life."

"Well, don't get too excited. It's one day at a time, you know."

Hobart reflexively wanted to tamp down expectations because suddenly, he felt an overwhelming desire to get high. He had been devoted to pot for so long, he wasn't at all sure the love affair should end. Alcohol was a second-rate substitute that could sometimes be a lovely exclamation mark, but he knew deep down, his problem was with both.

Walking down those steep basements steps at the shabby Pentecostal Church on the East Side, where he was pretty sure no one would know him, felt like a humiliating defeat. But somehow, Mimi made it feel like a win. On the other hand, he was mortified that Cressida knew. Hobart peered around to the side to see if he could catch a view of Cressida from where he sat, in order to see how she was taking the news, but there was silence from the kitchen.

"Oh, don't worry Hobart, she 'gets it.' In fact, I am certain it will even change the way she thinks about you."

Hobart felt embarrassed for Mimi to be talking about Cressida to him when she was in the next room, but the continued silence caused him to wonder if indeed she was still in the kitchen. He stood up and peeked around the kitchen door and saw her leaning against the refrigerator with her head down. She realized she was not alone, and their eyes met for a nanosecond before she disappeared up the back stairs. Hobart nervously looked back into the dining room at Mimi.

"I am so sorry, Mimi, I didn't mean to create drama here. I came to visit you and share prayers and peace. Please forgive me. We can try again another day perhaps."

"Oh Hobart, you do not understand. I am so heartened by this visit; you have no idea. I feel like a bird in flight right now! Sharing Communion with Ruthie, sharing you with Ruthie, it was just perfect."

Hobart didn't understand, but he knew he needed to get out of there and to a meeting sooner rather than later.

He didn't know what had happened or why he felt so flushed with the urge to get high, but he recognized the danger zone.

"How about I come back later this week, Mimi, just to prove I can visit on a day other than Tuesday?" He chuckled as authentically as he could and stood up. Then, he bent down and hugged Mimi as she kissed him on the cheek.

"Thank you, Hobart. Now, you better get to that meeting."

Hobart cocked his head in bewilderment that Mimi knew what was going on inside him. But rather than say anything or ask, he retreated at the opportunity.

Chapter Nine

"Alone"

The Brick Street – *The narrow one-way, one-block street connecting two busier thoroughfares is a canyon cutting through tall buildings, but meticulously manicured by the establishments located there with attractive planters and faux antique signage and lighting fixtures.*

Harrison stood outside *the spot* with his face pressed up against the glass. He instinctively felt the need to see who was there before opening the door. When he entered, he immediately scanned the panoramic view. In addition to all the unfamiliar faces scattered at tables and occupying the lounge furniture, he saw Wilma sitting by herself, tapping away at a computer on the far side of the cafe from Bernie, who sat staring into an iPad glowing up at him. Hobart was at his usual station in the darkness, holding a cup of coffee and looking up into the ceiling. Cressida was at a table by the window on the same side of the room as Hobart, reading her phone. Toward the middle of *the spot,* Google, Enid, Hopi, and someone next to him were talking animatedly around a large round table full of plates and cups.

He wanted to sit with Wilma but was afraid to, especially with Bernie there. He didn't want to hang out with Google just then, although he did have something he wanted to talk to Hopi about. Cressida would probably get pissed off if he didn't sit down with her. He headed to the bar and ordered a double redeye to put off his decision. As Harrison walked between tables, there were friendly waves and catcalls from Hopi and his friend, which caused Cressida to look up and nod, and Wilma to look his way with an expression he couldn't quite interpret. He noted Hobart never changed positions nor took notice of his entrance.

Table 86 – *just to the right of the table, someone had spilled a mint mocha with whipped cream that is now partially dried and swarming with sugar ants.*

Harrison, steaming paper cup in hand, wandered over and sat with Hobart. As he sat down, he noted that Cressida looked at him curiously, but without the anticipated scowl.

"Yo, 'Ho,' what's happening?"

"Hmmm, not sure 'Ho' is the best moniker these days, but not much. What's up with you?"

"What's your take on hookin' up?"

Hobart looked at Harrison without answering. He suspected Harrison was laughing at him, but couldn't be sure.

"You know, like 'friends with benefits.'" Harrison filled in. "What's your rap on it? I mean, I know that you've done it, but now that you're a priesty and all, is it still cool?"

Hobart could sometimes be comfortable in his own skin but not often among his peers, especially when the culture of his profession crinkled loudly up against the popular culture of his friends and acquaintances. He also had to be careful because he was held to a different standard now, by both church-goers and the unchurched alike. It was a weird and twisted logic he had to navigate, no matter what he actually thought and believed.

"You want my permission to fuck your brains out, Harry?"

"No, man, I'm not looking for permission for anything. I am just checking out different perspectives - an investigation, you might say."

"Okay, I'll take you at your word. Old school church frowns on it, so does new school church. But, there are progressives that recognize we live in an overly sexualized culture and hooking up is a symptom of a corporate problem, not simply an individual offense. But, I'll tell you this, Harry - what I know now that I didn't know before, just from experience, is that it is not harmless."

"Say more, bro."

"Well, it's a lot like pot. It's not cool to say that pot is addictive because everyone wants to make reefer legal, and to suggest there is a hazard in it will harsh the mellow of stoners. I should know, right? But pot is addictive, at least for some people, and those folks can get very dependent upon it, just like any narcotic. Sex among friends with no intent of a more sustained intimacy is hazardous, too, even though no one wants to acknowledge it. Forget the STD's for a minute; I'm just talking about what happens when we put our bodies inside one another. There is a bonding that happens, or should happen, and if it doesn't, or isn't acknowledged and reverenced, then a kind of violence has been done. No, it won't kill you, but do it enough and you get deadened to the pain. There is a kind of numbing that has to go on in order to get naked and have sex with people whom we have no intention of being emotionally intimate with." Hobart paused to look at Harry, who seemed to be tucked within his own thoughts, then added, "I'd go so far as to say that sex has a metaphysical dimension, and its magical mojo is diminished without the reverence and care it deserves."

Harrison was taken aback. He expected more of a stoner answer, even though he had recently come to realize there was more to Hobart than stoner. He wasn't quite ready for Hobart's challenge.

"Whoa, slow down, 'Father.' You really think casual sex is dangerous, like harmful? It seems mostly cool to me."

"Look, I'm the last person to be preaching about the dos and don'ts of sex. And I'm not saying it's the big deal that the Old Time Religion folks do, but you asked. Here, do this: don't need to tell me who it is, but think about the last person you had sex with."

Harrison had to work hard not to look over at Wilma. In his mind's eye, she was sitting there, so beautiful and lovely, working away at her computer, and then, without the slightest effort, the memory of her breasts released into the open air filled his thoughts. "Yeah, got it."

"Now, the very next time you saw her, was everything just as cool as before?"

Harrison flashed to only a few minutes before, when he and Wilma locked eyes and he wasn't sure about the content of her expression. He wasn't sure what he wanted his look to say, either. "Mmm, not sure."

"What do you mean you're not sure?"

"Well, like, it was cool, but maybe it wasn't. I don't know yet. We haven't actually, like, *talked* yet. We've seen each other across the room, but we haven't actually, like, you know, hung out. So, I'm not sure."

"Think about that for a minute. You were inside one another's bodies and as intimate as you could possibly be with another person physically, but instead of drawing you closer into emotional intimacy, it parked a distance in which you're not quite sure what is safe and what isn't. Is that right?"

"Well yeah, for now. But like, we'll talk, and then we'll find out."

"All I'm saying is that sexual intimacy ought to lead directly to emotional intimacy and that one without the other is hazardous." Then, as if he had forgotten something important, added, "I'm not saying it is morally wrong or you'll go to hell or anything like that. I'm just saying it is hazardous, not innocent. You know? Instead of nurturing intimacy like we want, it can end up a harpoon that leaves us bleeding. So, something intended to enhance ends up diminishing?" Hobart's voice tilted upward in a question at the end, which he hoped would make it sound less like preaching.

"Interesting theory, and I'll be testing it out. I'll get back to you with the data."

Table 69 – *seamless, black molded vinyl table for two with solid molded black vinyl chairs.*

Harrison stood up and took his coffee over to Cressida's table.

"Hey," he said as he sat down.

"Hey," she said back.

"What's up?" Harrison muttered.

"Not much," Cressida muttered back without looking up from her phone.

"How's your mom?"

At that, Cressida looked up. "She..." began then paused, "about the same."

"What? You were going say something else. What was it?"

"She really likes Peedad, er, Hobart," It was almost a whisper. "I was there today when he came over and I heard them talking, and it was like they were long lost friends talking about the secrets and mysteries of life. It just felt, I dunno, like, real. You know?"

"Dude's a mystery. He's a stoner, but someone put an underground chamber in there somewhere, and out of it comes weird shit. Good shit, I think, but kind of weird."

"Not anymore," she responded matter of factly.

"What do you mean, 'not anymore?'"

"He's not a stoner anymore. He gave it up. Finished. Just like that."

"Whoa, Peedad not a stoner?" He whispered a little too loudly. "That's gonna take some getting used to. I guess it's not surprising if you think about it, being a minister and all. Still. I told you, weird shit."

"Yeah, weird." Then, Cressida looked over at Hobart and studied his face as best she could from where she was sitting. He was leaning back in his chair against the wall, his lips chewing on a paper coffee cup, his eyes looking down. As she stared at him, suddenly, he looked up and caught her eyes. They both looked away.

Table 14 – *four chairs, two ladder-back with woven straw seats and two black hairpin metal chairs with black padding, both with some exposed stuffing.*

Wilma was apoplectic. She wanted Harrison to come to her table *right now,* and yet, she was afraid he was going to. Bernie was looking miserable and she didn't want to make him more so. But still, she didn't like Harrison being over there with that purple chick, either. It made her miserable.

Table 12 – *"Fuck" carved with crooked letters into the high gloss red paint on the table top, and "Fuck you, too!" just below it.*

Bernie was morose, but becoming less so. His reflex for any amount of pain was to get numb, and right now, he could feel the cocoon pulling in around him. The deeper he went into the tunnel, the less he felt, and that felt good. He was sensing a solution to his problems.

Table 27 – *a faded blue canvas patio table umbrella has mysteriously appeared in the center hole and Google has raised it in spite of Enid's superstitious dread of opening an umbrella inside.*

Google was still angry with Harrison. In truth, he was still hurt. He watched as Harry flit from table to table, and wondered if he had the balls to land at his.

Enid was watching, too, but she was hoping Harrison would visit their table because she wanted Google to make up with Harry and smooth things out. Google had been on a nonstop, manic Wikipedia rave ever since Harrison challenged his way of thinking, and even though she thought Harry had been rude, she also knew he was one of Google's most steadfast friends.

Table 86 – *the remains on the floor of the spilled mint mocha with whipped cream has now hardened beyond consumption. The ants have disappeared.*

One, 'meaning.' Two, 'death.' Three...why can't I ever remember that third one? Hobart was trying to reconstruct his therapy session from earlier that morning and struggled to figure out how he had wandered into the cesspool he referred to as "Wellhead Number One." *Aloneness, ha*! Wellhead Number Three was "aloneness." "meaning" was Number Two, and death an ugly Number One.

Yash Arjun, his Indian therapist with two first names, was a Geneva-trained Jungian with skin the color of milky coffee and massive, bulging eyes reminiscent of Yoda. In fact, Hobart often thought of him as Yoda, and not just because Yash's big ears curled out a little at the top. It was also the awkward, upside-down way Yash had of stating the obvious Hobart had overlooked on its head, and then placing it in the middle of the room for inspection.

'Death,' 'meaning,' and 'aloneness' were echoes that came back again and again in therapy because Yash said they were 'The Big Three' everyone had to contend with in life, and if he, Hobart, wanted to be a spiritual guide, then he was required to enter the dark hallway of each one and greet the angels and demons waiting for him there.

Hobart wondered out loud in his session that morning whether or not he needed to take a break from therapy while he struggled to get sober. In Alcoholics Anonymous, people talked about the need for at least six months of sobriety before attempting to contend with therapy issues, and at least a year before getting entangled in romance, if there were no current commitments already. Yash asked what was unnerving him.

"I just don't know if I can do this. My stomach is a mishmash of anxiety all the time and I can hardly stay in my own skin. I want to jump out and run away like the

Gingerbread Man. I'm no good to anyone else right now, and that feels shitty, too. I want to be there for Mimi when she dies, but I don't know if I can stand it."

"Stand what?"

"It. You know, IT. Death."

"What's not to stand?"

Hobart was stunned by the question. At first, it made him angry. Then, he scoffed inside at what a stupid question it was. Then, he couldn't answer it.

"'Stand it,' is such an interesting expression. Does it mean you will stand it up like a cut out figure, or does it mean stand on top of it like a victor?'"

Hobart remembered staring at Yash like he was an alien. *What the fuck is wrong with you?* he said to himself. And that is when Hobart knew the innocent little singsong man in front of him had just lifted the lid on Wellhead Number One.

"I don't know if I can stand it when she leaves, if I am there in the room. I won't be able to tolerate the..." he wanted a word, but the one that came to his thoughts seemed too obvious, "pain."

"What's to tolerate? You feel pain, so what?"

"So, it hurts!"

"Yes, and then?"

"It hurts more."

"And then?"

"And then, what? It hurts until it doesn't?"

"Yes."

"What are you trying to say, 'shit happens? People die, get over it?'" Hobart looked incredulous.

Yash sat silent. Hobart hated that. It happened when Yash wanted him to answer his own question, or when Yash simply wouldn't answer his question for whatever mysterious, dumb, stupid, therapist reason.

"Okay, people die. Is that what you want me to say?" *The fucking Yoda look,* he grimaced to himself, *those half-mast eyes content to wait as long as it takes.*

"I'm afraid, okay?"

"Okay. Good. What are you afraid of?" Yash asked it flatly.

"Seeing Mimi die, just go away, turn cold. I've never been that near death. I've never seen death. I don't want to. And Cressida. Shit, what about Cressida? She'll be beyond herself."

"What is frightening about death to you?"

"Are you serious? What's not to be scared of? Aren't you afraid of dying?"

"We are not speaking of my fears just now."

Silence. Hobart was Jell-O inside. He realized he was shivering, literally shaking, as if gripped by an icy cold.

"What are you feeling, Hobart?"

"Cold," he said through chattering teeth. "I feel really really cold. And shaky."

"Deathly cold?"

"Yes. I feel cold like Mimi will feel when her life...disappears," he trailed off. Hobart touched his arm with his fingers and his skin felt clammy, lifeless.

"That, my friend, is a courageous act of empathy. You have actually put yourself in Mimi's place when she dies and are overcome by the cold of life extinguished. Very brave."

Hobart shivered in the red, upholstered wingback chair. He felt a chilled bead of sweat roll down his forehead, then another. Sweating as he shivered, Hobart wondered if he was going crazy.

Wellhead Number One was his fear of death. As long as he could remember, he had been terrified of it. He did not understand how other people weren't preoccupied by death, too. It made him afraid of the dark, and as he got older, that evoked shame. When the other kids did ordinary kid things, like jumping off heights or riding bikes fast down steep hills, he lagged behind, timid. He was cautious, even when he didn't want to be. But it wasn't just death he feared. It was pain, too. The anticipation of it was enough to keep him from taking risks.

"Hobart, while you are there in the cold, what is so frightening about death?"

He shivered again. "It's dark, and so lonely."

"Ah." It was a sound more than a word.

Hobart could feel the terror of being alone in the dark for eternity. It was sheer horror. He desperately wanted to be high. Smoking pot drove any hint of this feeling far away. He wanted to make it go away. He resolved to get high as soon as he got done with his session. Harrison had a small stash he kept 'just in case.' He hated this; he hated himself.

"When you can be alone with yourself, and not be afraid, then, you will no longer fear death."

"That's easy. I can be with myself just fine when I'm stoned."

"Of course. That is how you manage your feelings, but they are mismanaged. You move further and further away from yourself. Your task is to learn to feel what you feel and not run away."

"Just hurt? Just fear? Just shiver? That sounds like hell."

"No, it is life. For someone who fears death, it seems you fear life even more."

Hobart felt pressure behind his eyes and, before he could steel himself against it, tears were rolling down his cheeks and he heard himself sobbing out loud. He was embarrassed and ashamed and covered his face with his hands.

Yash remained silent and still, sitting across from him in a matching red chair.

Finally, after several unsuccessful attempts to speak, Hobart grimaced, "I'm just so fucking sick of being afraid."

"Good," Yash whispered, "very good."

Instead of getting high, Hobart wandered to *the spot* and took his place in the darkened corner. Leaning against the wall on two legs of the chair, chewing the lip of his paper cup, Hobart had entered a strange chamber of emotion he had previously only associated with being stoned: peace. It was a different kind of peace than the wasted continuum of sensations that rolled in waves through him during various forms of inebriation. The peace he now felt was in the midst of all the things that made him nervous. Where he sat inside himself, there was calm at the eye of the storm. All the nasties were still swirling around him in the air, but a hammock of unknown proportions cradled him inside. When he and Cressida locked eyes, he looked away because he didn't want to leave the peace he was feeling, not yet, not after having finally arrived.

Chapter Ten

"Awkward"

The Spot Entrance – *the large, thick window panes facing the street are layered with a chaotic patchwork of overlapping flyers, posters, and announcements.*

Miss Landrace charged through the glass doors of *the spot,* entering the cafe in a whirlwind of manic agitation, her head swiveling left and right as she turned around and around, looking in every direction. Her old-lady heels clicked the wooden boards and, in the dizzying motion, it seemed as if she would tumble over.

"Harry? Harrison Jordan, are you in here?" It was a broadcast more than a yell, a plea to the universe from which she hoped a voice would answer back.

Harrison froze. Cressida looked up in shock. Wilma's eyes left the computer screen even while her fingers continued tapping. Still on the far side of the cafe from Wilma, an increasingly lethargic Bernie peered up as well. In fact, all eyes in the crowded Caffeination Journey were fixed on the stumbling Miss Landrace.

Sheepishly, Harrison stood up with slumped shoulders and raised his hand, offering a small, feeble wave.

"Shhh, don't bring her here," Cressida seethed through her teeth. "Go up there."

But Harrison didn't move. Miss Landrace nearly flew to their table, arms waving, heels smacking, hips wobbling. With every step, she muttered out loud with obvious excitement tinging her unintelligible words.

Table 74 – *a kidney shaped table with pink vinyl fabric glued to the top, stretched and pinched at the sides like a beer cap, with two matching pink upholstered chairs.*

"Harrison Jordan, I have news!" she exclaimed. "Oh, hello there, Ruthie. Harrison, you will never believe what has happened. I am getting married! Married, Harry. Isn't it marvelous and simply unbelievable? Oh, Harrison, it is just thrilling!"

With the announcement, Miss Landrace grabbed Harrison's limp body as tightly as a small child wraps both arms around a giant stuffed animal, and then she squeezed. Harrison's eyes widened as if his insides were coming out, and he looked down at Cressida for help. Cressida was snickering until Miss Landrace let go, then nearly pushed Harrison down into his chair and pulled one up for herself from an adjoining table. As if all in one motion, she sat down between Cressida and Harry.

"Harrison, I want you to walk me down the aisle." Miss Landrace was beaming as she grabbed Harrison's hands and squeezed. Harrison was stunned speechless. Eventually, he recovered enough to object.

"But Miss Landrace, don't you want someone in your family? I mean, Miss Landrace, I was your student and, well, we hadn't seen one another for a while, and, I dunno, walking you down the aisle seems like such an honor, and..." He was sputtering and putting together any words of objection he could think of in that terrible moment.

"Oh, Harrison, you have always been so shy and modest." Cressida snorted out loud but Miss Landrace ignored it. "I do not have any family since Daddy died. It's just me. I want you to represent all my students because they are my family. It was Hobart's idea - don't you think it's wonderful?"

Harry glanced over at Hobart, who was chuckling from his corner table. *Sonofabitch*! Harry hoped Hobart could read his mind.

"I am going to invite all my former students still in town, you, too, Ruthie, and the teachers, of course, and Dr. Withnow, the new assistant principal. And Hobart will perform the ceremony and it will be grand!"

"Was this sudden, Miss Landrace?" Cressida felt a smirk but it sounded sincere.

"Well, yes it was Ruthie, thank you for asking, dear. Milton Robert Beasley - everyone calls him Bobby - and I dated in high school. Oh, it was quite the romance. But three weeks before our senior prom, Bobby burned his draft card and Daddy wouldn't let me see him anymore! He went away to college and that was that, we never saw each other again except for our twenty-fifth reunion, but that doesn't count. Anyway, Bobby's wife passed last year and we reconnected on Facebook. Well, you know how these things work today. It just went crazy!"

Harrison's mind was racing down two tracks. On the first one, he was listening to Miss Landrace and trying to picture Bobby, wondering what kind of a sorry bastard he was. On the other track, he had taken a fast train for the exit, searching for any possible excuse to get out of walking down the aisle with Miss Landrace.

"I've never been in a wedding before, Miss Landrace, I won't know what to do. In fact, I don't think I have ever been to an actual wedding. Shouldn't you have someone older and more experienced than me?" Glancing at Cressida, he noticed that, while she retained a straight face, her body was jiggling on the outside from the giggles filling her insides.

"Harry, you are so sweet to worry about that, but Hobart will tell us what to do. I've never been married before either," and with that, she broke out into a loud cackle that lassoed the attention of all nearby tables.

As soon as Miss Landrace left the cafe, Harrison made a beeline for Hobart.

Table 86 – *each captain's chair sports a different college seal and varied in color and style. Hobart always sits in the "Colgate" chair.*

"You son of a bitch, I can't believe you did that to me."

"Whoa, Harrison. Chill. Sit down for a minute." Harrison glared at Hobart as he sat down opposite him in a red-faced huff.

"I know it's awkward," Hobart began, "but have a little compassion. She's got no one. I just thought if we could get enough of her former students together, it would mean a great deal to her and, you know, feel something like family. Honestly, I thought you'd be kind enough to do it."

"Oh, yeah, sure, butter me up with compliments, schmoozer."

"Well, there's also her house, if kindness isn't persuasive."

"What about it?"

"She's going to ask you to house sit for her."

"What? Where is she going?"

"Bobby lives in California, and she's moving out there, lock, stock, and barrel. But she doesn't want to sell her house because it holds so many memories, and she can't bring herself to rent it yet. So, in the meantime, until she knows what she wants to do, she is going to ask if you will live in it...rent-free. Just utilities."

"Are you shitting me? That's awesome!"

"Yeah, I'm a little jealous, to tell you the truth, but you were her favorite."

Harrison stood up in a daze evoked by his good fortune as it swirled amidst the awkward public intimacy of walking his strange and sad former Latin teacher down the aisle. *Does everything happen for a reason?* He was going to ponder this anew.

Behind Table 91 – *the corner where the black wall meets the dark blue wall, underneath the black light that casts a purple glow.*

Cressida was glad Hobart had left, and was surprisingly pleased when he went out of his way to walk by her table and say goodbye. Now, she could sit in her favorite seat in *the spot.* It was the corner behind where Hobart usually sat. It was dark, underneath a shadow produced by the glow of the black light fixture protruding from the wall. Sometimes, she had to wipe spider webs out of the corner and scuff yuck from the floor before she sat down. Most people could not see her there, when she sat on the floor in the corner, and those who did would think it so weird they would never bother her. Except Hobart, who would probably ask what was wrong.

Nothing was wrong. Or maybe everything was wrong, but that was nothing new. It was her safe place where she could be in public alone and watch the world from inside herself and not be distracted by anyone or anything. Maybe that's what meditation was, she wondered.

Cressida was thinking about changing her name back to Ruth before her mom died, but she didn't know why. Was it for her mom? Or was something changing in her? Something was changing all right, and it was life. She couldn't even imagine the world without her mom in it –

it was a thoughtwall, as Harrison called them. She couldn't even make her thoughts go there.

She felt confused by almost everything these days. As much as she was angry, Cressida admitted to herself there on the floor in the shadow that she found it comforting the last time Hobart visited her mom. Strangely, she had also been feeling the desire to pull up a chair at his table, but couldn't bring herself to do it. Shame, she recognized, because everyone else would think it was just too weird. Embarrassment, too, but she couldn't figure out why. Dread as well, because what would they talk about? *Oh, well, don't be silly,* she concluded, *there is no way that's ever going to happen.*

Table 27 – *the umbrella is gone and in its place, a closed oversized stripped golf umbrella, its curved wooden handle sticking up from the middle of the table.*

"Hey." Harrison tried to say it nonchalantly as he passed by Google's and Enid's table, as if he wasn't laden with a heavy cocktail of emotions.

"Did you ever wonder," Google looked up from his screen and spoke as if there had been no suspension of their previous unpleasant conversation, "why you got to be one of the chosen few?"

Harrison stopped. The question caught him off-guard because he wasn't expecting any conversation, and would have been happy with a civil "Hey!" in return. He wasn't exactly sure what Google was driving at =, though he had a suspicion that sent an immediate ring of heat inside his collar. He started to speak, then realized he was looking down at Google and didn't want to start off on the wrong foot. He grabbed an empty chair from the next table and sat down.

"What few?"

"Have you ever wondered why you were one of the few African-Americans that got to go to an elite college instead of the many that languish on the streets of big cities or in some hellhole bayou down South?"

"You know, Google, that's just ignorant." Harrison stopped himself and backed up. Even though he was pissed off, he did not want to make the tension worse between them.

"Excuse me. Look, there are almost two and half million African-Americans that go to college every year, and eight hundred and fifty thousand of us end up in private colleges. *Two and half million*, Google. That may not be the majority, but it doesn't qualify as a chosen few. In fact, of all the ethnic and racial minorities, there is a higher percentage of brothas and sistas going to private colleges than any other group. Fuck what gets reported in the news media; those are the facts. The idea that my only choice as a black man is to become Barack Obama, Notorious B.I.G., or a hophead speedballin' is a racist veneer that's part of the problem. You don't believe that, so why you going there?"

"I'm just making a point, that's all. Don't play the race card," Google said dryly as if it was not a slap in the face.

Harrison wanted to smack Google. He stared at him, not knowing what to say. Google sat there, his hairy bellybutton poking out of the bottom of his too-tight shirt and his big body bleeding over the chair's edges. Nothing about Google really fit. His clothes were too small. His glasses had big, thick black frames taped at one corner and sat crooked on his face. His curly hair was a mattress of unsprung coils, too much for his smallish head. In the midst of anger, he felt a small twinge of compassion for his friend who walked through life with too big a brain and too big a body to fit the world around him, plus a personality disorder that often made him difficult to love.

This was Harrison Jordan's focus-on-the-details technique that had more than once managed his anger and even rage. He discovered it on his first day in his family's new suburban neighborhood when he was twelve and happily riding his bike down his new street and checking out the houses and kids. A cop cruiser blasted a short whine of its siren and flashed its lights from behind him, almost causing him to jump off his bicycle in fright. With kids from all over the neighborhood watching, the cop pulled up alongside him and called out the passenger window a familiar bark demanding to know what he was doing around there. When he told the officer he lived in the neighborhood, the cop squinted his eyes and looked him up and down, then asked his address. Harrison didn't know his address, and even if he had, he was so embarrassed in front of all the other kids he had not met yet, white kids, that he probably would have forgotten.

He found himself staring at the officer and noticing the man was missing an incisor tooth. As he looked closer, he could see that the man was really quite unpleasant to look at, with severely pocked cheeks from long ago acne scars. He began to see the man's face as a teenager, covered with oozing zits, and could easily imagine the cruelty of classmates mercilessly humiliating him. Amidst the fear and rage coursing through his blood, Harrison also felt a small candle of compassion, and it allowed him to keep his wits about him. That was the first time he discovered the technique - it had worked many times since. In the Target store near his parents' exurban neighborhood, he was the only person of color and found himself being followed from a distance through the aisles. During the other three times, he had been pulled over by cops in the same neighborhood, "just checking." Now, with his friend, who, no matter how close they were, still stood on the opposite side of a deep river. Compassion was the bridge.

"Google, you played the race card. I'm playing the wild card." He said it more gently than he felt it. "I am sorry for what I said the other day, for bringing up your diagnosis. It was insensitive of me to do it in the middle of an intellectual discussion as if it wasn't personal. And that's what you're doing now. I don't know if you are doing it on purpose or not. But what I know is that you and I can't talk about issues from a ten-thousand-foot perspective when they are so deeply personal. It's just going to piss us both off."

"How come we can't talk about race without you getting pissed off?" Google said with the same erudite tone as if talking about foreign policy.

"How come we can't talk about mental health without you freakin' out?" Harrison knew it was a childish retort, but it just came out. "Okay, never mind that. I'll talk about race, and I don't always get pissed off, by the way. All I'm sayin' is that white people talk about blacks like there's a few of us living in their neighborhood, and all the rest are scraping by or on the street shootin' up. Yes, there is a higher rate of poverty among African-Americans, and yes, fewer of us go to college and especially elite colleges, but that's old news. What do you expect after four hundred years of slavery and then another century of pretend liberation? But the fact is, poverty doesn't make people shitheads and assholes. There are millions of people, black *and* white, living in poverty and also loving, sweet, kind, and productive citizens. And there are millions of people that live somewhere in between desperate poverty and the violence of the streets, and the neighborhood where I live. That's all I'm sayin'. Don't make it one dimensional when it's not."

Google did something he almost never did. He took his computer off his lap, closed it, and set it aside. Then, he looked at Harrison. Enid shifted in her seat ever so slightly and, with her big eyes opened wide, looked at him.

"Got it."

There was a pause, and Harrison looked at Google and wondered what he meant. Then, Google went on.

"Your mom came from big money and the whitest of privilege. Your dad ran like Usain Bolt out of the 'hood' and grabbed that shiny Ivy League ring. Did you ever wonder what would have happened to you, if that had never happened?"

"I wouldn't be born."

"Yeah, okay, but don't you ever wonder about why that happened and why you got so lucky?"

"But that's what I'm talking about, man. What makes me so lucky? There are millions of people who don't have as much money as my family, and they're happy. They have people that love them and who they love, and they do stuff they think is important and pretty cool. Just 'cause my folks have money doesn't make me the winner. You see what I mean? If I believed in a god, it sure as hell wouldn't be one that rewards a few people with wealth and privilege. I'd hate that kind of god."

"All I'm saying, brah, is you got the slick for a reason and you're supposed to do something with it. Whoever's pouring the gravy gave you some extra and it's cause they want you to do something with it. That's all."

"Dude, that's a giant millstone you just hung around my shoulders."

"I didn't put it there, man, the universe did. Maybe God did – you should ask your friend, Peedad. All I know is you got it, and there's a switch somewhere waiting for you to turn a dark place light. It's not a weight, it's just the way it is."

Harrison sighed. He was having a hard time staying angry because, besides Google's sleepy racism, he was also voicing something Harrison had been feeling vaguely himself. He didn't like it, neither the feeling nor his certifiably crazy friend seeing it and saying it out loud.

Table 12 – *"Rasta Forever" written with obsessive neatness using a black sharpie appears at the middle of the table.*

The stinkbug was back. It was the wrong time of year for stinkbugs and Bernie contemplated how artificial environments create artificial life cycles. He was in an artificial environment and it was killing him. Just exactly how he was supposed to change it was a thoughtwall that made Bernie's world feel smaller and darker.

Chapter Eleven

Ruptures

Chapter Eleven

"Ruptures"

Table 14 – *someone left a New York Yankees baseball cap hanging on one of the ladder-back chairs.*

"But whyyyyyie?"

It came out like a four-year-old and Bernie knew it, but even so, he couldn't help it. A wounded animal was screaming inside and, more than anything else in the whole world, he wanted to release it into the open air. Yet, the only thing to come out was a little boy's whine. Bernie was the one who should have been concerned about how it sounded to the people seated a few tables away, but it was Wilma who looked around to check if anyone was listening.

"I am done. Bernie, don't beg, it's gross." She didn't mean it as harshly as it sounded, but she was exasperated with the whining and him following her. He embarrassed her, especially when Harrison's friends could see and hear his driveling.

Bernie almost revealed to her that he was drowning. Vicodin and vodka were long, boney digits of the Zombie hand, moldering flesh hanging off exposed sinew and wrapped with a vice grip around each of his wrists, pulling him down into a thick, black, bubbling ooze. He opened his mouth to tell her, but all that came out was another whine.

Wilma exhaled a half huff, half sigh, reminiscent of a middle school mean girl. She scooted her chair out from under the table and stood up.

"Bernie, I am sorry. You need to get your shit together. You only have one week left to finish your dissertation or everything you have worked for these past five years will be for nothing. I am a distraction. Get out of here and finish. Really, Bernie, you've got to finish."

Wilma walked to the island to order a Pumpkin Spice Latte to-go so she could get the hell out of *the spot.* She was shaken, as much by her own cruelty and anger as by Bernie's antics. She watched the barista make her latte, swirling the foam into a pumpkin shaped design, and then shaking whatever the amber brown powder was on top. She paid for it and turned briskly around, trying not to look at Bernie as she exited, but her eyes went there anyway. To her surprise, he was gone. She stopped in her tracks. He had been flopped face-down into his arms on the table when she walked away, and she had assumed he would still be in the same position when she left. Wilma scanned the large, cavernous room. She saw Harrison's friends, Google and Enid, talking to each other across the table while looking at their respective screens. She saw his friend Hopi lounging with that woman Cressida, their backs on opposite arms of the couch and their bare feet in each other's laps. Professor Sanger was with a handful of faculty and students from the Anthropology department. There were not a ton of people compared to most mid-mornings at *the spot.* Harrison's minister friend was at his usual table beneath the ribbon of darkness strung over the back part of the cafe. No Bernie.

Table 86 – *the spilled mint mocha with whipped cream is now a permanent part of the ambience appearing as a darkened spot on the wooden floor somewhat in the shape of Florida, or a penis, depending upon which mindset views it.*

"You're Harrison's friend, right?" Wilma had walked right past Cressida and Hopi on her way to Hobart's table, and when she did, she got the distinct feeling that Cressida was tracking her.

Hobart stood up to be polite. "Yes, Hobart Wilson," he stuck his hand out, though it seemed awkwardly professional when it was toward a beautiful woman so near his own age. As he did, he caught himself looking right past her luscious red hair, hanging loosely on her shoulders, toward Cressida. To his surprise, Cressida was staring directly at him. It gave Hobart a jolt and unnerved him. He grabbed hold of himself and retrieved his attention by looking Wilma in her luminous green eyes.

"Wilma," she said curtly, all business.

"Do you want to sit down?"

"Thank you." Wilma sat, both hands wrapped around the tall paper cup as if it was already mid-winter. "You're a minister?"

"Yes, UCC. That's United –"

"I know. Can I ask you a question?"

"Of course."

"Do you know Bernie Weinberg?"

"I know who he is; everyone here is familiar with Bernie. He's almost a fixture. Ha, I guess quite a few of us are."

"I used to be with Bernie."

"Yes, I saw you two together quite a bit, but I didn't know you had stopped dating."

"*I* broke up with *him*. There's something going on with him, and I don't know what it is. To tell you the truth, I'm worried about him. For one thing, his dissertation is due this week, without any opportunity for another extension, and it only needs a little effort on his part to finish. But I don't think he is going to. I think he is stuck in some crazy place and can't get out of it. I don't even know what I'm saying, it's just, well, I'm worried about him."

"Do you think it is a fear of success, some kind of self-defeating psychological dysfunction, or is something else going on?"

"I don't know. One of the things that kept happening was that he would stand me up. We'd have a plan and he'd be a no-show, without a call or anything. It happened four times, and that was after his being late a bunch of times. It was incredibly disrespectful and why I broke up with him. I won't be treated like that."

"Is Bernie one of those people who is chronically late, or was this a stranger, more unpredictable behavior?"

"No, he's not really like that. He is always on time for teaching, and rarely, if ever, misses a department meeting or other work responsibilities. That's why it was so shocking at first."

"This may seem like a strange question, but does Bernie drink a lot? Alcohol, I mean? Or get stoned a lot?"

"Hmmm, not really. I mean he likes to drink when we're out – or when we *were* out. He would get a little buzzed, but nothing sloppy or gross. No, not crazy."

"Just thought I would ask because sometimes, otherwise uncharacteristic lateness or neglect can be symptomatic of a drinking or substance problem that has crossed the line. Is he depressed?"

"He's something, but I don't know if I would call it 'depressed.'"

"Depression doesn't always look the way people imagine it is supposed to look, with moping and immobilized behavior. Erratic sleep, an inability to complete even ordinary tasks, emotional numbness, or even being captured by a single emotion like anxiety, not eating; worse, a sudden calmness or detachment."

"Uh, I did the detaching. But yeah, Bernie doesn't eat much anymore, and I would say that anxiety was the primary staple of his emotional diet. Sleeping is weird, though. Sometimes at night, he would be restless, but then, in the daytime, he would fall asleep sitting up."

"I'm not a shrink, so I can't diagnose that kind of thing, but I would agree that the behavior you are describing has something underneath it that is concerning. Do you know if he has a circle of friends who could be enlisted to help? Are you interested in helping?"

Wilma fell silent. She didn't know if she wanted to help. She wanted to be done with Bernie, but she did care about him. *Did she want to help*? She didn't know how to answer. Maybe.

Sensing an internal conflict, Hobart offered her an out. "Have you mentioned any of this to your department chair? Maybe someone at the school could reach out?"

"That's a good idea. Yes, that's perfect. Thank you. Harrison said you were good to talk with, and I appreciate your listening." With that, Wilma stood up before Hobart could get to his feet, turned around, and walked toward the door that led into the bricked street.

Hobart watched her leave without getting up or saying goodbye. Stunned by the abruptness, he heard himself say out loud, "What an odd woman". He also thought, but did not say out loud, *so beautiful - so odd.* Then, he felt someone staring at him. Sure enough, Cressida, still on the couch with an open book in her hands, had her cattish gaze fixed on him. He smiled meekly before looking down at his computer screen. *What's going on with he*r?

Black Couch Number 2 – *black Gorilla tape in the pattern of a medical stitch dominates the left arm of the couch.*

"Mom thought you were coming to dinner last night, asshole."

It was an icicle that stabbed deep into Harrison's chest.

"Oh shit, I'm sorry. Fuck, I just forgot. Miss Landrace wanted me to come over and see her house and talk about the wedding. She went on for two hours and by the end of it, I just forgot. I'm sorry."

Cressida said nothing. She just stared at him with a look that would have killed a lesser man.

"What's up?" Harrison nodded in Hopi's direction. Hopi looked at Cressida as if to get permission to answer.

"Life's up. You?" Hopi said it with a straight face that registered slight worry.

"Straight on, bro. I'm going to be living in a sweet house. Landrace has some butt-ugly furniture but otherwise, the house is streaming. All I got to do is cut the grass and pay the gas and electric. And walk her down the aisle, of course."

Hopi couldn't help but snort.

"Eat shit, Harry. You're not smiling your way out of this." Cressida said it with a look that drilled into him.

"Lighten up."

The sound that came out of Cressida curdled the cream in Google's red-eye. It was part wounded scream, part angry snarl, part woeful wail. The sound was not especially loud, but it traveled through walls and pierced windows, laying down a layer of hoarfrost on everything it touched. Harrison bore the full force of it, and he moved visibly backward while Hopi's knees and arms pulled inward in self-protection. In the time it took for the sound to reach Hobart and ricochet back to Harry, Cressida was gone.

"Whoa, what was that?" Hopi remained curled into a cannonball. "That felt almost supernatural, man."

"F-u-c-k," was all Harrison could say in a hoarse whisper. Cressida had just amputated him from her life without warning and he knew it. The next time he saw Cressida in *the spot* or anywhere else, it would be as if they had never been introduced. Never mind their history, he had just been severed like a gangrenous limb.

Harry felt hurt and angry, knocked off balance. Then, he started to worry. Mimi was dying, and he wanted to be able to see her. He didn't want Mimi to think he was not coming around because he didn't care. Still, how could he visit if Cressida was going to be the way he knew she could be? The thought made him angrier, and more scared. Harrison got up and went with urgency to Hobart.

Table 86 - *covered with a chaotic patchwork of books and papers.*

"What was that?" Hobart asked before Harrison could speak.

"That was Cressida cutting me out of her life because I had the nerve to forget dinner with her mom last night." He said it with stinging sarcasm. "Hobart, man, it came out of nowhere. I've seen her do this to other people, but always to people that deserved it – jerks that were mean to her, or abusive. I'm her best friend, or was, and she cut me off without any real argument or anything. I mean, I don't think there was anything else."

"You look rattled, H."

"Yeah, I feel rattled. Freaky. She's one powerful chick, if you know what I mean."

"Yeah, I'm beginning to. But look, Harry, her mom's dying and if that wasn't bad enough, without her mom, she is alone in this world. She's got nobody, at least nobody she knows of."

"What do you mean?"

"Nothing." Hobart was curt; he tried to grab back what he had let slip. "I just mean there is no one else on the horizon behind her or ahead of her that she is connected to by blood or adoption."

"Then why's she cutting me off? I'm her oldest and best friend. It's stupid – crazy girl."

"I don't know Cressida like you do, but it seems to me that is what she learned to do in order to protect herself. She's a castle, and when pain approaches, she raises the drawbridge, fills the moat with acid, and readies the archers. For a woman who's not that old, she has suffered a great deal of pain. A lot of it is self-inflicted, but even more of it rained upon her through no fault of her own."

Harrison was quiet for a moment as he thought about being with Cressida through all the times of injury and healing. In seventh grade, she had been one of four girls sexually abused by Mr. Rochester, their English teacher and the girl's track coach. No one was supposed to know who it was, but everyone did. The other three girls left the school, but Cressida stayed.

She had always been solitary, shy as a bird around the other kids on the playground. He remembered her from first grade, when she colored inside rather than be on the playground at recess. When she did go outside, she would swing by herself. In middle school, when some kids are the meanest - especially a certain knot of girls that seem to feed off of whatever suffering they can inflict on other girls - Cressida's isolation made her more vulnerable. That's when she went emo. She had only just emerged from the dark fingernails and lipstick, the black clothes and hair a few years ago. Purple was her bridge to color and she was creeping into ROYGBIV.

"Shit," Harrison said with a slump.

"Maybe this is a good time to help her change."

"What do you mean?"

"Well, maybe the castle thing doesn't work for her anymore. Maybe she needs friends around who won't accept that the drawbridge has been pulled up. Get a ladder and climb the wall!"

"What the fuck are you talking about dude? I'm lost in your metaphor."

"Don't take 'no' for an answer. Go to her; make her talk to you about why she's hurting. It will be terrible for a moment because she wants you to be scared away. Refuse to be scared. Cross the moat and ask her what's going on. Go to her house; visit with Mimi, keep the doors and windows open so she knows you want to remain her friend. Then, maybe she will come back out."

Harrison was quiet. He thought about Cressida's temper and what it was like to feel her wrath. He wasn't sure he was ready for that.

Red Upholstered Wingback Chair – *Yosh Ajun's alcove size office is just off the library in the Victorian house on Beecker Street, home of the Jungian Society.*

"I hate AA meetings; they make me nuts."

"Why is that, Hobart?" Yosh asked blandly.

"I'm not sure. I've been trying to put my finger on it. I mean, I like some of the people I've met, and being with other people going through the same things is really solid. Good, you know? But it feels like...like *church*."

Yosh raised one eyebrow higher than the other, but didn't say a word.

"But not the kind of church I'm comfortable in. More like a dogmatic 'Fundamentalist' church where everyone has to believe the same thing or risk hellfire, not to mention shunning. It has that same feel, a little bit anyway. You know what I mean?"

Yosh appeared to be weighing his response, and Hobart was curious about what was circulating in his therapist's thoughts.

"Our tolerance for ambiguity increases with security," Yosh replied without indication of emotion.

"Don't you find it difficult to be surrounded by people that think the words of the Big Book are the only way to get sober, and who spout truisms like "Easy does it" and "One step at a time," as if Jesus uttered them? You can't possibly go along with the kind of black-and-white thinking that passes for wisdom in an AA meeting."

The more he spoke, the more agitated he became, and Hobart knew he was overly exposed.

"The times I am aggravated by what other people say and think are usually the times I feel the most insecure about what I say and think."

"Oh, come on, don't give me that Yoda yap," he wanted to take it back as soon as he said it. Yosh wore his poker face and Hobart had no idea what his reaction was. It suddenly occurred to Hobart that he cared desperately what his reaction was. In fact, Hobart realized that he always cared what someone's reaction was, a sudden insight that caused him to slump down in his chair.

"What did you just see?" Yosh asked without the slightest hint of interest.

"I am too concerned about what other people think about me."

"And you don't like that?" Yosh said it with perfected innocence.

"I'm sitting in those meetings worried about what other people will think about what I say and whether or not they will think I'm getting sober or not, you know, *succeeding*. I gave up being an A student, but I'm still begging for the A's! God, I feel stupid."

"What does stupid *feel* like?"

"Humiliation. Stupid feels humiliating. Ugh."

"Are there other times you have felt humiliated like that?"

"I was raised on humiliation. Wasn't everyone?"

"Gosh, I don't think so. Who taught you humiliation?"

"Well, let's see. My dad, Mr. Ivy League, who expected me to be good at everything:

science, math, language, lacrosse, swimming, art, girls. I can't think of one thing I ever did that felt as though my dad thought it was good enough. He had this way of saying, 'I see,' while wrinkling his nose as if he had just encountered a bad smell. I got an A-minus in algebra and he said, 'I see.' We lost the state lacrosse championship, and when I called to tell him, he said, 'I see.' When my first girlfriend broke up with me and I told him, he said, 'I see.' When I didn't get into Harvard, even though he had gone to Stanford, he said, 'I see.'"

Each time, Hobart said, "I see," he slid a pinch further into the chair until it was as if gravity was pushing on him from above.

"Is your father there in the AA meetings with you?"

"I suppose he is, or at least that is what I'm afraid of. When I say anything, if it isn't what I'm supposed to say or isn't the way it is supposed to be said, I think they are thinking, 'I see.'" Hobart looked surprised then added, "Yeah, that's exactly how I feel most of the time in those meetings. Do you ever feel that way at meetings?"

Yosh stared back at Hobart, wondering whether or not to talk about himself. Finally, he did.

"Hobart, I have been going to AA and Al-Anon, and sometimes to Adult Children of Alcoholics meetings for thirty-seven years. I do not go to feel confirmed or understood. I go to be in the presence of people who have suffered some of the things I have, and who know what it is like to live inside a bottle. When I can allow myself to simply be present with them, I often discover I have been moved or helped or challenged in some way I hadn't expected."

"I get that. When I am with Mimi and I am able to just be with her and not try to 'help her' in some way, really knowing and accepting I am powerless in the face of her dying, it sometimes feels like we are occupying the same moment in a really cool way. Connecting, you know? Or something like that."

"Yes, connecting on a level that people rarely connect on. Now, your fear of rejection and judgment and humiliation, so generously bestowed upon you by your father, is keeping you from being fully present in those meetings. What do you care if someone is a Big Book fundamentalist and rigid as a telephone pole? He or she may also say something that helps you to wake up to something you were not conscious of before. The messenger need not be Jesus to bring you what you needed to hear."

"True. It's just that religious people piss me off."

At that, Yosh laughed a full belly laugh, and Hobart began to laugh too when he realized how ironic it was.

"You know what I mean. I mean *religious* people, as in superstitious or overly scrupulous or black-and-white thinking. All the things the spiritual-but-not-religious folks think about religion. What Ruth thinks about me, for example."

"And how does it make you feel that Ruth associates you with 'those people?'"

"Embarrassed. Humiliated, I guess. Like, 'I see.'"

"What do you think might happen if you tried to explain to Ruth why you became a minister, and described for her your spirituality?"

"Oh shit, no way." The very idea of it allowed a thousand fingers to crawl into his stomach and play piano on his anxiety.

"Who could you do that with?"

Hobart thought about it and was startled by the only face that came to him. "Mimi."

"Why Mimi?"

"I can't imagine an 'I see' on her lips or in her eyes. She is special that way. And besides, she has a deep spirit that welcomes other people to open themselves up, and she receives whatever they choose to reveal."

"What about Ruth? She didn't receive that characteristic from her mother?"

"Hmmm. She's been beat up and hurt and has an angry dog snarl as a result, but when I think about it, she does have an amazingly nonjudgmental capacity when she hasn't been hurt by the person. It isn't always obvious because she has an aggressiveness that Mimi doesn't have, but she really does have a deeply-dug basement with a great deal of room."

"Perhaps you could tell her?"

"Oh, I don't think so. I mean, in the right atmosphere and moment, sure, I can see her handling it, but if it wasn't, then it could go very wrong. And besides..."

Yosh allowed the silence and waited.

"I think I might care too much." With this, Hobart looked down and blushed.

"Caring too much, in your line of work, may be a professional hazard. But, our time is up."

Hobart hated when that happened because it usually took him ninety percent of the time just to get open enough to touch something that he needed to talk about. But then, bam, the time was up. It made him angry at Yosh for being so goddamned fastidious about the boundaries on time, and angry with himself for being such a putz that he couldn't just start talking about the stuff that really mattered without spending most of an hour talking around it. He made a note to himself that next time he would jump in faster.

Chapter Twelve

"Happily Ever After"

14 Sunset Acres – *the backyard of Miss Landrace's house bounded by a six-foot tall, white vinyl stockade fence.*

Google and Enid crashed the wedding. Harrison told Miss Landrace that Hopi needed them to help with DJ equipment. Neither Google nor Enid had ever been to a wedding before.

Harrison didn't see Miss Landrace until ten minutes before the ceremony was to begin. She was pink. Everything was pink. The trunk of her short squat body was shrink-wrapped in shiny, dark pink charmeuse layered by lighter pink tulle netting. At the waist, where the dress should have billowed out to grant her eggplant figure a more pleasing shape, the alternating layers of coral pink chiffon with the stiffer fuchsia organza only flared out a short way from her midsection, giving her a bell shape – her head, the ball on top, and her just visible feet, the clapper. The bride's pale greenish-blond hair had a streak of hot pink running through it, too, in homage to former students, and a pink, diamond-encrusted tiara created a trench in the meringue hairdo.

Fortunately, Harry saw Miss Landrace before she saw him. It allowed for a moment to erase the image of Miss Piggy in pink stiletto heels ready for a square dance, with him as Kermit on her arm.

"Oh, my, you did it up right, Miss Landrace!" Harry exclaimed.

An entourage of young women, former students all, surrounded her as Team Landrace. They wore a variety of expressions from horror to pride, the prideful ones looking unselfconscious in their own horrid costumes – matching canary yellow prom dresses that designated the bridal party.

The commingling of two bright colors was meant to evoke, a long ago dream of her deceased mother, a bouquet of yellow roses surrounding a single pink one. Miss Landrace was a single pink rose, on her way to matrimonial bliss.

"Oh Harrison, thank you. And you look so handsome all dressed up like that!"

Harrison returned to the image of Kermit outfitted like Rich Uncle Pennybags from the Monopoly board game. All he was missing was the cane. He had tried to talk Miss Landrace out of the monkey suit, especially the top hat, but to no avail. All the men sported a top hat, and it was little solace that his was black while the groom and groomsmen wore bright yellow ones to match their vests.

"If you guys are all ready, I just want to go check on Hopi to make sure the music is synced and we've got our cues down."

"Yes, of course. Thank you, Harrison. I'm sure your friends will do splendidly." Then, she turned back around to join in giggly excitement with her girls.

Hopi had already started the music, blasting Vivaldi's "Spring" as if it were Jay-Z or Lil Wayne.

"Dude, mellow, not loud!" Harrison reached in past Hopi and turned the volume to just above the crowd noise below. Miss Landrace insisted that the DJ and 'his crew,' as Harrison had referred to Google and Enid, operate from the second-story bedroom window that featured a shallow decorative balcony, too small to actually maneuver on. So, Hopi had to set his speakers on the balcony and position his table just behind them, with the effect that, from below in the yard, people could see the speakers, but Hopi's face could only be seen as it appeared out of the shadows now and again. Google and Enid had to peek out from either side of the window to watch.

It was late autumn and the trees were just slightly past their peak, yet with enough color and leaves to make for pleasing photographs and video. The grass was especially lush and green. Ms. Landrace's father had installed a complex sprinkler system complete with an automatic timer, and ever since then, the yard was the envy of the neighborhood. He had been obsessive about weeding it and keeping it in nearly golf-course-green condition. "This goddamn barefoot grass," he used to tout from all fours, wearing a pith helmet and pulling up dandelions by the root.

The yard was large enough that it fit sixteen rows of eight rented white chairs with a wide aisle down the middle. The reception was to be held later that afternoon at the Riviera Country Club, after plenty of time for a chauffeured limo tour of picturesque sights of the city, where the photographer planned to capture the wedding party. Everything seemed ready to go, and Harrison confirmed cues and music one more time with Hopi, who seemed impossibly cheerful as usual, and not nearly nervous enough to give Harrison a sense of comfort.

When Harrison got back downstairs to the living room where the bridal party had gathered, Hobart was rounding them up and going over what would happen one more time. When he saw Harrison, he nodded and motioned him over to stand next to him with Miss Landrace.

"I want to have a prayer before I go join the gentlemen and we get started. I know some of you probably aren't religious, so I invite you to join in at your own level of comfort and bless this moment with your well wishes, if not your prayers."

Harrison was feeling quite anxious and was awestruck by how calm and professional Hobart appeared. *What is that?* he wondered to himself. Hobart was in a zone that seemed vaguely familiar. He remembered a late-night conversation with Hobart when he had felt calmed without knowing how or why, but in that moment, it seemed as if Hobart was holding all of them together by the strength of his...whatever.

"Let us pray." Hobart paused. "Thank you, God, for the love of Pearl and Bobby, and bless their wedding day by showering them with the love of friends and family. Amen."

Pearl? Harrison had forgotten Miss Landrace's first name and would never have called her that in a million years. But Hobart said it as naturally as if he had known her as a family friend his whole life. Suddenly, Harrison recognized Hobart had become a thoughtwall.

"Okay, let's do it!" Hobart exclaimed with a grin.

An audible, collective sigh of relief exhaled as Hobart finished his prayer. It was the momentary repression of energy inflicted by the insertion of religion, disappearing as abruptly as it arrived. A solemn, but decidedly giddy bridal party then lined up in reverse order, the last to be first down the aisle with Harrison and Pearl at the end. Hobart nodded at the group and slipped out the porch door to meet the groom and groomsmen. Miss Beverley, the high school English teacher, and designated coordinator of everything associated with Miss Landrace's wedding day, stood at the kitchen door looking into the backyard visibly ready to give the "Go!" signal to each canary-yellow bridesmaid to promenade down the aisle.

"Gentlemen, let's have a prayer," Hobart said somewhat dutifully to the men. They were sequestered in the garage. He looked around the room at the seven men dressed as Rich Uncle Pennybags in their anachronistic tuxes, given a garish splash of color with yellow vests and top hats. Hobart remembered that the Monopoly character appeared on the "Chance" and "Community Chest" cards, and chuckled to himself.

More stiffly than the women, the men responded to Hobart's prompt to hold hands, but they were also more visibly quiet and focused as Hobart prayed with a solemn voice.

"Gracious God, we give you thanks for the love that brought Bobby and Pearl together for this day and we ask you to bless them, allowing them, if it is your will, to pass "Go" and collect their two hundred dollars. Amen."

There was a slight pause as the words registered before a loud cheer went up from the garage. The groom, who was as rotund as Miss Landrace and sported a bushy, reddish-grey beard, grabbed Hobart and raised him in a bear hug, then slapped him on the back and said, "Let's go, laddy!"

Hobart texted Hopi that it was time for the procession. Seamlessly, Vivaldi slipped into Pachelbel's "Canon in D" and a hush fell over the cacophonous crowd of a hundred and twenty guests. Heads turned up the aisle and back toward the house. The tall fence gate that crossed the full width of the asphalt drive opened with a grand gesture from Cressida, shockingly dressed in a brilliant, cobalt blue midi. The dress parted for her thigh, a slit reaching all the way up to her hip, with a wrap-around halter neck fully exposing her shoulders, collarbones, and the edges of her ample breasts. Cressida balanced it all effortlessly on matching heels that made her tall slender body a half-foot taller. Hobart suppressed a gasp as the gate opened and revealed the vixen in blue, who was looking directly at him the way a panther might.

A bead of sweat rolled down Hobart's temple as he passed within an inch of her, leading the procession of men toward the gazebo tent adorned with flowers at the far end of the lush green yard, framed in the colors of autumn, about to be accented with a bouquet of brilliant yellow flowers surrounding The Pink Rose.

"Canon in D" compelled the single file line of men to walk with a stately grace as they moved up the side aisle and took their position in a line facing the audience with Hobart under the tent's apex, Pearl's beloved Bobby to his right, and the six yellow and black groomsmen a phalanx of formality standing in the open air. All attention was now on Miss Beverly, who stood frozen under a trellis of pink and yellow carnations woven with stems of baby's breath and Galax leaves framing the kitchen door and leading out onto a small, white vinyl deck. The stately music played and the company looked on as the screen on the kitchen door remained closed with Miss Beverly frozen in place. Too much time had passed without even one of the yellow women appearing from the kitchen, and Hopi began to be nervous, unsure of what to do. He craned his neck over the speakers on the faux balcony in an effort to see what was happening. He looked out at Hobart for an indication of what to do, if anything. Hobart scanned the scene and got a sick feeling in his stomach. Minutes passed, and the congregation began to murmur quietly.

"Don't worry, it's okay, there is probably some confusion up there," Hobart whispered out of the side of his mouth to Bobby. Bobby was shifting his weight back and forth in the awkward gap as minutes passed.

"Excuse me, I'll be right back." Hobart started to walk up the center aisle toward the house, thought better of it, and then veered to the left up the side aisle.

"What's up?" He looked at Miss Beverly, who was still frozen in the same position with her hand on the door while facing the yard.

"She's crying," Miss Beverly whispered through lips that never moved.

"Okay, just hang loose for a moment."

Hobart moved Miss Beverly's rigid hand from the doorknob and opened the screen, entering the kitchen through the gaggle of whispering yellow canaries. He moved through the kitchen and turned the corner into the dining room, where Miss Landrace was seated and sobbing into a large, pale pink handkerchief. Harrison was standing awkwardly nearby in a pose of indecision, as if he did not know whether to reach out and comfort her or run for his life. Hobart couldn't help but give him a small huff as if he could have done more.

"Pearl, what's the matter, why are you crying?" Hobart immediately placed a hand upon her shoulder and squatted down to be at face level.

"Da-da-daddy. He's not here. I don't even know if he would have approved of Bobby and..." she began to sob uncontrollably.

"Oh Pearl, you are still grieving for your father. That's natural. Today of all days, you miss him terribly."

More loud sobs reached a crescendo as she buried her face into her hands.

"There is another man here who loves you deeply. He is waiting to hold you and take you into his life, just the two of you. Your father would surely be so happy for you."

"Oh I, I, I, I want to believe that, Ho-ho-hobart," she huffed and puffed between heaves. "I think he would, but I know that he and Bobby would have argued terribly about politics. Still," she sniffed and then blew her nose, "I want to believe they would have come to love and care for one another. I know," more sniffs and another extended blowing of the nose, "Mother would have adored him."

Just then, a rush of wind pushed into the dining room from the kitchen door opening swiftly, and a surprised communal gasp from the canaries was heard as footsteps barreled rapidly across the kitchen floor. Bobby's reddish beard and yellow vest and top hat paused momentarily in the archway between the kitchen and dining room as he took stock of what was happening. Then, without warning, he rushed forward, picked up Miss Landrace in a single swift motion and wrapped his mouth around hers. She hesitated, then fully engaged his mouth with hers, their tongues in furious rapture, their hands relentlessly moving up and down one another's torsos, then swaddling each other's ample posterior cheeks. Forgetting herself in the moment, Miss Landrace began to hump backwards and forwards until Hobart cleared his throat.

"I think we have a wedding," the young minister grinned.

Suddenly, Miss Landrace caught herself and eased back as Bobby gently released her while still holding her left hand. Slowly, gracefully, keeping his eyes drilled into her gaze, he leaned forward and tenderly kissed the back of her hand. She shuddered and let go of a soft sound, something akin to the aftermath of an orgasm.

"I'll be waiting for you, my love," he whispered.

Hobart looked at Miss Landrace and nodded questioningly. She nodded affirmatively. Hobart smiled and he and Bobby walked out side by side. As they did, Hobart gave Harrison a look that said, "Do it!"

"Nice job," Hobart whispered to Bobby as they descended the deck together and walked up the center aisle, "Canon in D" still playing its eternally looping stanzas. All eyes were on the two men, and their broad smiles communicated an assurance that all was well. Once again, the guests became quiet as Hopi wisely paused the music. Then with greater volume, he pressed on with Pachelbel.

Up the center aisle, the canaries walked, syncopated with precision by Miss Beverly. When the sixth young woman had taken her place, Miss Beverly closed the kitchen door and Hopi faded out "Canon in D." There was a graceful moment of silence in the back yard, and those who listened could hear birds chirping, a distant jet overhead, and muffled sounds of children playing down the street. The door opened. A sound so loud and piercing emerged that the startled guests collectively moved back on cue. From out the kitchen door, a fully-kilted bagpiper stepped into the sunlight as the first gulp of air rushed through his instrument, producing a lurid noise that could not be categorized as music. Then, the instrument's bellows filled and exhaled the music of "Scotland the Brave."

Slowly, the piper stepped forward and descended the steps as he played, followed by two kilted snare drummers, commencing an accompaniment. The three made their way down the deck stairs and moved in military formation to the side where they played the familiar bouncy tune. Then, on cue with the live music, a full orchestral accompaniment descended from above through the speakers as Hopi, Google, and Enid looked proudly down upon the company. A spontaneous cheer and applause went up from the guests, as if an unexpected display of fireworks had been released. Finally, there appeared on the deck the pink bride with young Harrison Jordan on her arm.

The piper and drums erased all the embarrassment Harrison had expected, along with the unexpected and touching resolution to Miss Landrace's meltdown. It was a glorious moment, and Harrison was filled with something that felt a lot like pride.

Cressida, too, realized she was gushing with joy and couldn't help but marvel that this was happening. Gone were all thoughts of her mother's illness and any animosity she had been feeling toward Harrison. She was utterly surprised by the sudden visitation of joy that pushed out everything except the strangely peaceful acknowledgement of affection she now felt for Hobart.

As they left the sidewalk and stepped upon the soft carpet of grass, Harrison's eye caught the figure of Wilma sitting tall in her chair and looking up the aisle at him with such rapture it raised a hard on. The night before, they "came out" as a couple to Harrison's friends, although they discovered it wasn't a big surprise. After she helped him clean up the apartment, they made love four times during the night. Images of Wilma's long, smooth, beautifully defined thighs melting down into thin, delicate ankles and pedicured feet made his stomach lurch. And her back! There, walking down the aisle with Miss Landrace on his arm, he thought of Wilma's slender, sculpted, curvaceous back with soft, red hair brushing her shoulders like an elegant Picasso line drawing of the perfect female torso. He heard himself sigh, even as he became aware of weight pulling down on his arm and Miss Landrace leaning sideways.

He wasn't sure what was happening, but with each step, she became more unsteady. He looked down and realized that her pink stiletto heels were sinking into the grass, something no one had thought about the night before at the rehearsal. Twice, she nearly pulled Harrison over as her ankles gave way and the violent wobbling almost upended her. As the music continued, Miss Landrace stopped, giggled, and held Harrison's arm as she leaned over and took off her shoes. A warm round of laughter greeted the gesture as she handed the pointy pink weapons to a blushing young man on the aisle who happened to be seated next to where she stood. On they went, the bride barefoot on soft grass.

Finally, they were gathered as rehearsed, a line of six yellow and black men to the right with a line of six very yellow women to the left, Bobby and Pearl facing each other and holding hands, with Hobart behind them facing the guests.

"Dearly beloved, we have gathered here today to bless this man and this woman in holy matrimony." Hobart said it with a big, toothy grin, glancing at the couple, then out at the company before them. From the back of the crowd, standing behind the last row of chairs, he saw the deep blue-clad body of Cressida and saw that she was smiling back at him. His mind went blank. Suddenly, he realized he was lost in the moment and had forgotten everything else as Bobby kindly touched his arm. His face turned the color of Miss Landrace's dress, and he cleared his throat to gather his thoughts and continue.

"By the way," he whispered to the couple, "I never told you, but this is my first wedding."

"Oh, you dear boy," Miss Landrace cooed.

Hobart continued leading the ceremony without further incident. Harrison read a difficult Shakespearean sonnet Miss Beverly had chosen and the theater director, Paul Carr, read "The Art of a Good Marriage" with more drama than Wilfred Arlan Peterson had probably intended. Everything was perfect as Hobart announced Bobby and

Pearl husband and wife and instructed Bobby that he could now kiss the bride. As they embraced and entered into an overly exuberant and slobbery kiss, Harrison suddenly felt wet. In fact, he felt a splash from behind him and liquid trickling down his pants. There was a loud gasp from the guests, and pandemonium ensued with chairs tipping over and people fleeing in every direction. From his vantage point in the middle of the scene, Hobart could see that the sprinkler system had just gone off. Underneath the chairs, the well-spaced grid of sprinkler heads had all risen by electrical impulse on cue and were spouting highly pressurized water upward. From behind the groomsmen and bridesmaids, a row of sprinklers was soaking the wedding party, except for Hobart. He was in the perfect spot to only receive a few sprinkles.

As soon as he realized what was happening, he grabbed Miss Landrace and pulled her to where he was standing to protect her from the torrent. It was too late for Bobby; he was completely drenched, his silky yellow vest and top hat streaked by the moisture. The scene was something out of a movie: elegantly dressed people running for their lives, chairs tipping over and landing on sprinkler heads causing them to spurt even more furiously, and chaos of every kind unleashed on what had just the moment before been an idyllic photo op. Hobart and Miss Landrace stood on the same spot as if on home plate, Hobart protecting her from the water raining down on his back.

"Oh, Daddy, how could you?" She said it into the ether as Hobart looked with horror at Google and Hopi running down the backdoor deck stairs and yelling, "Slip 'N Slide!" just before they leaped and slid down the center aisle on their backs.

Chapter Thirteen

"The Shivah"

"Tonight, *Melanerpes formicivorus* knocked on my door."

Bernie wrote it in his best block handwriting with a black Sharpie, but even under the influence, he could see that the letters were squiggly from his shaking and some of the letters even seemed lopsided. He crinkled up the lined notebook paper and tried again and again and again. No matter- he was too euphoric to care. That wasn't quite true. He cared deeply, but any connection with what he truly cared about was swimming in a warm, euphoric pool of single-malt scotch infused with Vicodin, followed by overwhelming drowsiness. The effects of the toxins mitigated against anything his will intended with an overwhelming desire for relaxation.

He was falling into the hollow of the tree he had for so long been pecking, and he knew there was only one more chance to finish what he started. He opened his computer. Silly thoughts about which font to use splashed against his attempts to focus. As soon as a thought was formed, it popped like the thin sheen of a bubble. *Wilma likes Calibri. Okay, that one.* He pecked his way down to what he imagined might be the middle of the page and typed:

Tonight, Melanerpes formicivorus knocked on my door.

Should he italicize Woody? Okay.

"Tonight, *Melanerpes formicivorus* knocked on my door."

His fingers were beginning to tingle with numbness so he knew he had to muster some urgency, even though he felt no hint of anything urgent. He typed the thoughts in his slowing brain incrementally: get out the mouse and plug it in because he was having difficulty using his fingers on the touchpad, direct the cursor up to "File" and pull it down, go to the second-to-the-last word in the drop-down menu - "Print." Every action took minutes, not seconds, although Bernie had no idea about the real-time pace of what he was doing.

He heard the printer scritching and scratching and tapping away in its dutiful performance and smiled. *Hang it on the door* he thought to himself, and battled to hold onto that thought long enough for the printer to reproduce one sentence. Now, just walk over to the printer, find scotch tape or a pushpin, and do it. Each command began as a straight line but immediately melted into a wet noodle.

Bernie had finished his dissertation, an act of indomitable will. He would be awarded a Ph.D. and the last sentence of his opus was: "Tonight, a *Melanerpes formicivorus* knocked on my door." *It would bring a tear to all who read it*, he smiled at the thought.

Bernie fell hard onto the floor as he struggled to reach the door. Grabbing the table next to the couch, he pulled himself up, only to have the table, lamp, and everything that had been left on the table, fly off and hit him. He fell again. The tingling numbness was now up higher than his knees and reaching from his fingers to his shoulders. It wasn't an unpleasant sensation, exactly, but it did make simple motor control difficult. Bernie wasn't defeated yet. He crawled to the door. He strained to reach up and open it. Grabbing each side of the door knob, he hoisted himself up. Unable to think beyond the exact moment he was in, Bernie hadn't counted on the door swinging him right to left, but he managed to hold on as the door sent him flying toward the wall. Still, after hitting the wall, which knocked the coat rack over, he held on. Smiling at his achievement, Bernie willed himself upright, took the piece of paper he had been holding with his lips, and taped it to the door in what felt like a gyrating pin-the-tale-on-the-donkey move. He fell down again.

Without warning, he vomited. It was a dry-heave followed by gagging, followed by another and more gagging. Finally, some yellow-green bile dribbled from his mouth and he paused there on all fours, panting like a dog. *This is not fun,* he thought. Though his breathing was as shallow as an old man's, he caught his breath the best that he could, raised a fully numb arm up around the back of the couch and pulled mightily. He was able to raise himself enough that he got the other numb hand to the top of the couch and pulled again. Up he rose, panting furiously, as if he was trying to keep up with Wilma on an elliptical machine. *Wilma,* the thought brought a feeling of warmth followed by melancholy. It was the last emotion he felt. Bernie fell to the floor on his back, a trickle of liquid draining from his mouth down his chin to the floor and a pungent cocktail of bodily fluids escaping out his lower orifices as his muscles released the last energy of his life.

Wilma arrived at Bernie's apartment to check on him and give him back his keys. The horror of what she was about to find punched her in the stomach the moment she reached the door. The piece of paper Bernie had posted to the door was taped crookedly only three feet from the floor. When she read it, she knew immediately what it meant. In folklore, a woodpecker knocking on the door was an omen of death.

She stood, shaking, afraid to go in. She knocked and knocked and knocked. Then, she began to sob, still not going inside, still knocking, desperately wanting Bernie to open the door. "Please, God," she pleaded between sobs.

Finally, her hand shaking like a drunk's, she wobbled the key into the lock and turned the bolt. The door only opened a foot before hitting something behind it and she screamed. Doors up and down the hallway opened and people emerged to stare at Wilma screaming and running in place and waving her arms, all at the same time. A neighbor forced the door wide enough to both see the body and squeeze through the opening.

"Call 911!" he shouted to anyone who could hear. Immediately, half a dozen cellphones glowed like emergency beacons on the side of the road. Within minutes, the first responders were present and cordoned off the area. Amidst the squawks of walkie-talkies and the barking of medical code, they prepared the body for transport as police arrived to interview Wilma and neighbors.

Table 12 – *no chairs, a small folded sign reads "Reserved for Bernie," and a single orange rose in a thin red vase sits lonely in the middle of the table.*

The news of Bernie's suicide sickened everyone it touched, whether or not they knew him well. Few of his friends and acquaintances had been touched by the death of a peer and no one wanted to fathom his despair. All of them felt some measure of guilt, and none more than Wilma.

She sobbed through the memorial at the college. She hadn't wanted to go because she felt responsible and as if everyone would be talking about her. Even so, she sat in the front row with the faculty and students of the Ornithology Department and cried loudly at times, especially as a string quartet played one of Bernie's favorite pieces, "The Lark Ascending." The Vaughan Williams music began with a melancholy solo violin echoing the birdsong, then blossomed into a romantic, orchestral, up-and-down flight of the Lark. No eye in the small, unadorned, interfaith collegiate chapel was dry.

Hobart attended, sitting in the back, even though he did not know Bernie. He showed up to support his dawning network of *spot* friends and old high school buddies, especially Cressida and Harrison, who were there mostly to support Wilma. Truth be told, each of them were floundering in shared grief and an ugly tangle of emotions. Besides Wilma, Google was the most obviously unnerved, as he had tried to commit suicide in college, and being so close to it now rattled him from the inside out. Hobart stared at the pew containing Harrison, Cressida, Google, Enid, and Hopi, sitting noticeably close to one another. Looking at their backs and watching their body language as the service progressed, his heart grew soft and envious. These long-time friends variously leaned into one another, placed a head on a shoulder or an arm around another. There was a sweetness to them, like watching children on a playground. Hobart ached to be part of such friendship.

Afterward, they all went to *the spot*, except for Harrison and Wilma. No one knew where the two of them had gone, but they also understood Wilma was too raw for public.

Table 14 – *Wilma's table with the yin-yang inlay, six ladder-back chairs with woven seats encircling the table for four.*

To Hobart's surprise and thrill, Cressida asked him to join their table. He was awestruck by how calm and confident she seemed when asking him. If he had asked her to do anything that was the least bit personal, he imagined himself stuttering helplessly. She even had the grace to make sure he knew everyone, which he did - even if only perfunctorily.

"I feel so bad for Wilma," Hopi said with the forlorn expression of a puppy.

"Yeah, what a guilt trip," Enid exhaled the words through perfectly straight, thin lips.

"I'd be pissed off if I were her."

Everyone looked at Cressida in amazement when she said it. Google looked especially shocked.

"Well," she shot back, "that's a fucking self-centered, shitty thing to do to people, that's all I'm saying. Believe me, I know life can be a shit sandwich, but how could you not think about your family and friends and what that's going to do to them?"

Google stiffened. Hobart recognized the body language and moved in to defuse the situation.

"Any death can evoke anger as well as sorrow; that's why grief is so hard. But remember, Bernie was obviously struggling with drug and alcohol addiction, and that had to have lessened his capacity to fight depression. Depression is a monster and both alcohol and oxycodone are depressants. So, instead of lifting him up, every time he consumed them – especially together – they were pushing him down and down and down. Who knows what started it all but, man, he must have been in a grim place.

Google's posture loosened slightly.

"It's dark, bra, it's a dark, dark place." He said it with a grim voice and looked down at his sandaled feet.

Cressida looked over at Google with a slight tilt of her head, as if trying to see him from a different angle. She knew Google was bipolar, but had never seen him in a deeply depressed state, and in fact, was hardly ever cognizant of his mental health struggles because he seemed so functional.

"I'm sorry, Google, I wasn't thinking," Cressida said softly.

"No prob, Angel Dust. If you haven't traveled down to Guttertown and lived there for a while, you don't know how hard it can be to hold on. Hope is a blossom that requires sunlight, and where Bernie was hanging, there ain't a single ray. Maybe Wilma was a bare bulb in an empty room. But it's not on her."

"I couldn't live without hope," Hopi chirped. "I have never been hopeless and hope I never am." The very thought of it erased the innocence from his face and darkened it.

"I've never lived without hope either, isn't that weird?" Cressida looked at Hobart as she said it, and everyone else suddenly felt as if they had been excused from the table. Hobart recognized the awkwardness ignited by Cressida's stunning and disarming intensity.

"How about you, Enid?" Hobart asked quickly, his eyes darting back and forth from Cressida to Enid. Cressida knew exactly what he was trying to do and it tickled her. She grinned deliciously.

"I would say," Enid drolled, "hope is a strategy employed by those with something difficult before them. I have employed it myself on occasion, but I prefer simply to see things as they are and live with them as best we can."

Silence followed Enid's exposition, as often happened. Hobart thought about the idea of hope as a strategy.

"I'm not sure I can agree with you about hope as a strategy, Enid." Hobart said it gently. Google, for the first time since he had answered Cressida, looked up from his feet and at Hobart. "When we make hope a strategy, I think it is really just wishful thinking. It's what we want to have happen rather than anything we might possibly expect to make happen. I really think hope is nascent in people, a built-in light as Google says. It can get knocked out of us or put under a bushel, but it's there. It's not about what we wish for, but more the knowledge that there is always another possibility to discover or try to make it happen."

"Ya, more like that," Hopi added triumphantly.

Enid raised one eyebrow and stuck her lips out slightly, as if to show she was thinking about it.

"The Bern went into a dark room with no oxygen and gave up hope. End of game. Drugs or no, he put a period at the end of his sentence." Google was grave as he said it, looking straight at Hobart to see what he would answer.

"If we go down that road – especially oxycodone and booze – there is a period at the end of the sentence waiting for us if someone or something else does not intervene. Bernie was just really good at hiding it, and that was his doom."

"But Hobart," Cressida started. It filled Hobart with warmth to hear her call him that instead of Peedad. "You did it. You're in recovery, why not Bernie?"

As soon as she saw the look on Hobart's face, she realized what she had done. He struggled for composure, but everyone could see the look of shock, the color of anger, the tinge of embarrassment or shame streaking his cheeks. Cressida gasped and held her hands to her mouth, and Hobart stiffened.

"That's another story, but I need to go just now. Thanks, you guys, for letting me hang for a while. This was a hard day."

He got up and left with as much gracefulness as he could muster under the circumstances, leaving a nearly full cappuccino and cinnamon roll behind.

"Shit," Cressida hissed under her breath.

"Dude's pretty cool, for that type," Google said, as if nothing awkward had just happened. In fact, for Google, nothing awkward had happened.

"Yes, surprisingly normal," Enid added, equally nonplused.

"Yeah, but what's that about recovery?" Hopi asked.

"Excuse me," Cressida said as she stood up, wiping a tear away and carrying both her and Hobart's dishes to the dirty dish trays.

Front Park – *third bench from the end, dark blue wooden slats with a view of the whole harbor.*

Wilma sat with her face in her hands, leaning hard on her elbows with Harrison's arm draped very lightly across her shoulder. They had been there for nearly two hours with few words between them, throwing bread and peanuts to the gulls and sparrows.

Harrison did not know what to do or say. He figured it was one of those times to just be present, and though she couldn't have articulated it then, Wilma was relieved not to talk. Harry realized he had only ever been to this spot with Cressida, and also in times of sorrow or anger for Cressida. It made him realize how often he practiced simply being present, and that caused him to wonder what the hell anyone could really do for anyone else when shit happened. Cressida's mom was dying, Google's life was on hold as he tried to find an even keel and navigate all the shrinks and medical prognostications and figured out his real limitations, and Wilma was wearing Bernie's suicide like a scarlet letter. *What the fuck can I do for any of these people?* his mind stuttered over the thought like a skip in the vinyl.

The breeze off the water was gentle and constant, and the noise of cars and people seemed far away, even though the park was but a small peninsula into the bay with downtown on its flank. Cormorants flew awkwardly above the water, then dove with force beneath the surface, reappearing yards away. Gulls wafted in the wind, lifting and dropping without moving their wings, crying their mournful sound. Harry suddenly remembered something Hobart had said, a little throwaway line that seemed like just another one of his weird little sayings. "Powerlessness is the portal of God's presence."

Harrison felt excited and frustrated all at the same time. A pinhole had punctured one of his thoughtwalls and a tiny ray of light pierced through, but he didn't know what it meant. It was something about the relationship between God and powerlessness, but what a ridiculous paradox. *A powerless God? God's powerlessness? God's presence in our powerlessness? What good is it for God to be present in our powerlessness if he or she doesn't do anything? A do-nothing God?*

The thoughts were racing through his brain at a hundred miles an hour when Wilma finally said something.

"I'm a practical person, Harrison," she began. "But I feel like I should quit the program and go someplace else and reapply to another doctoral program for next year. I think I could get in someplace, probably not as good as this one, but maybe that's just the cost of having been the ruin of Bernie. It's not practical, for sure, and my folks would just go nuts, but that's what I'm thinking, Harrison."

"First of all, you were not the ruin of Bernie. That's giving yourself a whole lot more power than you actually have," he heard himself saying it and, at the same time, bells went off in his own head. Harrison wanted to talk about power and powerlessness and God, but he knew he couldn't right then and there. But still, his stomach was jumping with the excitement of his thoughts. "My friend Hobart would call that 'stinking thinking.' He thinks all of us should go to some Al-anon meetings."

At that, Wilma turned fiercely toward Harrison, her eyes narrowed with wrinkles between her brows and a steep frown on her lips. But she didn't say anything, and after a pause, Harrison continued.

"All I'm saying is that Bernie had a secret he kept hidden and it killed him. As awful as that is, his addiction and depression shouldn't ruin your life, too."

Again, there was silence before Harry started again, delicately, tentatively, and softly. "Besides, Wilma, I wanted...I have been thinking, wanted, I know it's not good timing, but..."

Harrison reached over and put his hand on her thigh, which, for some reason, seemed less risky than taking her hand. "I wanted you to think about moving in with me when I go to Miss Landrance's house."

He said it, it was out, and he felt exhausted. He was exhausted. The grief and exposure surrounding Bernie's death was exhausting, and he felt as though he had been holding himself back and holding Wilma up all at the same time. "I know it's really early in our relationship, but honestly, I have never felt this way about anyone, ever. I don't even know how to describe how intense my feelings are. I just want to be with you every minute. I sound silly, I know...and I know this is a terrible time to be saying this, and I'm sorry."

Finally, he shut up. Ugh. It was a mistake, he was certain of it. Wilma's expression melted from fierceness to confusion to wonderment to watery eyes and a half smile, half frown. She turned toward him more fully and put one of her hands on his thigh.

"Oh, Harrison," was all she said. She didn't know what else to say. Her thoughts started jumbling up, bumper-to-bumper, until they were all at a standstill. Instead of saying anything, she wrapped both arms around his neck and pulled him close. Harrison took her into his arms, wrapping them around her ribs and holding tight. He didn't know what this meant, but it felt like the right thing to do. Wilma began to sob loudly, to really let loose in a way she hadn't done before. Harrison knew those deep, guttural sounds because he had heard them more than once being ripped up from Cressida's intestines on the end of a fishhook. Though they unnerved him, he wasn't scared, and he knew Wilma's tears had nothing to do with what he had just asked her.

Chapter Fourteen

No Palliative

Table 86 – *all but two chairs are missing, the two remaining are collegiate captain's chairs.*

Sobriety sucks. That was Hobart's conclusion after a particularly disturbing AA meeting. Ringing in his thoughts was a story he had heard, from someone not too much older than him. It was just one more story in an AA circle, around another dirty table, in another dingy church basement. But as the guy spoke it sounded so much like his own drunk-alogue that a brilliant light shone on his own self-centeredness, greed, and stinking thinking.

Christmas was coming, and in addition to Hobart feeling blue, everyone around him was Smurf. In AA meetings and in church, there was a thin veneer of pleasantness but under every smile and greeting was something grim. In spite of the unspoken pall of seasonal depression, church was willfully all about the festivities. Eighty poinsettia plants adorned the inside of the 1960s era A-framed church sanctuary. Red altar and pulpit hangings matched red banners hanging floor to ceiling on the walls, syncopated by electric candles as the centerpiece of fresh greenery on every windowsill. This was supposed to be a happy season, yet Hobart trudged around with depression weighted around his ankles, and he listened to other people whose loss of children or spouse cast a dark shadow on their holiday. The feel-good Christmassy atmosphere in church made it all the worse.

AA was no great joy, either. 'Sharing' never reached the height of real conversation in Hobart's estimation, and what he really wanted was a deep connection with someone. He'd had enough of trading stories. 'No talk-back' is the strict rule of most AA meetings, which meant cutting his bowels open, pulling out the guts and gore inside for everyone in the room to look at and smell, only to hear "Thank you for sharing, Hobart." Then, the next person would commit hari-kari and, "Thank you for sharing, Fred."

A beloved AA myth related how founder Bill "W." left the planet with these words on his lips: "Keep it simple." Hobart was overdosing on simplicity.

"Go easy, and if you can't go easy, go as easy as you can."

"It's when you act on faith that you actually have it."

"One day at a time."

"Keep coming back, it really works."

"Wherever you go, there you are."

"I only drank on special occasions, like the grand opening of a pack of cigarettes." "Without God, I can't. Without me, He won't."

"Expectations are resentments waiting to happen."

"Attitudes are contagious; is yours worth catching?"

"It's okay to look back, just don't stare."

"A resentment is hurting yourself with the hope that someone else will feel the pain." "Serenity is what we get when we stop hoping for a better past."

"We're either working on a recovery or we're working on a relapse."

"No one was ever too stupid to get sober."

It was that last one that always caught him short. Simplistic truisms and proverbs were tossed around in meetings and with happy glad handing afterward, and it made Hobart crazy. He was only half uncomfortable in the knowledge that his resistance to AA culture was from feeling too smart for formulaic thinking. He listened as woebegone ex-drunks talked at length about their struggle, unraveling horrific tales of inebriated disasters or recovery, threatened by gnarled and self-deceiving thoughts that then ended with a "but." "*But,* God don't close no door without opening a window." He knew it was coming, *but* it made him want to puke anyway.

His silent, seething judgement also raised the gholey-headed presence of guilt. Then, he questioned whether it was his intelligence that was getting in the way of sobriety. He ended up in an argument with himself.

Inevitably, he came out of the logjam that AA meetings created inside him, deciding that those truisms had enough practical wisdom buried in them to compensate for being wielded as an antidote for anything that troubled the mind and soul. Still, nearly every meeting was a grind inside his head as he worked toward hearing whatever nugget of truth was there to be mined, or for the serenity he hoped to feel. Slowing it all down and feeling *everything* was Hobart's challenge, as he struggled to emerge from his long-term career of self-numbing.

Yosh, and his tumultuous experiences of the mind in AA, kept hammering at him to "feel it." He spent the better part of a decade burying his feelings in the soft, creamy slush of being stoned or the etherized unselfconsciousness of drunkenness. Emotional pain, even the slightest discomfort, caused turmoil. Instinctively, he wanted to reach for something that would take it away or make him feel better. It was downright Pavlovian. Feel the slightest chink or kink or clump and immediately turn in search of something to mollify or take it away. When a problem appeared, he launched an intense search for its solution. No level of discomfort was small enough to keep him from losing his balance. Three months of sobriety had only made his emotions more intense, although he could feel the rollercoaster was slowing down, the ups less high and the downs less steep.

He was utterly lost in fishing those deep, disturbing waters of thought when startled by Cressida. She pulled the other chair out at table 86 and sat down across from him.

"So, I'm an asshole. I just want you to know I know. I'm really, really sorry, Hobart. It just came out, I guess because of the Bernie thing, and everything was so awful and lying around in plain sight, and I didn't think."

She started to put her hand out to touch his and then thought better of it.

"I won't deny I was angry and embarrassed. Walking up those stairs to my first meeting was the hardest, most humiliating thing I have ever done; or at least that's how I felt at the time. But even now, it's mine, something I can tell if I want, but no one else is supposed to."

"I get that. I'm sorry." Cressida blurted out.

"But I've been thinking about it since. I didn't tell you, you overheard it, and so you did not betray a trust or anything. I never told you directly and didn't ask you not to say anything, so I don't really have any right to expect something different."

"Oh, but I knew better anyway. You didn't have to say something."

"Yeah, I did. That's the point. People need to make things explicit with one another if they don't want to get all tangled up in each other's assumptions and crazy ideas. You never know what someone else is thinking if they don't say it. So, thanks, and I appreciate the awareness, but no offense taken."

"Man, how'd you get so grow'd up?"

"Ha, I feel about as grow'd up as a five-year-old on the first day of kindergarten. But going to meetings has a way of keeping it real. Sobriety requires brutal self-honesty, because the only way you can get so far down the rabbit hole in the first place is denial."

Hobart suddenly felt exposed and regretted saying so much. He pulled in and watched himself cross his arms as he leaned back and tipped the chair on its back two legs.

"So, I had a dream. You want to tell me what it means?"

Cressida didn't wait for him to respond; she simply launched into a description of her dream as Hobart was leaning back with his gaze affixed to her braless chest covered by the tight, thin veneer of a purple cotton halter.

"It started with a bluebird. It was in the grass, hopping around like it had a broken wing, but it didn't. When I went to help her, she flew away and flitted around, zooming in and out and up and down. It was a little crazy, the way dreams are. But then, the next thing I know, it's in my hand, and I realize it's not a bluebird at all. It's a bird with some kind of blue, glittery foil or something wrapped around it, but underneath the foil is a shrink-wrap that totally covers her body. Somehow, I know, the way you just know things in dreams, that I have to be very careful about unwrapping it or her feathers will be pulled out. So, I loosen the blue glittery foil around the edges and carefully pull away at the shrink-wrap, the way you do a band-aid. Then, as the shrink-wrap is coming off, the little bird lets out the silkiest sound of pleasure I've ever heard. It was more than "yummm," or even an orgasm groan. It was startling from this little bird. When I finally got it all unstuck, except for the head, I pull it off and out pops a robin. This bluebird was really a robin, and off she flies in total happiness. That's it. What's it mean?"

Hobart was speechless. It wasn't only that the dream was fascinating and dramatic, like Cressida herself, but she was sitting there of her own accord and telling him something intimate.

"Well, what's it mean?"

"I can't tell you what a dream means - that's something inside your own head. What my therapist says is that everything in a dream is *us* – kind of like all the pieces of an allegory. So, for example, the bluebird is you, and the robin is you, and the foil and shrink-wrap are part of you, and even you watching it all happen is you. Each element is a different part of you interacting with other parts of you."

"Huh, kind of like a prism? You know, the same light hits the glass but is reflected into a bunch of different directions and colors?"

Hobart hadn't thought of a dream as light before, but he liked the idea. "Yeah! Exactly, and the dream is our way of bringing to light something we normally keep from ourselves in the dark."

"Huh." Cressida considered her dream as parts of herself in conversation.

"Can you remember what your feelings were during the dream?" Hobart asked it gently.

"Oh yeah! When the foil and plastic came off, I was sure the robin would be disappointed to discover she was only a brown and rust-colored bird instead of the brilliant blue she had been. I felt disappointed for her, too. But she didn't! She made that sound like it was the most pleasurable experience of her life and flew away as happy as she could be."

"Nice. Which part of you was that?"

Cressida looked back at Hobart in shock. She suddenly felt completely naked and wanted to run away and hide.

"Never mind, you don't need to tell me," Hobart said, quickly registering her vulnerability. "Anyway, that's how you work a dream."

Cressida still sat across from Hobart and looked at him, or looked through him as if he wasn't really there. A drawn-out silence followed, in which Hobart had to sit on his hands and bite his tongue because discomfort rose in him like mercury in a thermometer.

"You know, Hobart, I like you after all. But I can't talk right now, so come back over to the house and see my mom sometime soon, okay?"

She stood up and left. Hobart suddenly felt as if he were about to have diarrhea and would lose the total contents of his bowels right there at table 86. He ran to the tunnel and made it just in time.

710 N. Dill – *dining room with hospital bed on one side, small kitchen style table in front of the window on the other side, with three chairs.*

"Hobart, you should feel honored that Ruthie is cooking for you," Mimi smiled. "I can't remember her ever cooking for any other boy."

"Shut up, Mom," came the voice through the open doorway into the kitchen.

"She's making the one recipe I taught her," Mimi whispered, "it's what she always wanted for her birthday when she was little. Chicken Cordon Bleu. She's very good at it."

Feeling awkward and embarrassed, and exceedingly strange at the turn of events, Hobart smiled weakly. "How are you feeling, Mimi?" he asked, to take the focus off him as much as anything else.

"You know, Hobart, it's very strange. Apart from the weakness, most of the time, I feel normal. I thought dying would have its own unique feeling, wouldn't you? But since I stopped chemo, I feel like myself. But, like I said, tired and weak, too."

Hobart wasn't sure what to say. In his seminary training, he had been a hospital chaplain for a summer and been around death, but never anyone he knew and felt close to. It was difficult for him to keep a professional detachment. Instead, he found himself pulled from two opposing directions – to get closer and to back away.

"It was so tragic what happened to that woodpecker boy, wasn't it?" Mimi said it with such feeling and innocence, it made Hobart's festering mix of emotions about Bernie's addiction and suicide all the starker.

"Yes, terrible. All of us are unnerved by it. Cressida's friend Harrison is really struggling because the woman he is seeing was once Bernie's girlfriend."

"Oh, yes, Ruthie told me. I haven't seen Harrison. He was supposed to come to dinner, but I guess he forgot. Ruthie," Mimi called, "you make sure Harry gets back over here, okay?"

After a silence, in a low raspy voice, Cressida answered, "Okay." Then, "Hey, minister dude, come in here and help set the table."

Mimi smiled at Hobart and he looked sheepishly back at her, shrugged his shoulders, and got up. He soon reappeared with a handful of silverware and napkins. "Fork on the left?" he whispered.

"Yes, and the knife on the inside on the right," Mimi whispered back.

"Anything else?" Hobart called to the kitchen.

"Nope," came the disembodied voice. Immediately, Cressida appeared with a lighter and lit three candles in the center of the small table.

"Mom, are you going to want to eat in bed or sit at the table?"

"At the table, if you'll help me down. But I want my robe on."

Cressida handed her mom the thin, pink robe which she put on over her pea green pajamas, and, with Hobart and Cressida on each side, Mimi stood up and walked to the table. Hobart seated her as if the Queen of England, then sat down himself. After much clinking and clanging, Cressida emerged with three plates, placing the first in front of her mom, the second in front of Hobart, and the third for herself.

Centered in the middle of his orange plate was an elegant, boneless breast of chicken folded in two with a thin slice of ham oozing cheesy sauce from out of the fold. On top, more cheesy sauce drizzled down the golden-kissed sides of white meat. On one edge of the plate were half a dozen pieces of bright green asparagus, clearly placed individually in a fortunate array and sprinkled with Parmesan. On the opposite edge of the plate was a gathering of roasted red potatoes in quarter pieces. The complimentary colors in association with the careful display of each food item evoked a smile from Hobart.

"Dessert is to die for," Cressida smiled across the table at Hobart.

Mimi quietly grasped both their hands, closed her eyes, and bowed her head. "Lord, make us mindful of the needs of others, and bless this food to our use and us to your service. Amen."

"Amen," Hobart answered quietly.

"Dig in, "Cressida smiled.

The forks and knives clinked the plates and ice clinked the water glasses but no one said a word until Hobart gave out an almost lyrical, "Yum!"

"This is delicious; I can't believe how good it is," he added.

"I told you," Mimi chirped.

Cressida grinned, "There's more if you want it."

Table 74 – *a kidney shaped table with pink vinyl fabric glued to the top, stretched and rippled down the sides like a beer cap, with two matching pink upholstered chairs.*

Wilma couldn't sit anywhere near table 12 or 14 and Harrison knew it. This was the first time she had been back at *the spot* in four weeks, and Harrison had been fretting about whether she would ever return. He was astonished when Wilma said she wanted to go to *the spot* after dinner that night.

They were taking their relationship one day at a time, just as Wilma was doing with her life. Neither of them had mentioned Harrison's offer to move in with him at Miss Landrace's house, and it felt to Harrison as if every day was a wait-and-see proposition. Tonight, returning to *the spot* seemed like progress.

Wilma held a sumptuous-looking salted caramel mocha with a raspberry turnover, while Harrison sipped a miniature cup filled with black oily espresso and nibbled on a giant peanut- butter chocolate chip cookie. They didn't speak as they people-watched the crowded café.

"Harry," Wilma said suddenly, "I've made a decision."

The somber sound of her voice filled Harrison with dread. He felt himself shaking, his abs tightening from the inside out.

"I don't know if you were serious or have had second thoughts in the last month, but if you think you still want to move in together...I want to."

"Oh my god! Yes! Of course!"

Harrison couldn't believe it. He had been steeling himself for just the opposite as the days went by with the pall of grief enveloping Wilma and, from its close proximity, himself. He had to will his arms not to wave and his legs not to leap.

Slowly, deliberately, Harrison uttered, "I'm surprised." He heard his voice crack with a high-pitched squeak. He cleared his throat and tried again. "I am surprised. I was afraid you had decided not to come back after Christmas."

Wilma teared up, one bead of moisture overflowing the corner of one eye and dripping silently down her cheek.

"I know I haven't been very good company the past month and I have to say, you have been the most amazing man I have ever known during the whole thing. You allowed me to be quiet and withdrawn, you talked when I felt like talking, you held me when I just wanted to be held, you didn't ask or urge me to make love, and all this time I knew I just couldn't. You have been, like, the perfect dance partner that knew exactly when to step, where, and how. I know I have been totally self-absorbed, but I want you to know that I have noticed you and been more aware than you will ever know of how well you treated me. If anyone has ever loved me, it has been you this past month. Not only that, you have taught me how to love, and I want the chance to love you like you have loved me."

Wilma took both of her hands and softly placed one on each of Harrison's cheeks. She leaned over and touched his mouth with her wet, salty, voluptuous lips, holding them on his with such tenderness that he thought he might melt. They opened their eyes at the same time, faces so close they could feel one another's breath. "I love you, Harrison Jordan."

Chapter Fifteen

"Connections"

"How do you know about thoughtwalls!" It was an exclamation more than a question, as Harrison's confusion and shock blared into the open.

"Cressida told me," was all Hobart said. He may have even felt smug because, if he was being honest, Hobart was frequently poked by feelings of competitiveness with Harrison. Cressida was the source of that internal pinch, to be sure, but Harrison was also what Hobart aspired to be – cool, respected by his peers, and seemingly unconcerned about recognition and achievement. Even so, Hobart realized that, while it was unlikely he would ever be cool like Harrison, now that he was a minister, the fantasy had gone completely limp.

Unbeknownst to Hobart, and not truly recognized by himself, Harrison envied Hobart. The minister part was way too foreign and weird, but he recognized Hobart was getting paid to think about shit, and that was Harrison's passion. Hobart had figured out a scam in which he hung out and could go tripping up thoughtwalls, kayaking down rivers of consciousness, and generally dance in the rave of the mind. Harrison wanted that job in the worst way, but working in a bookstore was as close as he had gotten to it. As it turned out, it wasn't very close.

"Man, I don't get why she's pissed at me. Who's been her best, and sometimes only, friend for more than a decade? Now, she's all cozy up in your space, even though she has thought of you as a useless stoner since junior high. The cosmos as we have known them are crumbling, and Cressida is the agent of chaos bringing it on."

It took all the emotional discipline Hobart had, which was not much, to keep from saying something condescending. Learning to be less passive-aggressive was another one of his goals from therapy. So, Hobart stopped himself. He searched his emotions for a way to stand on level ground with Harrison. Immediately, he felt his deep thirst for a real friend swell up in the middle of his throat.

"Too true. Everything and everyone seems to be changing. It's weird." Hobart paused and opened the next door, in spite of the tight, rusty hinge that didn't want to open. "I quit doing drugs."

"I heard that, dude. I don't know what to make of it. You've always been a stoner and even though we made fun of you for it, it was like, you know, like a clock that keeps time. It was kind of comforting." Then, Harrison realized what he had said. "But, hey, I mean, it's cool and everything. Was it hard?"

"No, it *'is'* hard. You remember Blake Bledsoe who moved to Alabama or Mississippi or Georgia, one of those places in ninth grade? I guess you would have been in seventh."

"Yeah, I remember him all right; he beat the shit out of me and stole my extra-large Reese's Peanut Butter Cup."

"Well, when we were in seventh grade, he asked me if I wanted to get high. I only vaguely knew what he was asking, but I wanted to be cool with him, so I said yes. I started smoking dope way back then. It was love at first toke. Feeling stoned became home. After high school, as best I can remember, I got stoned every day for almost ten years. The last six months has been like meeting myself in seventh grade again. It's rough."

"Whoa, I never thought of it like that, kind of Alice in Wonderland in reverse. But I heard you were going to AA?"

"Wow, it's really out there, huh? Well, I glommed onto booze, too, because I could do that in public and, you know, church life. In seminary, it was cool if you drank, but smoking dope was a no-no. So, I did one privately and the other publicly. I tried NA, but we're talking heavy drug shit in those groups. Being a stoner is a special category of in-between, but I can tell you, it's its own kind of prison."

"It's weird with the dope and alcohol and shit. Cressy and me, even in high school, it was the kind of thing we could take or leave. I kinda liked getting high and she was more partial to those sweet drinks, but she didn't like the feeling of being drunk. I didn't like feeling too stoned either, just a little buzzed. But then, there were other people who couldn't stop. I wonder what makes the difference?"

"Physiology and psychology, I guess; all I know is that when you start getting stoned on a regular basis when you're in seventh grade, the circuits get fried and re-directed, and there are some things that just don't work very well anymore. The longer I am straight and sober, the more regret and grief I feel for what could have been, might have been. But in the program, regrets are discouraged."

"Man, Hobart, it's just hard to imagine you in an AA meeting. I mean, I never thought about what one was like but, you know, seen them on television and movies. You sit back here in the press box and type away on sermons and shit, and people come and talk to you about their thoughtwalls, and all the time you're going to AA meetings and hanging your head among the alkies. It's like you're the cool dude one minute and down and out in the next scene."

Hobart was stunned that Harrison ever thought of him as cool and chagrined at the image of himself as indistinguishable from the crusty old-timers that populate some of the AA meetings he attended. He managed a chuckle.

"I think you got AA meetings all wrong. There is usually more laughter than somber confessions. I'm what they call a 'high-bottom drunk' because I didn't lose a job, a wife, wreck the car, or go to jail before I quit. When you hear those men and women talk about what they went through and what they lost, then everyone laughs in recognition of the utter craziness of the bizarre thinking that made such a life possible. It's cool. I don't mean chuckles, but belly laughs.

When you hear how deranged other people's thinking gets, and the terrible things it leads to, your own brand of insanity feels a little more manageable."

"Huh, you're right. I never thought of AA meetings and laughter going together. Interesting. But let me ask you, - changing the subject - what did Cressida tell you about thoughtwalls?"

"Oh, just that it was your term for getting stuck on a thought or perspective you want to get deeper into. I call them 'wellheads', 'cause I know there is a whole lot of shit down there that would explode if there wasn't a cork in it."

"Hmm, I don't think of it as the wall keeping something inside, I think of it as keeping me outside. It's like trying to find the beginning on a roll of clear plastic tape; if you find it, you can peel off another layer, but sometimes, no matter how hard you look, you can't find the damn thing."

"I wish my wellheads didn't feel so malevolent. I like your concept better – more curious than daunting."

"Yeah? Cool." Harrison felt pleased that he had said something that Hobart recognized as valuable, maybe even better than something he had thought of before.

710 North Dill Street – *front steps during a "January thaw" with the sun out and the temperature at a mild fifty.*

"She's getting worse, faster." Cressida said it fast as if ripping a Band-Aid off a scab.

"You think? She seems about the same to me," Hobart said with a high note at the end of the sentence.

"No, she never gets her energy back. Each setback takes her down a little bit more and she never quite gets back to where she was. For the past two weeks, it seems to have been going faster."

Hobart searched for something to say, but there was nothing to say. Without even thinking about it, he put his arm around Cressida's shoulder and squeezed. But then, he thought about it and pulled his arm away, even as she leaned into him slightly. The silence was full of everything they did not want to talk about.

"Will you do me a favor?" Cressida asked after what felt like a very long time.

"Sure, what?"

"Will you call me Ruth, or even Ruthie for a little bit? Just to try it out?"

Hobart turned and looked at her face as she looked into his. He tried to read those crystal eyes surrounded by thick, dark lines of makeup.

"Okay, why?"

"I dunno, exactly. My mom is the only person on earth who calls me that and...and she'll be gone. I guess I want to know if anyone else can call me that, or maybe even if I want everyone to start calling me that. I'm not sure."

"Okay, Ruth. Hmmm, I think maybe Ruthie at first. Okay, Ruthie. No, Ruth. Okay, Ruth."

There was another silence between them in which the winter birds sang and flitted bush to bush in the front yard. One of them was on the cracked sidewalk leading to the street, pecking at something.

"Ruth," Hobart said again, trying it on for size.

"I like that," Ruth answered. "I also like that the sun is out and it's warm enough to sit on the step and *breathe*."

"Yeah, relief."

"Hobart?"

"Yeah...Ruthie?"

"Will you tell me what my mom told you that she hasn't told me?"

Hobart was gripped by a frigid wind inside, this thought immediately froze in place. He wanted nothing more than to continue this walk into intimacy with Ruth, the new Cressida that only he seemed to know, but he was bound by a sacred trust. In his theological world, not much was absolute, which would have surprised his peers that lumped all Christianity into the evangelical and fundamentalist mold. But the bond between confessor and penitent was absolute and never to be broken. In fact, according to the rules that guarded the confessional, even the penitent could not bring up what was confessed to the confessor once absolution had been pronounced. It was to be as if it was gone completely, removed forever. That was its power.

"I can't," Hobart said in a pleading tone, ready to defend it against Cressida's angry onslaught.

"I didn't think so," She said it with a calm sadness that completely disarmed him. "You feel strong to me. Can I just lean on you, please?" Then, her small tilt toward his shoulder became a full-weighted lean with her head on his shoulder. In order to keep her from falling on his lap, he had to put his arm fully around her and hold her in place. The two of them sat there in silence, watching the sparrow hop and peck on the sidewalk.

Table 54 – *the smooth, clear resin covering the Brio train pieces completely concealed by two computers, open spiral notebooks, saucers, plates, coffee cups, and crumbs.*

"I have never seen you so excited," Wilma smiled at Harrison.

"I haven't been this excited, except when you said you would move in with me. It just feels so right; now all I have to do is figure out how."

"As soon as you said it, it was like, 'Of course!'"

"I know, right? Like, how long can something be right in front of you and you don't see it? Crazy. But this is the first thing that has ever felt like it fit, and even though I haven't started yet, I know it's right."

Wilma reached across the table and slipped his hand into hers, rubbed it, and beamed at Harrison. "I will help you any way I can. We can make the house just right, and you can have a schedule, and I will be as quiet as a mouse except when I look at you and want you naked right then and there." At that, they both laughed and gazed at each other, Harrison feeling a fullness he had rarely ever felt.

"Whew, that's intense." Harrison grinned. "I've been checking out MFA programs and there are three here in Creative Writing. There are also goo-gads of writing workshops and programs for people who are working and writing on the side – which I think is everyone except a few lucky authors that somehow blast off. The Internet has democratized writing, giving access to publishing that many wouldn't have had before, but also wreaked havoc on the profession. Like Indie musicians, it's hard to make a living from writing these days. But I don't even know what kind of writer I am yet."

"You'll figure it out. I don't know what kind of ornithologist I am either, or at least, I'm not sure about my concentration."

"Well, I know books, now I will learn how to write them. It just feels right. I have written so many ideas in my journal over the years that I thought I was preserving just to think about later. Now, I realize they are short stories, poems, even books just waiting to happen."

Just then, Google walked over from table 27, pulled a chair backwards between his legs, and sat down.

"The bra-man and sister shine, what's happening?"

"Goo, I decided what I'm going to do when I grow up! I am going to be a writer."

"Awesome. 'Thoughtwall Man becomes pioneer of the mind, leading a cavalcade into the new frontier.' Spike it dude." Google, Harrison, and Wilma slapped high-fives all around.

"You know, though, Harry, the wall you got to scale is shear and the ladder rickety."

"Whatd'ya mean?"

"So, like, these statistics are a few years old, but they haven't changed. In 2009, there were 1,052,803 books published in the United States. That's triple the number published in 2005, and yet, book sales peaked in 2007, then fell five percent. Still falling, I think. The average non-fiction book sells less than two-hundred and fifty copies, and less than three-thousand copies over its life-time. Worse yet, less than one percent of the books published each year will find their way to the shelf of a bookstore. Most books published today are only selling to the publisher's and the author's communities, and the author has to do most of the marketing, not the publisher. There's way more stars in the sky to reach for, but fewer people gazing, dude."

Harrison and Wilma were slumping in their chairs. No one said a word as Google's bucket of cold water dripped over the moment.

"But Harrison, my man, you have the goods. Your mind works, bra, and it worms in and out of places no one else can go. You've got the word, now, pass it on to the rest of us. We're waiting, dude, you can do it!"

With that, Google stood up, turned his chair around and pushed it back under the table. "Later, my ray of hope and light," he declared over his shoulder, heading back to table 27 and Enid, who was playing solitaire with actual playing cards instead of her phone.

Harrison and Wilma looked at each other and silently went back to their respective computers.

710 North Dill Street – *cluttered dining room with hospital bed.*

The table next to the bed was crowded with newspapers, books, Kleenex, and a giant pink water bottle with a ribbed purple straw sticking out. The two comfortable chairs in the room were occupied, one with dirty towels and sheets and the other with clean linens draping it. The dining room table had no extra leaves in it, which left it an oval shape big enough to host four ladder-back chairs, each of which had something hanging from or over it. Mimi was sleeping on her back with her torso propped up at a thirty-degree angle. Hobart walked lightly into the room, hesitated as he looked for a clear surface to sit on, then removed the clean linens and quietly placed them over one of the ladder-back chairs on top of a bright green sweater.

"It's chaos in here," Mimi said with a croak in her voice.

"Looks like my house," Hobart offered.

"I'm worried about Ruthie, Hobart. I think she is overwhelmed. She has to work, take care of me, and deal with the house. It's too much."

"Mimi, I have to say, I think Ruth is doing very well - considering. Really, your daughter is a rock – maybe a little molten inside, but that just gives her warmth." He smiled, and she smiled back.

"You two are getting close, aren't you?"

Hobart blushed and didn't say anything.

"Well, I'm glad. If there were two people ever meant for each other, it is you and Ruthie. Just don't hurry it. Let time show you mercy and grace. That first growing season between two people needs lots of tenderness so that it becomes lush and rooted. Enjoy it; let it seep deep into each of you before enjoying any of its fruits. Walk in the rain, but don't devour each other. Hold hands, but don't try to fill every moment. Talk deep into the night, but don't rush to tell every secret you know. I envy the two of you."

Hobart did not know what to say. Was he the pastor or the one being ministered to? He never really knew with Mimi and had given up trying to hold the boundaries.

"Um, Mimi? Remember that thing you wanted to share with Cress...Ruth, before...you die?" The word sounded so loud in the room, even though his voice was soft. Hobart could hardly breathe. "Well, I think it is time. Not that it's your time, but it's time for her. I think she is ready."

"Oh, Hobart, I don't know. I may not be ready. To tell you the truth, I kind of want to tell her, then exit, you know what I mean?"

Tears welled up in Hobart's eyes as he said, "Mimi, you are more ready to die than we are to let you go. But yeah, I know what you mean. Two things about that, though: First, you don't get to choose when death comes, and second, maybe it would be good if she had some time with you to process it a little rather than have it be a hit and run."

"Sometimes, Hobart, you're wise beyond your years,"

Chapter Sixteen

Brokenness

Behind Table 91 and from Table 86 – *the corner where the black wall meets the dark blue wall, and in the "Colgate" captain's chair at the table where the Che quote carved into the table is now traced with red marker.*

"Are you going to sit back there all day?" Hobart said over his shoulder.

"Maybe."

"Are there still sugar ants crawling around back there?"

"Maybe."

"You want me to leave you alone?"

"Maybe...not."

Hobart got up and walked over into the shadows of the dark corner, beneath the purple glow of the black light, and slid down with his back against the wall, making a thud as he landed next to Ruth. Before he could say anything, Harrison arrived and did the same thing on the other side of Cressida.

"We're ganging up on you," Hobart said.

"What is this?" Ruth looked one way then the other.

"I need you to like me again," Harrison said plaintively.

"Fuck you."

"Do you even remember what you're angry about?" Hobart asked.

Ruth glared at him, but there was a glimmer of doubt that flickered through her stare. "Come on, Cressy, whatever I did, I'm sorry. I just need to get right with you, and I need to see your mom. Please?"

"Just 'cause I don't remember right now doesn't mean I won't remember later. I'm all blocked up and confused right now, so don't think I won't remember what you did, whatever it was, Harrison Jordan."

She looked at him fiercely, but within moments, her eyes softened. Tears welled up without a sound, and one small bead rolled from the outside corner of her left eye and down her cheek. Harrison watched it leave a track of glistening purple light from her eye to her lip. Then, he noticed she was not wearing makeup. Gone were the dark lines of black that had always outlined her eyes and the thick black glue that had always laden her eyelashes. Her face looked naked, strangely plain. But the more Harrison looked, the more he could see how extraordinary her eyes and face actually were, and then it was as if he had never seen her with makeup. He was taken aback and marveled at the moment.

"You're not wearing makeup."

"Yeah, so?"

"I just noticed. I've never seen you without makeup before."

"Yeah? What's your point?"

"No, no point. I mean, you look great. I'm just, I don't know, shocked. But really, it's amazing. You look fantastic without makeup. I mean, you looked great with it; I'm just, you know, like, what's up? That's a big change."

"It's been coming. But today was the day."

"Wow, somehow, that seems big, like even more than when you started wearing colors."

"Can we talk about something else?" It was a statement more than a question, her voice strong and steady.

"Yeah, right. Okay." Harrison was clearly unnerved and, at the same time, feeling the presence of détente. "So, maybe I could come over tonight and see Mimi?"

"Not tonight, Harry, I've got a date with her to talk. How about tomorrow?"

"Sure, okay. I work until three. Hey, do you guys want to have dinner with Wilma and me, then go over to Miss Landrace's house? You haven't seen it yet."

Ruth and Hobart turned and looked at each other. They had never done anything socially together; that would acknowledge the dawning intimacy between them. It was startling to have Harrison act like it was perfectly natural.

"Sure." Ruth said sharply, looking at Hobart as if it was a challenge.

"Uh, um, I guess, maybe, sure," Hobart stuttered.

"Great. How about tomorrow, after I visit Mimi?"

"Yep," Ruth agreed.

"Um, okay then," Hobart uttered hesitantly.

"Cool." Harrison sprang up and was off before Hobart could even get a clear thought in his head about what was happening.

"Awkward," she said, looking straight ahead.

"A little," he said, looking at the floor for ants.

Table 86 – *the spot is nearly empty of customers at the dinner hour and before the evening rush.*

"Can I ask you a personal question?" Harrison Jordan posed it with an unusual tone of earnestness that caused Hobart to smile.

"Since when do you ask if you can ask? Shoot."

"I don't get the whole church thing."

"That's a statement, not a question."

"I mean, I don't exactly get why you are a minister. Church is so, well, so straight. You know, like clothes your parents wear that you wouldn't be caught dead in."

"I'm a thoughtwall?"

"Yeah! You are a thoughtwall. But then again, like you said once, all of us are really just getting to know each other all over again. Growing up together, there were things we never knew or even thought to ask about each other, and connecting again like this, well, those things are sort of glaring now. But I mean, really, you were our stoner and now you're our priest. Really?"

Hobart let out a chuckle that muffled the pain.

"Weren't you a religion major or something?" Hobart asked, nudging the conversation away from himself.

"Minor, religion *minor*. And honestly, that's just because I could get it cheap. I had already taken three courses and, heading into my senior year, realized that if I took one more, I would have a minor as well as a double-major." Harrison grinned, the boy who just gulped a forbidden cookie.

"What was you major, English?"

"Nah, I wish. I should have, looking back at it. Sociology and Math."

"No way."

"True. I always loved math but wasn't interested in any of the professions that use it a lot. Like Alfred North Whitehead, I discovered that delving into the mathematical nature of the universe blew my mind open, and then I could stare at infinity. But sociology was grounding, and discovering the intricacies of human nature became one of those attraction-repulsion things."

"But where did religion fit in?" Hobart found himself authentically curious.

"That's the thing, I know hardly anything about modern organized religion. I took weird, esoteric courses: 'African Animist Religions,' 'Ancient Chinese Buddhism, the roots of Falun Gong,' 'Native American Religion Before the Missionaries,' and 'Moses: Jewish and Muslim Prophet.' What you do might as well be Voodoo for all I know."

Hobart looked Harry in the eyes, penetrating the glass in search of something soft enough to feel safe. He looked away, down to the right, scratching for a memory. Then, Hobart's eyes stared straight ahead, stuck in neutral. Finally, with a small shudder, he wrestled free and spoke.

"Did you ever try walking around in your dad's shoes when you were a kid?"

"Oh, yeah, I remember doing that!" They both chuckled.

"That's what I'm doing, Harry."

Harrison stared at Hobart, wondering if he was going to say something more, while Hobart stared at the Che quote carved into the table top.

Hobart heard the echo of Yosh's words, "When you make your soul known to no one but yourself, your soul has no air to breathe." Then, just before he spoke again, he imagined he could hear his soul take a giant gulp and inhale.

"Healing is not an individual sport." Hobart said it definitively, as if it was obvious and needed no more explanation.

"Okay..." Harrison said it with intentional tentativeness, giving Hobart a bridge to say more.

"Well, I think, to people on the outside of something, the people on the inside all look alike. I mean, the stereotype of an AA meeting is of a bunch of derelicts and other gruff, working-class guys sitting around talking about how hard it is to stay sober. And 'church' looks like a bunch of people in suits, ties, and dresses, with polished shoes, singing nineteenth century hymns and getting yelled at from the pulpit. To anyone on the outside, there is nothing in those stereotypes that looks the least bit attractive. Right?"

"I guess not," Harrison chuckled.

"On the inside, to the people who are there and have sunk their teeth into it, it looks and feels completely different from how it appears to those on the outside. In each case, it is about healing and recovery."

"I get 'healing and recovery' with AA, but what are people in church recovering from?"

"Life. All kinds of shit. I don't know anyone, in church or out, that isn't in need of healing from something, or in hopes of recovering from one kind of wound or another."

Hobart waited for Harry to object, but he didn't.

"Think about Bernie," Hobart asked, and it jolted Harry to sit more upright. "He was the epitome of someone in need of healing and recovery, and, if he had been able to reach out and ask for help, he might be alive and healing at this moment. It's being trapped inside that makes us fragile, and the ones who can hazard the risk to move outside with it, paradoxically, become more resilient."

"Oh man, Bernie. I shudder when I think of what it was like to be in his head." Harry shook his head to clear the image.

"And he didn't have to be there, at least not all by himself."

"Why was he, do you think?"

"Shame is powerful. He was ashamed of himself. Who knows for what, or where the root of his shame came from – and maybe it was all coming from him without help from others, but I doubt it. Shame is powerful. It keeps us from opening our heart to allow for healing. And that's what AA and church do when they are at their best: host an open-air market for healing."

Harry thought about his images of church and AA, and they didn't look anything like the kind of thing Hobart was intimating.

"You've got a church of sorts." Hobart broke into Harry's silence.

"What? Who?"

"You've got church," Hobart reiterated, "with Google and Enid, Hopi and Wilma, and of course, Ruth. I mean Cressida. I watch you guys and listen to what's going on between you, and it feels like church in the making. A small community of healing and recovery from life's bumps and bruises."

"Calling us 'church' is a stretch, dude."

"I don't know, think about it. You talk openly with one another about things that matter, life, and even death stuff sometimes. You and Google had a falling out because you hurt him deeply, and what happened? You came back to it and understood each other, and healing that wound brought you closer. The same thing just happened between you and Cressida. But you also play together, and make meaning together, and laugh. You truly *see* each other, too. You know one another's tender places and dysfunctions and wounds. Most of the time, you honor what you know rather than using it to your own advantage against one another. You have a community with one another. The deeper it is, the more it approaches what I call spiritual. What I mean by spiritual community is one that transforms the people in it. The whole becomes greater than the sum of its parts and, almost miraculously, it is woven into something the participants don't even know is being fashioned."

"Hmmm." Harrison Jordan was speechless, lulled into a mesmerizing reflection as he peered up at this thoughtwall.

Several minutes of silence passed, long enough that Hobart went back to looking at his computer screen. Then Harrison added, "You forgot someone."

"Huh?"

"You forgot someone when you were describing our 'church.'"

"Who?"

"You."

Even though Hobart felt like an outsider, as he always had, as soon as Harrison said it, he knew it to be true. Hobart did feel like part of that community, the little *spot* community. Both Harry and Ruth had intentionally brought him into it. Hobart chuckled over the thought of his membership in '*the spot* church'.

Then, Hobart grimaced slightly, sitting as he did on the recognition that he had not really answered Harrison's question. Even though his new profession felt like a shoe many sizes too big for him, it also felt like something he would be able to grow into. At the same time, he did not know how to explain it to Harry or anyone else. Fortunately, he had distracted Harrison Jordan with a new thoughtwall.

Table 27 – *new red and green striped umbrella raised with white Christmas tree lights strung from its ribs.*

"Like the new glow, bro?" Google shouted across the cafe at Hopi and his friend standing at the bar making an order. Hopi waved back, and the man with him smiled. "Looks like the Hopi has a new cuddle-boy, Enid. You ask the questions cause you're sneakier than me."

Enid looked back at Google with a face that to anyone else looked expressionless, but that he could see was a grimace. Within minutes, Hopi and his friend approached, holding hands and seeming almost to skip with exuberance.

"Hi guys!" Hopi exclaimed, "This is Raoul. Raoul, meet Google and Enid."

"Yo, Ra, how's it hanging?"

"Nice to meet you, Raoul," Enid added.

"Hi. This is a cool place, I've never been to the Caffeination Journey before. How long has it been here?"

"Dude," Google snorted, "since Sarah was a triceratops. If you look at the floor, it's got moss and mold on it from when the troops came home after the first World War."

"Noooo!" Hopi oozed. "He's kidding, Raoul. But it has been here awhile. Everyone just calls it '*the spot*.'"

"You guys gonna sit?" Enid asked.

"Sure!" Hopi exclaimed in his routine chirp. He and Raoul put their coffees on the clear table top and pulled up chairs under the umbrella. "Where's everybody else?"

"Dunno," Google said glibly, "but I think there's something happening at Mimi's. The Ho was looking anxious as he said he was headed over there to meet Cressy. Of course, he may just have been anxious about meeting Cressy."

They all laughed except Raoul, who looked curious.

"Hobart is a minister," Enid explained, "and he's been hanging around our friend, Cressida, a lot lately. Like, we're thinking something's up, even though Hobart doesn't know something's up. In fact, he may be the only one who doesn't know something is up. But our friend Cressida is a handful..."

"And then some!" Hopi interjected.

"Yes," Enid explained placidly. "Cressida is a person of somewhat uneven emotions that often crinkle the air like static electricity wherever she is standing."

More laughter ensued, and Raoul shook his head dramatically as if he understood perfectly.

"Ra-man, or can I just call you 'Noodle' for short?" Google said, looking straight at Raoul, but continuing before he received a response. "Where are you from?"

Enid looked at Google again, expressionless to everyone else, but with a signal that told Google he was butting in after inviting her to pry.

"I recently moved here from Buffalo, New York." He answered with extreme earnestness, his large brown eyes opened widely.

"What brings you to our fair city?" Enid invited, almost warmly.

"I just got a job with the newspaper. I'm a journalist and I'll be doing the arts beat."

"How cool is that!" Hopi blurted.

"Pretty cool," Enid drolled.

"And how did the Hop-ster and the Ra-man meet?" Google grinned professorially.

"OkCupid, of course!" they both said, simultaneously and with the same note and degree of enthusiasm as if Siamese twins.

"Honestly, it was love at first date," Raoul hummed.

"So true," Hopi said dreamily and grabbed Raoul's hand again.

"How lovely for you," Enid extolled with a dry voice and straight lips. "Google and I had a similar experience in the dark."

Raoul grinned, but it was clear he wasn't quite sure how much to grin. "We're going to Alice's tonight," Raoul then declared.

"Yeah, there's a new show there that everyone says is like 'Lips' in NYC and we can hardly wait," Hopi enthused. "But we better get going, too, cause we've also got reservations at Hubbub's for dinner first. I'm starved!"

With that, Hopi and Raoul jumped up from their chairs as if synchronized divers, each taking hold of their coffee at the exact same moment and finishing off what was left with the exact same motion. "Bye, then!" Hopi shouted.

"See ya, nice to meet ya!" Raoul rhymed. Holding hands, they never looked back as they left the cafe.

"Wow, peas in a pod," Enid said with a rush of almost discernible excitement.

"Yep, the Hop-ster found himself and fell in love!"

Chapter Seventeen

Unearthed

710 North Dill Street – *the living room.*

"It was the sixteenth night in a row he came home drunk," Mimi's voice was grim. She took a sip from the pink water bottle on the stand next to the over-stuffed red chair in the living room. Ruth sat on the matching ottoman, situated at an angle while holding her mom's hands. Ruth's knees pointed higher than her lap as her long legs were parked awkwardly in the small space between the ottoman and chair.

Hobart sat in the corner of the beige and yellow couch across the room from them, almost fully enveloped in a shadow cast by a single lamp in the opposite corner from mother and daughter. The squirrel in his stomach was a cuddled yearning to be right next to both of them, up close in the heat of their fierce love for one another. But Hobart was the outsider tonight, the strange presence allowing a dangerous truth to bloom under the cover of its silent witness.

"I had been counting them. Your father had been a binge drinker when we got married, getting drunk on occasion, which allowed me to tell myself it was just what young men do. But the binges got closer together and he became more violent as they did."

Mimi shifted her hips, as if a pain had settled in one and she wanted to shift it to the other. Hobart was suddenly gripped by how skeletal she was, shocked by what seemed so sudden a loss of weight.

"He hit me for no reason, just because he was angry inside. He hit me in places the bruises wouldn't show – the back, my stomach...ribs. He broke two of my ribs when I was pregnant with you, and the fact he couldn't kick me in the stomach made him angrier still. He shoved me, pushed me down, and slapped me. All I could do was try to protect you inside me, cover you with my arms and leave my head exposed."

"But didn't anyone know? What about your doctor? Wasn't there anyone you could call, Mom?"

"Oh Ruthie, I've looked back a thousand times and kicked myself for not doing something, calling someone. I was ashamed, and scared, of course. He usually didn't hurt me unless he was drunk, but I was afraid to provoke him. I suppose, losing both my parents so young, I didn't really know how to ask for help or who to get help from. I covered up the bruises as best I could. I didn't go to the doctor 'cause we didn't have money. Honey, I can't explain it. I should have done something, I should have, but I just couldn't. I don't know why, even now, telling you, I don't know why."

Mimi began to sob and lean into Ruth. Ruth leaned back into Mimi and cried louder. In a tangled heap overflowing both red chair and ottoman, they heaved in and out as Hobart fought the urge to cross the room and hold them both.

This is where his training kicked in, steel girders holding in his every instinct to 'do something.' *Simple presence*, he said to himself. *Just be present.* He had been taught the discipline of presence in his pastoral internship at the hospital, learning to resist the temptation to "do" in order to allow the patient to lead. It was a painful lesson in powerlessness, when the object was not to fix anything but to simply be with another person in their suffering or in their joy. Anything he might do at that moment would be a distraction from what Mimi and Ruth needed to do together. He was only a witness to the burning bush, taking off his shoes in the present of the sacred and listening in silence.

"After you were born," Mimi's voice was hoarse and raspy as she gathered the strength to continue, "everything changed." Mimi reached up and cupped Ruth's face in her hands. "You changed me."

"How, Mommy, how?"

"For whatever reason, I wasn't able to protect myself or run away. But, after you were born, I knew that I had to protect you."

She fell silent and pulled back within herself, as if remembering terrible moments, an anguished pain distorting her face in the silence. Ruth leaned back in recognition that she didn't belong inside those memories, but Hobart could tell that the grip on her mother's hands had tightened.

"We were so poor, you can't even imagine. I had nowhere to run and nothing to run with. I couldn't even buy diapers without him. He wouldn't give me any money and I couldn't leave the house without his permission. When he went to work, I was told to stay inside or in the backyard. I had been hit for walking down the block. I was so afraid. I just kept playing over in my head what my options were, night after night and day after day. Then, one day, when you were four months old and wouldn't stop crying, he started screaming at you. He grabbed you from my arms and I couldn't stop him. He put his face right in your face and screamed. It was the kill-or-be-killed scream of a wounded animal spilling out of his awful soul. All I could do was hover around the two of you, begging for him to give you back. I was terrified and so powerless."

"If I tried to grab you it would provoke him more, and if I tried to hurt him, I wouldn't succeed and you would pay the price. Oh my God, I can't describe the clawing inside or the horror on the outside of that moment."

"Oh, Momma, I never knew it was like that. I'm so sorry," and again, they collapsed into one another's tears. Hobart rose up from the couch and sat down again. The rawness was blanketed under the comforter of the darkened room, and though he did not know it, Hobart's presence gave both women a sense of safety in which to enter further and further into their pain.

"That is when I knew what I had to do, Ruthie. I decided then and there. It took weeks for me to decide how to do it, but it was that moment that gave me the conviction. He threw you at me and left to go get drunker. I held you in my arms and we cried together until we both fell asleep."

"On that sixteenth night of coming home drunk, he passed out on the bed. He was out cold. God help me Ruthie, I draped a pillowcase over his head to restrict the splatter and I crushed his skull with a short-handled sledgehammer."

Ruth's gasp was loud and unrestrained. Her hands pulled back to cover her mouth. She was shaking with noises coming from her mouth, but no audible words. Her feet began to tap the floor as if what was filling up her body needed some motion to escape. She stood up and immediately sat down again. Mimi held her face in her hands, her elbows holding the weight on her thighs.

Ruth stood up again and walked to the other side of the room and back. She sat down facing her mom, then stood up and went over to the couch and looked down at Hobart, but said nothing. Then, she went back and sat down facing her mom again. As if an involuntary motion, her hands reached out and grasped both of Mimi's arms around the biceps.

"Momma, what did you do? What happened? I can't believe you're telling me this. This isn't you. Momma, that really happened?"

Mimi slowly unfolded and looked at her daughter. Pale, thin, face splotched from crying, Mimi now looked deadened as she spoke the words. "Yes, Ruth, I murdered your father. I really did do it and nobody but you and Hobart know it."

"Why, Mommy, why are you telling me this? This is awful. Why did you tell me this?"

Then, she whirled around at Hobart with an indescribable look of anguish. "And why did you tell *him*?"

"Oh, oh, oh," the guttural noises crawled from Mimi's bowels into her throat before dripping slowly out her mouth. With the appearance of her physical frailty, it made Hobart think of a wounded animal that had slinked away to die. "I'm so sorry, Ruthie. It is a burden to you, I know, and one I had to unload before I die. Hobart is the first minister I ever met that I could trust with it. He helped me so much, so much." She looked over at Hobart for the first time since the conversation began, her eyes watery and worried, but still able to communicate gratitude in that horrid moment.

"I have been afraid that somehow, someday, you might find out or figure it out, and then I wouldn't be there to explain."

A half hour of stillness emptied the room of extreme anguish. Ruth had moved to the other chair opposite her mom while Hobart remained tucked in the corner of the couch. No one spoke. No one moved. The only sounds were of an occasional car passing outside, its headlights streaking the room with white light and making the shadowy dimness seem all the darker in its aftermath.

"Then what happened?" Ruth finally asked.

"I had planned this part a hundred times without ever recognizing how difficult it would be, especially while still caring for you. Your father had a piano dolly, just a rectangular frame on four wheels. I put a square piece of plywood on it, wrapped his bloody head in a plastic bag tied around his neck. I pulled him off the bed onto the dolly. It was much more difficult than I had imagined and I started to panic, wondering if the whole thing was a mistake, and that I couldn't really make the plan work. You were asleep, and that was a mercy. I finally had to kind of hog-tie his arms and legs in order for the dolly to work, and I wheeled it to the kitchen door that led down into the attached garage."

"There were three steps down into the garage. I didn't dare turn on the light in the garage because the windows were broken, and there were even some gaps in the walls boards where someone could have seen the commotion. I was terrified and sweating like I had never sweat before or since. I worried about waking you, and I feared someone seeing what I was doing. I couldn't bear the thought of being separated from you, or of you growing up an orphan like me. It probably gave me the adrenaline I needed to get it done."

"Somehow, I got the dolly down the three steps and up to the back of the car with the trunk open. I used a rope tied to his waist and one of the ceiling joists as a pulley and was able to hoist him up enough to swing him into the trunk. I left the rope on his waist and pulled the other end down from the rafter and threw it on top of the body. Then, I put a shovel in the car and you in the nasty used child seat and drove into the country."

"Thank God you never woke up. You just kept sleeping. I knew of a place from when I was a little girl, before my parents died, that I hoped was just the same as it had always been. Since I could never leave the house and hadn't gone any place in years, I started to worry that maybe people had built houses there and then I wouldn't know where to go. But it really was just the same as it had been."

"I played hide and seek with my parents when we were camping there. It is one of the few clear memories I have with them. I remember my mom getting frantic because they couldn't find me, and my dad calling angrily for me to come out. I had found a little hollow in the earth, a mini ravine covered by ferns, and they couldn't see me.

"The night was becoming gray with the slightest tinge of pink on the horizon when we arrived. I found the spot where I had hidden as a little girl, pulled the car up to it, opened the trunk and pulled on the rope. It was an intense struggle, but he finally rolled out and I could roll him downhill into the little valley. It took more than two hours to cover him with earth and you were crying before I had finished - hungry, I imagine. I covered the area with dead leaves and made it look as natural as possible before driving home."

"Didn't anyone wonder what had happened to him?" Ruth finally asked, only a little incredulous.

Mimi looked at Ruth with dried eyes, shrunken and stiff, bird-like and exhausted. Hobart began to be concerned about her physical stamina, and whether or not he should now intervene and help Ruth get her back to bed. He hesitated, and she began to talk again.

"Sad to say, his disappearance hardly caused a blip. His work called, of course, and when I told them he hadn't come home from the bar, I suppose they figured he'd run off. Somehow, no blood got on the trunk of the car. I guess I had planned that well enough. I suppose if there had been a big investigation, they might have found something on the floor. Every time I watch CSI reruns, it makes me quiver to think what would have happened to you if I had been caught. But either way, no matter what I did, you were at risk."

"Dad didn't have any family?" Suddenly, the word "Dad" felt different in her mouth. It burned. She was molten with rage at what he had done to her mother. But then, something shifted inside and she felt a deeper sorrow than she had ever known. She never truly had a "dad" – she never had a father that loved her.

"Honestly, Ruthie, I never met his family. You have some relations, though. They live in Michigan, or at least they used to. He had a son and a daughter before we married, and he had two sisters, too. I don't know what kind of people they are, but I suspect one day, you will want to find out. The family name is Spencer and they lived in a little town in Antrim County, name of Mancelona. Like I said, I don't know anything about the people or the place, but no one ever inquired as to what had happened to their son or brother."

Ruth moved back to the ottoman facing her mom. She reached out and took her hands, and they sat there facing each other in silence. Several minutes went by before Ruth looked up at her mom, "You must be exhausted, let me help you back to bed."

Mimi locked her daughter's gaze in her own, and asked with dire somberness, "Forgive me."

Ruth stared backed, addled and confused. "For what, Momma, what do I have to forgive you for?"

"Taking your father. Never knowing your father. Murdering a man. Oh my God, the horror of it! Even telling you now. I just don't know," and she broke into loud wailing and sobs.

"Oh, Mommy, please," Ruth embraced her mother as if she were a small child. Hobart desperately wanted to breach the distance and envelope them both so they wouldn't hurt anymore. Still, he sat.

"Tell me you forgive me," Mimi's whimper filtered up from the heaving lump of bodies, "Please, tell me you forgive me."

"Mommy, I forgive you. You're forgiven, isn't she, Hobart?" And, for the first time since he sat in shadow in the corner of the couch, Ruth looked at him. It was a wounded look of desperation, an urgent pleading for him to make it all better and take away the pain.

Who am I to forgive? The thought nearly paralyzed Hobart in the very moment he was finally needed. Practicing presence had forced him into the safety of his head and away from the raw pain of emotions that he was so unpracticed at enduring without dope. Ruth's urgency and the immediacy of the question caught him off guard, and he began to think instead of respond. Seminary discussions over arcane ideas about absolution for murder and other extreme sins populated his thoughts and caused him to pause.

"Hobart!" Ruth nearly screamed it.

"Of course," he jumped and blurted out. "God holds you in love, Mimi, you know it is true. There is no unforgivable sin, and no unforgiving God. You are loved, Mimi, deeply and completely loved."

He held his breath. Hobart wasn't sure what he should have said, or if what he said was powerful enough to stand up to the moment, but for once, he spoke from his gut, without knowing what to say in advance. Ruth had knocked it out of him.

Standing outside himself, he watched as he rose slowly and stepped to the other side of the room. He knelt down on both knees at the side of the red chair. He leaned over and spread his arms around Mimi and Ruth, and gently kissed Mimi on the side of her head just above the ear. "You deserve every good thing, Mimi, and God holds you now and always in the healing arms of His love."

Then, he leaned slightly the other way and very lightly kissed Ruth on her cheek, just at the peak of her cheekbone below the eye. Then, without words, he stood up. "Maybe it is time to get you back in bed, Mimi, you look as if you are physically uncomfortable."

Both women looked up at him as if they were children and he the adult. It was an unnerving moment for Hobart because he realized they needed to feel someone was there with a grounded presence, but he felt so small and so weak.

"Come on, Mom, let me help you."

Hobart helped Ruth lift Mimi from the chair, but then stepped away as Ruth escorted her into the next room. He picked up the pink water bottle with the purple straw and the book of prayers that were on the table next to the red chair, and carried them to the dining room and placed them on the table next to the hospital bed. He then went into the kitchen to allow Mimi the privacy of getting into bed without him in the room.

In the kitchen, he leaned against the counter and looked around, feeling slightly awkward, discerning how much time to allow before returning to the dining room. The letters of his name caught his eye. On the kitchen table was a notepad with his name written on it. "Hobart!" it read, in what he imagined was Ruth's writing. Immediately, he felt ashamed for the thrill that raced through him and caused his heart to pick up speed. This was not the time, he told himself, to have such feelings.

710 North Dill Street – *the front steps on the same cold, frosty night.*

Hobart leaned against the left railing of the front step, his arms crossed to warm himself, even though he was wrapped in his down winter coat, scarf, and knit hat. Ruth leaned against the right railing opposite him, but their feet touched in the small space of the front stoop. Ruth had pulled on her calf-length, down-filled coat to go on the front step to talk with Hobart before he left, but now, she zipped it up as they stared at each other.

"I don't know what to do, Hobart. I feel like everything has been shattered. It's a nightmare, a bad dream, and no matter what I do, I can't wake up."

"If you want, Ruth, if it will help, I'll sleep in the living room chair tonight and you can go upstairs and get some sleep. Your mom's not going to wake up. She was exhausted."

"Yeah, I think I would like that, if you don't mind. I'm tired of feeling alone. After all the years of making myself feel okay about feeling alone, I just don't want to feel alone any more." Then, she straightened up and leaned forward into Hobart so that he would hold her, which, with some hesitation at first, he did.

Chapter Eighteen

Wellhead Number Two

Jungian Society House on Beecker Street – *Red Upholstered Wingback Chairs*

"Well, suppose I'm wrong and God doesn't forgive her?"

Hobart sat there feeling like he had just asked the question to a statue of Mary and expected her to respond. There were moments when those big round Gibbon eyes, lips with a default setting that curled upward, ignited his anger.

Yash could sit there, looking content, for as long as it took for Hobart to voice the thing that was eating him up inside. It pissed him off! He struggled and suffered and Yash just sat there without a care in the world.

"Well? I don't really know what God thinks; what if I'm wrong?"

"Yes, what if you are wrong?"

"No, man, I just asked you."

"And I asked you back," Yash smiled serenely.

"Fuck. I don't know, okay? I don't know, that is why I am asking you. Do you know?"

"How would I know what God thinks? I do not even know what you think."

Hobart sank, slouching as far into the stiff cushions as he could. *Did anyone really know? Of course not*, he silently answered his own question.

"Why did you make up an answer to the question if you did not actually know?"

"The look on her face was awful, and the urgency in her voice, pleading for my help to sooth Mimi's anguish. How could I not answer? It was a moment screaming for an answer, so I gave the only one I knew to give, even though I didn't really know. It's what I hope."

"You thought you were saving Ruth from her pain, and saving her mother from her guilt and fear. Why did you feel that it was up to you to save them from those feelings?"

Hobart was incredulous. *Was that even a real question*?

"What the fuck, Yash? When people are drowning in front of you, you don't just let them."

"Yes, indeed, you reach out and give them a hand. But were they really drowning, or was it your anguish you were trying to do something about?"

"Mine? It wasn't me that murdered my husband, and it wasn't me whose mother just told me she killed my father. My anguish was only empathy, sympathy."

"Was it?"

Hobart stared at Yash. *Was it*? He went back to the living room, and in his mind sat in the corner of the couch. What had he been feeling? He was a detective of the mind now, searching for clues, when it reached out from the corner of the couch and slapped him in the face. *Powerlessness*.

"No, it wasn't just empathy," Hobart drawled in baritone. "I felt powerless and I needed to feel powerful." It felt like a confession, even though he knew Yash didn't care one way or another.

"Was there anything else you might have said or done that would have been more honest than giving an answer that was not yours to give?"

"Well, that is not exactly true. It was mine to give. The Church grants me the power to offer absolution and that is what I did."

"Then what is the problem?"

"I don't really believe the Church has that kind of power. I just mouthed something I don't really believe."

"What else might have you said or done that, today, sitting here with me, would feel more authentic?"

Hobart again replayed the scene in his mind, and suddenly realized that Mimi had not asked for God's forgiveness, but for Ruth's. It was Ruth that turned and asked Hobart to declare forgiveness, even though she had already said she forgave her mom. Maybe no one was asking about God's forgiveness; maybe all he was being asked to do was confirm Ruth's forgiveness and declare his willingness to confirm that in the absence of other options, she had done the right thing to protect her child and herself.

"I was the one who brought God into it! Jesus, I can't believe I did that! In the moment of panic, the first thing I did was reach for the God-stick. I could have just echoed that Ruth's forgiveness had been spoken, or even invited Ruth to say it again. I could have told Mimi I thought she had been brave and done the right thing under the circumstances; even if murder is wrong, she was lost in a morass of wrong choices. I could have recognized that Mimi needs to forgive herself and said so out loud. In fact, sitting here right now, I realize that my work is unfinished there and I need to help Mimi forgive herself, if possible, before she dies."

Yash smiled a little beyond his natural grin.

"You know, though," Hobart went on after pausing for several moments, "that doesn't answer the bigger question. Does God forgive us? How do we know? Do I ever get to know?"

Yash's eyes grew even bigger than normal and boomeranged the question back to Hobart.

There was Wellhead Number Two, and he was afraid that if he really lifted the lid and poked his head all the way inside, it would be empty. Yash would say the question was his to determine, but Hobart wanted there to be something more universal and more objective. He wanted there to be a mountain of God from which he could carry down the sacred tablets with The Meaning of Life etched into them. Otherwise, in the absence of something that solid and enduring, he feared an empty well and a meaningless existence.

"Yosh, you know your Trinity of 'death,' 'meaning,' and 'aloneness' are all connected, don't you? I'm afraid it would be possible to fall into any one of them and get lost. Floating around in them, if you got lost, there would be nothing to stop you from drifting away weightlessly and alone into the black emptiness of space."

"True. But what is your alternative to such space exploration? Will you live under a sky of pretend answers, breathing a false atmosphere? Or will you risk the discovery of answers you want to search for, which of course, means risking that there are no answers?"

Hobart knew the answer but he didn't like it.

710 N. Dill Street – *small green 'TV room' off the kitchen with two small recliners and a flat screen television in a built-in bookshelf.*

"Sometimes I want to call you 'Ho,' but that doesn't sound so good, so then I think, 'Bart.' But that makes me think of Simpson. I need a new, cuddlier name for you."

Ruth sat back in the green recliner covered in thick, woven fabric with large, beige nubs bulging between the threads, clicked the handle that raised her feet, and smiled like a child on a swing.

"Hobart's not so cuddly, right? Maybe that's how I got 'Peedad' as a kid."

"That's not how you got Peedad, I heard the stories."

"Okay, okay, never mind."

"It'll come to me, a name. All of us have at least a thousand names, but we give up looking for them too early. We only know two of yours so far."

"Now that you're Ruth, I kind of miss 'Cressida.' But only sometimes."

"Well, you should still call me Cress in public because I haven't, like, totally decided." Then, after a pause, "I'm so glad Harrison is coming over tonight. It is so heavy here. Last night...never mind, I don't even want to talk about it."

"Yeah, I saw my therapist this morning and I was so tired, I wasn't sure I could think straight."

"Did you talk about it? Last night, I mean?"

"Yeah, some."

"What'd your therapist say?"

Hobart was silent, frozen with regret for having brought it up and fear that he would now say the wrong thing.

"What'd he say?"

"It's complicated. It wasn't really about you or your mom, it was about me."

"Yeah, but you never talk about *you.* Did you know that?"

"Sure I do."

"No, not really. You ask a lot of questions about everybody else. And you listen. Man, you are a really good listener. But you never talk about *you.*"

The frost line went deeper, all the way to Hobart's toes. He felt naked and under a bright light. His insides were solidifying. The hardness at his center squeezed every thought he might speak out of his mind.

"Well, you got nothing to say about having nothing to say? What's the deal with you, anyway?"

Hobart looked at Ruth, then away as panic fluttered through the hardened mass.

"No, really, you are good at getting other people to talk about themselves but you're like a secret code no one can break. What gives? It's not really fair, you know."

Words he might use to respond dripped into his thoughts slowly, but he couldn't get them to move through his lips. He wanted to say something, but couldn't.

"Are you there? Hello?"

"I-am-not-very-good-at-talking-about-myself," he spattered with machine-gun staccato.

"No kidding," Ruth quipped dryly. Then, with a softer tone, she said, "It scares you, right? Not being in control scares you."

Even more than the softness of her tone, it was her recognizing him that began the meltdown. She had liquefied the frozenness inside with a sentence, and now, it was seeping out his eyes and out his nose. Ruth was as startled as he was by the suddenness and ferocity of his tears.

Hobart was a mess and he didn't know what to do. He was sobbing out loud like a blabbering idiot, his body heaving up and down. He wanted to run away and hide. He didn't know whether to cover his eyes, get up and leave, or shrug his shoulders to let her know he didn't know what was happening, either.

The drywall compound that had always hardened the shell and kept him inside himself had suddenly turned gelatinous, and he was melting away. Hobart was as befuddled about what was happening to him as he was embarrassed by it, but part of him still retained the ability to be curious about what was happening.

"I think...I, I, um..." he was sputtering between gasps for air and wiping away tears.

"It's okay, I'm sorry, Hobart," she said it with such tenderness that another, deeper layer of tears exploded upward.

Neither of them attempted to say anything else as Hobart cried and snuffled and snorted his way through five minutes of crying out loud. Ruth didn't know what was happening or why he was really crying, and she felt embarrassed for him, as well as deeply sympathetic. She remembered how much his presence the night before had felt like a solid wall for her to lean on, and how knowing he was downstairs sleeping allowed her to collapse into the very deep sleep she had so desperately needed. Sitting there as he sobbed, Ruth was determined to do the same for him, even though she wasn't sure what to do.

"Whew!" Hobart finally said with a feigned chuckle. "Well, I guess maybe that was a little therapy hangover or something."

Ruth instinctively reached over to hold his hand, and that caused Hobart to get soft inside again. He could feel more tears rising up, so he pulled his hand away.

"Ruth, I'm not very good at talking about myself and honestly, not many people have ever noticed or cared. More than once you have touched me – I don't know, I guess listened to me - in a way no one else ever has. I think just now, and yeah, softened up by some pretty heavy therapy and not to mention last night, you touched a very tender place in me. I self-medicated myself into numbness for so long, I don't know what all is in there, but it seems to be melting. Holy shit."

"It's okay, I like that you cried."

"I'm really sorry for this. I didn't mean to, and you have so much you're dealing with right now, I can't believe I just dumped on you. I'm really sorry." Hobart wanted to jump up and run out the door.

"No really, it's really, really okay. I'm sick of crying and falling apart and shit. This is way better," she chuckled. "Besides, fair's fair. You've been so incredible with me, even when I was being an asshole to you. So, it's cool, really."

Hobart relaxed into the chair and breathed deeply and slowly in his best yogic breathing. He was struck by how crying like that brought about the same sense of freshness as negative ions in the air after a rain. His thoughts raced in that direction until Ruth started talking again.

"What's it like going to AA?"

"It depends," he said with fake nonchalance. Then, he thought better of it and answered truthfully. "Most of the time, I have to talk myself into going. I think I hate it until I get there. Then, I sit with thoughts and feelings, spinning around like a hamster on a treadmill inside my head and guts, while I listen to other people say brilliant things or unload their woe. I listen, I judge, I beat myself up for judging, and listen and judge some more. Then, I think about what to say and how to say it so I don't sound stupid, or in a way that everyone knows I'm really sober and getting more sober the way I'm supposed to. I beat myself up for judging myself and try to be spontaneous and authentic, and that doesn't work, so I judge myself some more. Then, almost always, somebody says something that makes everyone start laughing, because we all recognize it in ourselves. And almost always, there is a lot of that kind of great belly laughter that isn't from meanness, but from healing, in the way it recognizes the truth of something and finds it funny. Then, we stand up and say The Lord's Prayer together, and I leave, glad I went. But the next time, it starts out just the same. Crazy, huh?"

"Wow, that sounds kind of cool. Hard, but cool."

"Yeah, that's what it is, hard - but cool."

After a pause, "What if you didn't go?"

"Hmmm, I sometimes wonder that, too. I know people who got sober and stayed that way and don't go, and they seem fine. Then, there are others that slip away and they go right back to it. I don't know. You know, I haven't been at this very long, so I'm not going to find out. 'Keep coming back' is the slogan and that's what I'm doing now, one day at a time."

"What if I went?"

"You, why? You don't even drink or do drugs. Why would you go?"

"I dunno, to find out about it. I mean, my dad was a drunk, I guess. I got it in me, right? Maybe I want to know you better."

Hobart felt a sheet of hot skin wrap his cheeks at the same time the squirrel below shook its tail and tickled the lining of his stomach.

"Then you would want to go to ACOA or Al-anon. ACOA stands for Adult Children of Alcoholics and from what I hear, it's pretty cool. They deal with how the alcoholic shaped the family culture and the individual relationships in the family. The whole co-dependency thing points to how the presence of an alcoholic in a family, even generations back, has an impact on those in the future because of the bad behavior a family system learns to incorporate in response to the presence of the drunk. It happens in organizations, too. In fact, in seminary, we learned about how to identify the effects of an alcoholic minister in the past on the current congregational culture. It's really weird - like DNA carrying forward certain traits."

Ruth was only slightly interested in what Hobart was saying, but she thought he was so cute when a subject that no one else would be interested in, except maybe Harrison Jordan, got him juiced up and enthused. She listened to the music in his voice trip up the scale and down again as he unfolded what he thought was fascinating. It made her smile, and seeing her smile caused Hobart to imagine she found the subject fascinating.

The sound of Mimi coughing interrupted Hobart. He paused and they looked at one another, waiting to see if they should get up. But Mimi went quiet again and they relaxed.

"This feels like quicksand, Hobart." She whispered it so her mom wouldn't hear.

"What do you mean?" Hobart whispered back.

"THIS, my mom dying. Every step feels like the suction is pulling me down and I can never get my foot above the glop and mush. It's like tramping through a marsh, and you just keep sinking further and further instead of getting anywhere." Then, going limp, she said thinly, "I'm so tired."

Hobart wanted to put his hand on her face and stroke it, but he knew that was not what a minister should do in the situation. He could envision his hand moving slowly between them and softly brushing her face, but he also bristled at the image in his mind, knowing he was Mimi's minister, not a man on a date. It caused him to sit up a little straighter, even as his voice softened.

"It's grief," he whispered. "Grief is that kind of heavy fog that settles in and around everything, wraps you up, and sucks every bit of energy from you. And it comes and goes in waves."

"How do you know about grief, Hobart?" She said it plaintively, anticipating a sad story.

Hobart was silent, then lowered his head as he responded, "I don't, really. It's just what I've been told by people who have it. I've never lost anyone really close to me. In fact, your mom will be the first person I have known well who..."

"You're grieving, too, aren't you Hobart? You love my mom, too, don't you?"

"I do. I really do. Your mom is really easy to love."

Ruth grinned, "Yeah, she is. My mom is really easy to love."

With that, Ruth reached over and took Hobart's hand and held it in hers as she placed her head on the arm of his chair, closed her eyes, and fell asleep. Hobart felt warm and wary, and wondered what he would do – what he should do.

Chapter Nineteen

Musical Chairs

Harrison's Apartment – *above the garage, behind a suburban ranch on moving day.*

Google was flying high. Even though there was nothing he hated more than moving, and especially helping other people move, Harrison and Wilma moving into Miss Landrace's house had created an opportunity for him that he never saw coming. Harrison arranged for Google and Enid to move into the garage apartment on the Jordan property, and to become caretakers of the property since Harrison's parents spent more and more time at one of their other two homes – one in Florida and the other on Cape Cod. It was a double move-in day. Google and Enid were to help Harrison and Wilma move into Miss Landrace's, and they, in turn would help Google and Enid move into the freshly empty garage apartment.

The fifteen-foot U-Haul truck was backed up the driveway, and its pullout ramp strategically placed at the bottom of the wooden decking and steps descending from the second-floor garage apartment doorway. Google stood inside the open bed of the truck, watching Harrison and Wilma bring the last piece of furniture down the steps, a queen size mattress. In the blink of an eye, Harrison, who was backing down the steps first and struggling to hold up his end of the mattress, slipped and fell into the stairs. Wilma was caught totally off guard. It was a latex mattress and too heavy for them in the first place, so Wilma was totally powerless to stop the onslaught. Harrison went down flat against the stairs and his shirtless, muscular, and sweaty back made for a perfect slide down which the mattress glided on its way toward Google.

Wilma was distraught as she rushed to Harrison. Harrison was positioned awkwardly, half kneeling and half sitting while sucking air. The breath had been knocked out of him and there was panic on his face. Even so, Google couldn't keep from laughing. Wilma's hands didn't know where to go, whether to hold Harrison or stroke him, but her face was a tortured twist of flesh pulled in the competing directions of anguish for Harrison and fury at Google.

Just then, Enid stepped out of the apartment door onto the deck and looked down upon the scene of Harrison gasping, Google wheezing, Wilma flapping, and the mattress leaning with one end on the ramp and the other end against the truck as if someone had rested it there before loading.

"Must be a yoga break," she wondered aloud in her most innocent monotone. Enid turned around and went back into the apartment.

It was almost completely empty now, and Enid could see how she might want to arrange their furniture as she looked across the large, open area with the small, open kitchen at the opposite end. In between was a nasty cleanup.

Harrison was a slob, even with Wilma hanging regularly. The nicely-finished wooden floor was a Rorschach test of crusty, sticky spots and debris she would have to get on her hands and knees to scrub off. But first, she needed to finish sweeping.

Enid had already swept half of the room, leaving piles of dust and debris to scoop up later with the dustpan. It was not pleasant: a dried used condom, a brown, dry apple core, half a smushed Reese's peanut butter cup, a once white, now gray sock somewhat stiff from who- knows-what, and crumpled paper wrappers, notes, and unidentifiable objects populated the piles along with heaps of dust bunnies, hair tangles, and dirt. Enid was glad it was an open room because it felt like it would be easier to clean. Both she and Google liked clean. She wondered if she could bargain with the others for her to stay behind and clean while they proceeded with the move.

Enid also wondered about Wilma. Harrison was a filthy slob. He didn't look like it, and that was the irony. Google looked like he lived in a pig sty because he wore T-shirts that were too small and allowed his belly to bulge out like custard from a Boston Cream Pie, and the zipper on his ragged jeans was broken, and he didn't always wear underwear which, because of his fragile clothing, could sometimes be discerned by the public. But Google was obsessive about order and it had hardly taken Enid any time at all to train him to be clean as well as orderly.

Harrison, on the other hand, always wore clean clothes and was generally presentable to nearly any judge of appropriateness. Standing there, surveying the nastiness that had taken root underneath the cluttered chaos that was Harrison Jordan's unruly mess, Enid pondered the contrast. *Wilma*, she thought, *is going to kick his ass.*

To Enid's way of thinking, Wilma was put together. Whether dressed for work or play, in old clothes or new, she was one of those people who knew how to put combinations of colors and textiles together to look as bright and shiny as a new car. In fact, Enid thought Wilma was hot, and couldn't help feeling slightly aroused from time to time when she walked by. She knew that Wilma was going to change Harrison's way of life or go crazy trying. The corner of her pencil-thin lips curled slightly to the right in a wry smile as she thought about being a fly on the wall for that carnival.

Wilma wanted to strangle Google. *What is wrong with him?* she grimaced to herself as she bent down to inspect Harrison. Wilma felt Harrison to make sure he was okay and concluded he just had the wind knocked out of him. When she looked back at Google, he had already hoisted the mattress up to the truck and was talking vigorously to himself while tying it snug against the chaotic stack of items that had gone into the truck before it.

What is wrong with Enid? her thoughts wondered. It was clear what Google's problems were, and they were legion, but what was wrong with Enid that she was in love with him, or at least living with him? Was it a relationship of convenience? Did she have some kind of hidden mental health problem? *Maybe she grew up in some really pathetic, dysfunctional family and simply doesn't know any better*, she was telling herself when a flash of memory stormed through her thoughts. It was the image of Bernie's body sprawled on the floor as she saw it through the cracked door. Wilma suddenly realized she had been in love, or minimally infatuated with someone with deep mental health problems.

The acknowledgement turned her cold.

Wilma literally stopped and sat down on the stairs next to Harrison, who was still trying to recover. Her face cupped in her hands and elbows leaning hard on her knees, she stared at Google. She felt an unintended thawing of her icy feelings toward Google, warmed by a small glow of affection she felt for Enid. As Wilma watched Google talking to himself with abandon and happily looping, twisting, and tying the rope, snatches of memories with Bernie flitted through her thoughts. She remembered his goofy, quirky way of doing simple everyday things, and the strange, awkward way he had of expressing himself. The memories evoked a tender grin, even as they poked through the skim coat of distance over the pain of grief. Wilma suddenly realized a tear had streaked down her cheek and landed on her grin. She licked the saltiness and wiped away the track with her finger. *I get it, Enid*, she thought to herself.

Harrison was feeling bruises on his ribs and pain throbbing from his sternum as he also worked to get his breathing back to normal. His butt rested on the very edge of a step while his legs were elongated over several steps below, and his torso and arms rested on several more above. Wilma was next to him and had already pronounced him safe before sitting down herself. *She must be exhausted, poor thing,* he thought in the midst of other notions racing through his head.

What have I done? was another thought as he stared at Google working away and talking up a storm to no one in particular. This was his parents' house, and he had convinced them that Google and Enid would make good caretakers. *Would they? Was this going to end well?* he began to wonder. He trusted Google with friendship and loved the fierce brilliance of his mind, but Harrison found himself worrying about whether or not Google would make good decisions regarding his parents' property. The consequences of a Google bad decision could be grim.

But, there's Enid, he reassured himself. *I'm glad Wilma and I are well matched and I don't really need her the way Google needs Enid,* he reasoned. Just then, a niggling thought announced itself as it bore through the multi-layered highways of thought in Harrison's brain that were constantly busy with traffic. *I do need her.* He did not know if needing someone was a good thing or a bad thing, or maybe both. Until recently, until Wilma, he had thought it was a bad thing. It was more important to be self-sufficient; Cressida had helped him learn that. But now, he was leaning the other way, seeing that *need* allowed for vulnerability, and that mutual vulnerability could lead to intimacy. Still, it was a hazardous move, Harrison thought to himself as he looked up at Wilma, who was grinning down at Google.

"The problem with Harrison," Google said to himself, "is that he gets stuck in his thoughts and that keeps him from learning from his experience. Harrison isn't sure about whether he made a good decision or not when he invited Enid and me to take this place." At that, Google chuckled out loud. "But he reassures himself that Enid will make up for any lapses in judgment I might have. He might be right about that, except that I also know a great deal about everything that needs knowing around here: electrical, structural, habitat. And what Harrison forgets," Google announced to no one in particular, "is that I know people who know stuff, so if I don't know, I know who to ask. I'm not just a bro, I'm a bro-network."

Google laughed out loud to himself again and tightened the cinch on two half-hitches. "I was an Eagle Scout, after all."

With his back to Wilma, Harrison, and Enid, who was now watching from the top step, Google pulled the rope tight to make sure that it would hold the tightly packed contents of the truck in place. His white, belt-less painter pants were at half-mast, revealing a plumber's smile grinning back at the group behind him. Google continued his conversation with himself out loud.

"Wilma thinks Harrison needs her more than she needs him, while Harrison thinks it is an arrangement among equals. Silly Harrison. Relationships are never equal; they flow up and down and back and forth, and each person takes turns being leader and follower, lover and loved, needy and needed. At least, that's how it works in a good relationship, and even someone as crazy as I am knows that. One of these days, Wilma will figure it out too. She's smart when her need to control gets out of the way. But everyone has control needs, which is why Harrison stays in his head. Enid's right, they've got a lot to learn, and they probably will because they rub each other in all the right and wrong places." Then, looking over his shoulder to Harrison, "Yo, Bro, we got this one!"

Google, as he often did, was thinking out loud for all the world to hear. Neither Wilma nor Harrison heard, however, because they were lost in their own thoughts and had long ago stopped paying attention to Google's chatter. But Enid did, and from her perch, she caught Google's eye and they smiled at one another.

14 Sunset Acres – *Miss Landrace's house, later on moving in day.*

The day progressed.

"No Harry, the bed needs to be against *this* wall. You want the bed against an *insid*e wall so it will be warmer in winter, and besides, the window is too low to put the bed in front of."

"Who made up that rule? What'd you mean, 'too low?' Just 'cause it covers up the windowsill is no reason. It is much more artistic over *there*."

"Harry, trust me, *no one* puts a bed in front of a window – at least not if the bed is higher than the windowsill. Besides, that would mean all the street noises would be right in our ears. This way, putting it over *here* it won't be quite so loud."

Google stood in silence, steadying his end of the heavy latex mattress as it rested on the floor, his half in the hallway and Harrison's end in the bedroom. He could see Wilma through the crack in the door, hands on her hips with her face leaning out a little way beyond her feet. He looked back at Harrison, who was slump-shouldered and hanging on the mattress, and could tell that Harrison knew he had already lost the argument.

"Harry-bra, this ain't your ditch to die in; live to fight another day, dude," he whispered secretly on the other side of the mattress from where Wilma was dictating.

Harrison craned his neck around the mattress to look back at Google and roll his eyes.

"Okay. I mean, really, what difference does it make?" With that, Harrison lifted his end of the mattress, and Google followed.

A low-intensity combat ensued, fought room-to-room, from bedroom to kitchen to living room. By the time they reached the room that would be their study, Harrison had learned that Wilma was tougher and more persistent than he was, and she did not give up even on the most minute detail of furniture placement. Even lamps had a special order to them in the system of Wilma-rian Feng Shui, so try as he might to render an adaptation, he met steep resistance all along the way. He would discover that hanging photographs and art was an even more relentless enterprise in the face of Wilma's punctiliousness.

When Enid carried the last plastic tub in from the truck, she found Harrison sitting on the living room floor with his back against the outside wall, from which he could look through the dining room to the kitchen and into the hallway that lead to the master bedroom. Wilma was sitting on an ottoman, hunched over, leaning with her cheeks cupped in her hands and elbows on her knees. She could hear Google chatting to himself upstairs in the bathroom.

"This is the last thing! You're in!" She announced it with her usual muted punctuation. Harrison and Wilma did not react, move, or respond. "What's a matter, you guys?"

"Look! This is all of our stuff and it doesn't begin to fill the house." Wilma grimaced.

"Yay, we don't have that much stuff, I guess. I mean, we've both been living in studio apartments and this is a whole house! 'HELLO,'" he shouted as if it would echo.

"HELLO!" came a response from upstairs. Enid grinned, filled with affection for the man on the toilet up above.

"Well, kids, I guess you'll have to grow into it."

With that, she went into the kitchen, got a drink, slurping directly from the faucet, and went outside.

"I suddenly feel kinda scared, Wilma."

Wilma didn't move from her hunched-over perch. "About what, Harry?"

Harrison paused. He wasn't sure he wanted to say, realizing he hadn't really meant to say that he was scared out loud. He felt much safer in his head where it was mostly quiet, even when there were multiple racing thoughts. At least in his head, he knew he was safe, but letting thoughts escape in words almost always felt risky. Mentioning the way he felt was even scarier, and he was feeling stunned now that he had said out loud. He looked at Wilma, who was looking back at him, as if evaluating the disposition of a sleeping dog.

"This feels so...so grown up."

"Yea, it does." She said it in total synchronicity. "*This* does too."

"Whatdaya mean, "this?"

"*This*, you and me. Moving in together. In a house."

"Oh, yea, I guess it does." Then after a pause, "Too grown up?"

Wilma looked at him intently as she responded, "If I have to be grown up, I'm glad it's with you." Then, in an amazingly seamless and graceful move, she unfolded herself forward, landing with her hips wedged between Harrison's legs and curled with her head on his chest. She exhaled a purr of such deep and guttural pleasure, it warmed Harrison from the inside out. He wished Google was not upstairs.

They sat in silence on the floor of the living room, Wilma with her eyes closed and Harrison's darting around the room. *She is so tough and still so sweet*, he thought to himself. Joy and fear formed a braided barber's pole twisting inside him. He closed his eyes and relaxed into the moment. Soon, the sound of the upstairs toilet flushing signaled it was time to move Google and Enid into his old apartment.

Harrison's Apartment, now Google's and Enid's – *above the garage, behind a suburban ranch.*

As they drove up, Harrison was shocked to see a bright red flag with the black silhouette of Che hanging over the banister of the decking outside the second-floor entrance to the garage apartment.

"You can't have that hanging out there!" Harrison yelled at Google, who was driving the truck.

"Dude, it's my home."

"No, it's my parent's home, and you're living in the apartment as the caretaker. Listen, Google, you gotta play this really straight. This is Republican Nation out here, and my folks, although they are cool, are not *that* cool. Promise me you are going to leave a small, quiet footprint that my mom and dad and their neighbors are not going to see or hear."

"Bra, you're sizing the Google with a straightjacket, you know that? Okay, I'll be cool: low tide, sweet grass, mellow moon, peace out. Life's good, and the Harry 'rents will never know we're here."

Google eased the truck to a halt and waited for Wilma to drive around it from behind, where she and Enid were following in Wilma's tidy blue Fiat. He turned the truck and angled it as Harrison went outside to give direction so they could extend the ramp to the first white wooden step.

It was about four in the afternoon, slightly warm for mid-March, and a clear sky. They had about an hour and a half of light left, so Enid convinced everyone to simply unload the truck and place all but the biggest furniture items on the driveway while she cleaned Harrison's former apartment. When Harry had helped Google bring up the bed, dresser, couch, and dining table, Enid gave him and Wilma their release so she could finish cleaning and have Google to herself in their new home.

As Google trudged the last box of books up the stairs, Enid was cleaning the last kitchen cupboard. Google gave a loud sigh as he closed the door with his butt, and then, with a grand gesture, set it down in the vicinity of the other boxes clumped in formations around an open space. Enid put her sponge down on the counter and walked quietly over to the bed she had already made. She turned to look at Google. Slowly, Enid reached her arm around to the back of her neck and lowered it again, allowing her simple dress to fall to the floor around her ankles. She stepped out of the clump of material at her feet and stood, with no bra and burnt-orange panties, her palms up toward Google, who looked back with bemused restraint.

"Take me, Carl Prichard, and consummate our new home."

Chapter Twenty

"Spring"

Mimi insisted on being moved to a Hospice unit, rather than dying at home. Ruth had protested vigorously with tears, believing that her mother's dignity would be preserved with privacy. But Mimi did not want her daughter acting as nurse and nurse's aide while death abused even the pretense of grace by a thousand cuts. In a rare instance of denying Ruth anything in her young adulthood, Mimi's wishes won out.

Hobart didn't know what to expect. Rev. Miller had confused him when he told Hobart that Hospice was his favorite place to visit as a pastor. How could that be true? In his mind, he had imagined a long hallway with dozens of dark rooms, in which patients groaned and families cried. That image was dispelled when he turned off the busy suburban thoroughfare and drove down a long, leafy drive into a large cul-de-sac with parking in the middle, circled by Tudor style cottages. It was early April, following a week of unseasonable warmth and daily rain, so the trees were bursting with new green shoots, with some stems now fully flowering. Crocuses had come and gone, with tulips and daffodils now owning the field of stylishly landscaped buildings.

Hobart put his rusty, gray Jeep convertible in park and stepped on the emergency brake, which was his habit, whether needed or not. The door was already off for the season and lying across the back seat. He sat still and took a deep breath, filling his lungs with the scent of wet soil, blossoming trees, and, he now recognized, hyacinths. He looked around to see where the hyacinths were and saw an entire bank of cobalt blue bordering one quarter of the circular lot. *What the hell?* he exclaimed inside his head, stuttering over the contrast of vibrant colors and fresh life surrounding the cottages of death.

Still in his car, he took stock of the scene.

Large maples, oaks, and beech trees hovered over the cottages. It struck him that someone went to a lot of trouble to preserve those trees while building the cottages, which could not have been more than five years old. It felt like a park headquarters more than a place where dozens, or even scores of people were dying. The cottages themselves looked like a Disney movie where the woodsman or Snow White lived. White stucco banded with dark wooden beams and steeply angled roofs with softly rounded points. *Which one of these is Mimi in?* he wondered. He pulled out a scrap of orange paper he had written directions on, but all he had scribbled was, "third cottage." There were six. *Hmmm, one of the two middle ones.*

As he swiveled out and unfolded himself, standing up straight in full sunlight, he looked toward the middle two cottages shrouded in shade. Each cottage appeared to have three sections, each with its own egress. At the center of each building was an obvious main entrance and signage with information that meant little to him. As he approached the building he had guessed would be "number three" he read the sign, "Hunt Cottage" and below it, "Given in loving memory and with thanksgiving for Pearl Hunt." He took a deep breath and opened the door.

Expecting dark hallways in spite of the lush grounds and architecture, he was confronted by a light and airy open foyer with a huge fish tank against one wall and an ignited gas fireplace opposite it, reflections of flames dancing in the glass of the fish tank. In between was a desk with a woman smiling back at him.

"Good morning."

"Morning," Hobart replied.

"Can I help you?"

"Yes, I am looking for Mimi Friuth."

"Hallway 3," the woman smiled, and pointed to the left side.

Hobart realized that the foyer enjoined three hallways and he was now facing up the third one, which was, in fact, dark. But it was not anything like his imagination. Instead, it was deeply carpeted and wrapped in earth tones, aglow with subdued yellow lighting that might be found in any residence, rather than an institutional setting. There were only two rooms off this hallway, one across from the other. One room had no door and was an open space with a small kitchenette, accompanied by table and chairs. A sign read, "Dear Families, please clean up after each use, and please take all items from the refrigerator that you have brought. Thank you." He turned to the other door, which was seventy percent closed. He knocked gently. There was no response, so he knocked a little louder.

"Come in," the familiar voice croaked.

Slowly, Hobart opened the door and surveyed the scene. To his surprise, it was not a hospital room - more like a hotel. Music was playing from an mp3 player on a cherry nightstand next to the bed. The bed was queen-size, and on it, under a fluffy maroon down comforter and sitting up, supported by half a dozen squishy pillows, sat a smiling Mimi.

"Not what you expected?" Mimi was chuckling.

"Is it that obvious?"

"It's the way everyone looks when the first enter, at least so far."

"Yea, it's pretty nice. The Vivaldi is a nice touch, too. Is it 'Spring?'"

"No, 'Fall', I think. It is so soothing. Don't tell Ruthie, but I enjoy my music so much more than hers!"

"No surprise there, Mimi. I think I do, too. Dirty guitar is not my idea of beauty. Do you mind if I sit down for a little bit?"

"Of course not, Hobart, I've been hoping you would come. Please," and she pointed to an overstuffed leather recliner angled next to the bed. He sat down and continued looking around the room. There was a chair rail bordering the room with the wall painted a deep maroon below and a light rose above. The furniture was all matching cherry with a television hanging from the wall. There were two large windows with maroon patterned curtains flung fully open, and a wild chaos of multi-colored bird feeders of many styles visible from every angle. An entire aviary of birds was flitting from one feeder to the next in a raucous display of hungry competition.

"Wow, what a show!"

"Isn't it wonderful? I can't stop watching them." Mimi's face was glowing, her eyes brighter than he had seen them in weeks.

"You almost look happy," he regretted saying it as soon as he heard it come out.

"Instead of like I'm dying? Oh, well, I'm proof you can find happiness anywhere." The light left her face as she smiled weakly.

"I'm sorry, I didn't mean it that way. I meant, you don't look like you're in pain, and your enjoyment of the show outside is on your face."

"This is the best I have felt in weeks, maybe longer. I gave up trying to be brave and resist the morphine. Instead, I welcome it whenever they offer. And really, this bed is to die for – I don't mean that," which made them both chuckle. "Maybe I'll surprise everybody and hang out here for a long time. Maybe they'll have to kick me out because I refuse to die, I like this bed so much – especially compared to that other one."

"Listen," she continued gravely, reaching out, taking Hobart's hand, "I need you to really help Ruthie. I know you two have gotten close, but I know her. She will pull into her shell, put her head down like a horse charging uphill, and not realize she is sinking. When she gets like this, she also becomes very difficult to help, pushing people away with anger and outbursts. You are a tender soul, Hobart, and that might scare you away. But please, don't let it scare you. It just means she is really needy and can't say it."

"I am here for both of you, Mimi, really I am." Then, he remembered he was supposed to reflect back what she said rather than jump in and fix the problem. "I mean...you sound worried."

"Worried? Not really. Ruth isn't as invincible as she wants everyone to think, but truly, she is very strong. I'm not worried for her; I just want to protect her from as much pain as I can. You never stop wanting to protect your children, Hobart. If they hurt, you hurt. It's funny, I'm dying, but I am more concerned about Ruthie not hurting than I am for myself. Maybe that sounds crazy to you."

"It sounds like love to me."

"You're a sweet boy, Hobart," then, she added quickly, "although, I know you are a man. I just say that, you know."

There was a pause and Mimi closed her eyes.

"Would you like me to go so you can rest?" Hobart asked earnestly, even though he didn't really want to go.

"If you don't mind, Hobart, it would be nice if you just sat here with me for a little while. I am very tired all of the sudden, but it feels good to have you here. Ruth will be off work after lunch, but you probably know that already..." She drifted off to sleep.

Hobart leaned back in the recliner and watched Mimi sleep. He noticed the lines in her face, how few there were except around her eyes – starbursts of lines moving away from the corners of her eyes. They were laugh wrinkles that matched the ones at the corner of her mouth where she smiled. "What an amazing woman," he heard himself say out loud without meaning to.

"Mmmm, thank you, Ho..." the words drifted out of her mouth through the glow of morphine and into thin air.

He continued to stare at Mimi.

Her cheeks were smooth with high cheekbones like Cressida's, but much more rounded and soft below. Her skin had a naturally reddish tone, even after remaining untouched by the sun for a very long time. Mimi's eyes, even more so when closed, were a perfect almond shape and placed gracefully apart, separated by a delicate nose that drew little attention to itself. Her neck was long, and somehow showed little sign of aging, remarkably little. He watched the pulse in her neck, as a vein twitched up and down in rhythm with her heart. *That will stop*, he thought to himself, *that tick in her neck will just end.*

It was a sobering thought, and he shook his head. Just then, a woman entered the room and peeked around the chair. Hobart looked up and started to move.

"Don't get up," she whispered. "I was just checking in - I'm the chaplain."

"Oh, hey, nice to meet you, I'm Mimi's minister," he whispered back. "Can we go in the hallway?"

Hobart got out of the chair and walked with the middle-aged woman into the hall, where they entered the kitchenette area across from Mimi's room.

"I'm Hobart Wilson, North Street UCC." He held his hand out and she shook it.

"Andrea Mitchell, nice to meet you."

"Listen, this is my first time dealing with Hospice and I have to admit I do not know what to expect. What happens, anyway?"

"How long have you known the family?"

"I've been visiting Mimi for the past nine months, and I went to school with her daughter."

"Oh, I see, so this is personal for you, as well."

Hobart suddenly felt exposed. "Yea, I guess it is."

"Well, Hobart, no two people are alike when they die. Nor is there any way to make predictions about how long it will take, although there are certainly stages of the body breaking down and vital signs that begin to tell us whether the end is near. But again, the human body has an amazing strength and doesn't give up without a fight, even when a person has otherwise let go. But the greatest gift you and her daughter can give is your permission for her to let go when she is ready. Your acceptance will help her acceptance. Just from what little I have seen of Mimi, if she knows her family is okay, then she will be far more at peace herself."

"So, no one can say whether it is two days or two weeks?"

"That's right. There will come a time when it is more obvious. When that happens, the nurses will make sure to keep her daughter informed. No one dies alone here."

Hobart felt his phone vibrating in his pants pocket and reached to see if it was a call. It was a text from Ruth: *How's Mom?*

"Excuse me, this is her daughter now. I just want to respond." *With chaplain, she's sleeping.* He started to put his phone back in his pocket, but another text arrived. *What's with a chaplain, YOU da man.* He chuckled and tucked it away.

"I am around most weekdays, sometime during the seven-to-three shift, and The Rev. Anne Potter makes calls from three to eleven. We are also on call, if needed. If you or Mimi's family need anything, don't hesitate. If someone needs a break and you want someone to be with Mimi, please let us know."

"Thank you, Andrea. I appreciate it. You have a tough job here."

"Oh, this is an amazing place and I love it. You will probably come to discover that Hospice is a very special place, and what happens here is full of blessings."

She smiled and walked quietly down the hall toward the foyer. *Full of blessings?*

Hobart crossed the hall and settled back into the chair, but immediately he felt his stomach growl. Hunger was not a common occurrence for him. He understood the concept of fasting, but never practiced it himself. The idea was for the mind to control the urges of body instead of the other way around, but for so long, he had been controlled by the urge to get baked or shitfaced that the idea of willfully experiencing hunger was a mountain someone else could climb. He was torn. He wanted to stay there, be relaxed, and just sit with Mimi. Something about the idea of finding peace along with a dying person, especially Mimi, appealed to him. It felt like what he was *supposed* to do. But he was hungry, agitated, and restless.

He brushed a bug away from his ear, then again. It was annoying. He used his whole hand to swat it away this time. Suddenly, he realized it wasn't a bug but someone blowing on him. He jerked around to see Ruth's face bulging to restrain laughter, her finger holding back her lips as if to say, "shhh." She reached down and grabbed his hand, pulling him into the hallway.

"What are you doing?" he whispered fiercely once in the hallway.

"I want lunch," she said, laughing and giddy in a way that didn't match a home of death. Hobart felt somber, and he had been trying to wear his best grown-up minister temperament while in Hospice. Ruth was pulling on him like a little girl at play with her best friend in the backyard. It rankled Hobart. He frowned and stiffened.

"What?" she whined.

"Ruth!" he pleaded, straightening up and pulling away, acutely aware that such personal and playful banter was inappropriate to the professional relationship and distance he was supposed to maintain. It was instinctive, as if seminary evaluators and the professional boundary police were watching him. Ruth ignited instantly.

"What the fuck is wrong with you, Hobart?"

"Shhh, you can't say that in here," he half-pleaded, half-scolded.

"I can fucking say anything I want in here, for Christ's sake. This is where my mother is dying and I can fucking say 'fuck, fuck, fuck' if I want!" Then, she threw his hand she had been pulling back at him, and stormed into her mother's room and closed the door.

Shit, Hobart said to himself. He stood in the hallway with his face burning, beads of sweat beginning to drip down his forehead. He looked around to see if anyone was looking, and wondered if the woman out in the foyer had heard Ruth swear. He worried that Andrea the chaplain might have heard the interaction and gotten the wrong impression about his relationship with Ruth. *What was his relationship with Ruth?* The thought boxed him in as he stood motionless.

Finally, he stepped into the kitchenette and sat down at the table. He had to do something about Ruth, he realized. He couldn't sit on the fence like he had been. He needed to re-establish the boundaries so it was clear that he, Hobart, was Mimi's minister and not Ruth's playmate. But the thought of giving up the bubbling warmth in his bowels that rumbled up to his throat every time he was with her was immediately depressing. That was not what he was *supposed* to be feeling. Maybe, some day, there would be a time for that, but not now. Mimi was dying and he was a minister, and whether Ruth knew it or not, she needed a minister, too. He was settled about it. He would re-assert boundaries and keep himself, and Ruth, under control. He sat up straight, ready for the dawn of a new day when he heard the whisper in his head, *You faker.*

Just then, the door across the hall opened slowly. Ruth's face squeezed through. Her extremely prismatic blue eyes traced perfectly by black lines penetrated him; her thin black eyebrows slightly furrowed were made more emphatic by the shape of lush black hair curving around her cheeks. "P-l-e-a-s-e, I n-e-e-d you," she mouthed without sound. Faster than any thought that might have moved through his brain, he was up and across the hall. Before he knew it, he was in the chair, and Ruth was sitting on his lap holding his hands that were holding her around the waist. Hobart felt fully present and no longer hungry.

Chapter Twenty-One

"Gratitude"

Harrison Jordan, Hobart, Ruth, and Rev. Miller shared the shadows of a darkened room, the buttery light of a single lamp in the corner casting its glow over them and the other objects in the room. Mimi's breathing was steep, the gurgling of mucus clogging her throat sounded between heaves.

Harrison leaned against the window sill, the curtains pulled closed against the dark night outside. Ruth sat on the bed next to her mom, holding her hand and occasionally stroking her forehead. Hobart stood slightly behind Rev. Miller, shuffling awkwardly, as if he had no place in the room where he was supposed to be. Rev. Miller stood at the bed on the opposite side from Ruth, holding Mimi's limp hand. His eyes were closed and his lips moved without sound.

Then, Rev. Miller let go of Mimi's hand, slipped into the pocket of his dark suit coat, and retrieved a small, round, shiny brass cylinder. As he unscrewed it, a strong, sweet fragrance was unleashed in the room. Harrison, Ruth, and Hobart suddenly snapped to attention as the smell drew them in.

"What is that?" Ruth asked, obvious curiosity intermingled with alarm.

"It is holy oil, Ruth, mixed with myrrh. I wanted to anoint your mother before I leave, if that is alright with you."

Ruth cocked her head and stared at him. After a pause, she nodded. Rev. Miller pressed one thumb into the brass cylinder and raised his hand over her mother's head. Very slowly, almost sensuously, he traced the sign of the cross on her forehead, leaving a glistening track of oil as he did. In a deep, hushed voice he prayed:

"Into your hands, O merciful Savior, we commend Mimi. Acknowledge, we humbly beseech you, a sheep of your own fold, a lamb of your own flock, a child of your own redeeming. Receive her into the arms of your mercy, into the blessed rest of everlasting peace, and into the glorious company of the saints in light. Amen."

Then, after screwing the lid back on the cylinder and slipping it back into his pocket, the graying minister looked around the room and held out both hands in opposite directions.

"Could we hold hands and say The Lord's Prayer together?"

Harrison Jordan moved next to Ruth and held her hand, holding out his other hand to Hobart, who had moved to the foot of the bed. In a circle around Mimi, with Ruth and the senior minister each holding one of Mimi's hands, they prayed:

"Our Father, who art in heaven, hallowed be thy name, thy kingdom come, thy will be done, on Earth as it is in heaven. Give us this day our daily bread, and forgive us our trespasses as we forgive those who tress –" Ruth burst into tears as the prayer went on with only two male voices, "trespass against us. And lead us not into temptation, but deliver us from evil. For thine is the kingdom, and the power, and the glory, now and forever. Amen."

Rev. Miller bent down and kissed Mimi on the forehead, "Peace be with you, dear." Then, he leaned over and gave Ruth a peck on the forehead as well. Finally, he turned and faced Hobart. Looking at him intently, he finally reached out and hugged him, pulling the slightly stiffened young man into his chest. Then, without saying anything else, he left the room.

"Was that like, 'Last Rights' or what?" Harrison whispered to Hobart.

"Yea."

"Huh," Harrison muttered to himself.

"Sit here, will you, Hobie?" Ruth gestured to Hobart, motioning to the corner of the bed unoccupied by her curled legs and next to the outline of Mimi's feet under the covers. Harrison leaned back against the window sill as Hobart moved into place. Ruth, still holding her mother's hand, reached out and took Hobart's hand with the other one.

"Hey, Harry, remember when we stole cigarettes from old man Hutch's deck and smoked 'em behind the garage?" Ruth looked over at Harrison.

Harrison chuckled, "Yea, and your mom caught us!"

"What happened?" Hobart asked.

"Nothing," Ruth laughed, "we got sick and my mom thought that was punishment enough."

"And it was for me!" Harrison chimed in.

It was quiet again before Ruth added, "You know what she did after the 'Jerk' Chamberlin thing?"

Both Harrison and Hobart were shocked to hear the memory spoken out loud, especially from Ruth, and they looked at each other.

"I don't know how she heard about it, but she came up to my room that night where I had shut myself in. I wouldn't eat or talk or do anything except cry and scream, and play music really, really loud. She let me go crazy like that, never told me to shut up or calm down or anything. Then, finally, she just came into my room and sat on the bed. She leaned against the wall, I remember, and just hung out there. I dithered and puttied around, still alternately crying and yelling, Mom just sitting there. Finally, I don't know how long it was, I just went and laid down. Then, she laid down, too, next to me, and just held me. All night. We never talked, but I slept, and she was still there when I woke up the next morning."

"Mom," she said, looking down at Mimi, "you are the best mom in the whole world, and I am going to miss you so much, but it's okay, you can let go, if you want." Then, Ruth leaned down and sobbed with her face right next to Mimi's cheek. Hobart sobbed, squeezing Ruth's hand, and Harrison cried out loud, too.

By the time morning light began to leak through curtains, Harrison had gone home, but promising to be back early, and both Hobart and Ruth were in separate chairs on the right side of the bed. Nurses and aides had come and gone checking on Mimi, delivering morphine, and offering drinks and encouragement to both Ruth and Hobart.

Mimi's breathing had become intermittent with what seemed like long moments of emptiness between them. The gurgling was mostly gone, the nurses having suctioned her throat several times during the night. Ruth and Hobart leaned back in their respective chairs with their hands flopped over the arms, touching one another in between. Now and again, Ruth would lean forward and take her mother's hand, but it seemed to her that her mom was already distant. She plopped back into the chair each time, undecided about what to do and how to sit.

Hobart kept watching the tick in Mimi's neck. It was demonstrably slower now. Her skin seemed to have become translucent and the blue vein almost luminous beneath the surface. Mimi would heave another breath, followed by silence, then Hobart would catch himself holding his breath. He had to let it out before she inhaled again and he wondered what, if anything, was happening inside Mimi's head.

It went on like that for hours. Mimi became thinner and paler with each passing minute. The beautiful woman, who looked so young for her age, had disappeared and was replaced by an older, hollowed version. Ruth seemed to be growing more desperate and agitated. She moved from the bed to the chair, then back to the bed; holding Mimi's hand, then brushing her forehead, then sitting and staring at her mother. Hobart had gotten Ruth to tell him stories about her mom and her growing up throughout the night, but now, there seemed nothing to say as the cavity of sleeplessness and grief emptied them both. He wondered if there would even be any tears left at the end, but that turned out to be a silly thought.

It was mid-morning, and Hobart had pulled the curtains open on the stage of manic bird life exploding on the other side of the glass. Harrison had called to say he was on his way and asked if they wanted coffee and food. Ruth was lying next to her mother, an arm around Mimi's waist and her face near to her mother's shoulder. Hobart had only just sat down when he watched, as if in slow motion, the tick in her neck melt into nothingness. It just happened. He saw the tick and watched it slip beneath the surface and never rise again. Ruth gasped and sat up on one elbow looking at her mother. Immediately, Mimi's color changed. Ruth shrank away as her mother's skin turned stone cold. Hobart reached over and touched Mimi and was penetrated by the chill. He rose immediately, and they both froze, looking at each other for a long second. Then, Ruth began to cry.

She got on all fours on the bed in an effort to get off the bed and stand up, but she began sobbing uncontrollably, wobbling and unable to pull herself up. Hobart went around to her side of the bed and placed both hands tenderly around her waist, helping her off. She stood, but immediately threw her arms around Hobart's neck and collapsed into his arms. There, she wept loudly, choking and sniffling and bursting into tears again. Hobart held her, firmly but tenderly, allowing her body to expand and contract with ease. He could feel the weight strung around his neck, but he strengthened his legs to hold on for as long as she needed him to.

At that moment, Harrison's silhouette appeared in the doorway and stopped on a dime. Hobart looked at him, his chin on the top of Ruth's buried face, and then down at Mimi. Harry walked gingerly toward the couple, rubbernecking in shock at the lifeless body on his way. He put one arm around Ruth and another around Hobart's waist as if to steady him too. Ruth never looked up from deep in Hobart's chest, but she knew it was Harry.

A nurse had heard the familiar groan and wail and came in to register death. Another woman joined her and they spoke in hushed tones, one looking at her watch. Take as much time as you want, they assured Ruth, and when she was finished, they would ready Mimi's body for transport.

Ruth was incapable of making a decision about when it was time to leave her mother. They would start to leave the room, and then she would turn back and cry some more, reaching out to touch her but then not wanting to. Hobart stayed close without directing her in any way. Finally, his arm around her shoulder, he asked, "Are you ready now?"

Ruth slumped in resignation and leaned into his shoulder. "Let's go."

North United Church of Christ – *a sunny colonial sanctuary, dark stained wood with white painted trim and clear windows.*

None of *the spot* entourage except Ruth had ever sat in those church pews before; in fact, no one other than Harrison Jordan had been to a church service since childhood except for Bernie's memorial at the collegiate chapel. Even so, there was nothing about the unfamiliarity that intimidated them.

The pews were twelve-foot long natural oak benches with a thick, high back that joined the seat at a right angle, without cushions or padding to ease the experience. In the first pew, though it could easily seat eight or ten, Harrison sat next to Ruth. He wore his best skinny jeans, a white shirt with small, thin red lines forming a check pattern that Wilma had ironed for him, a narrow, black wool tie, grey tweed jacket with black suede elbow patches, and pointed, brown shoes that needed polishing. Ruth wore a little, sleeveless black dress that fell to mid-thigh, and purple tights. She had her old black boots with all the laces on that she hadn't worn in almost a year, and no makeup at all. Looking at her, without seeming to look at her, Hobart thought how beautiful her face was, even now with blotches of red and the salt tracks of tears.

In the pew behind them, Google had the aisle seat and Enid next to him. Then came Hopi and his new best friend, Raoul, sitting perfectly straight and holding hands. Next to the happy couple was Wilma with Miss Landrace, now Mrs. Beasley, and her husband Bobby, who were in town for a visit and there to support Harrison.

"Hey, does Peedad always wear a dress?" Google whispered loudly to Enid. Ruth's head pivoted without moving her body and said tartly, "Hobart."

"Yeah, Hobart. Does he always wear a dress in church?"

Wilma leaned across Hopi and Raoul, and whispered back, "It's not a dress, it is an 'alb.'"

"How do you know that?" Hopi chirped.

"My brother is an Episcopal priest in Cleveland."

"I never took you for religious," Google said through pursed lips, one eyebrow raised high above the other.

"Not. Episcopalians aren't religious. Besides, he did that on his own. We only went to church on Christmas and Easter."

"Does everyone get candy on Easter in Church?" Hopi asked, thinking he might have to try it out.

"No, only little kids," Wilma said authoritatively.

"Travashamocory!"

"Shh!" The hiss came from behind them, and on cue, the entire pew turned around to see who was shushing them. It was a grim-faced woman dressed in black with a black doily bobby pinned on her head. Again, on cue, all their heads turned back around and continued on with the conversation.

"Why does he wear an alb dress?" Google whispered loudly enough to be heard at *the spot.*

"I dunno, I guess it's like an academic robe and hood we wear at graduations and special events. Just dress-up, I guess." Wilma answered but continued pondering the question.

"Does he have any clothes on under there?" Raoul asked without the slightest hint of innocence.

"Dude, you can see his pants and shoes, look." Enid replied with a hint of agitation.

Harrison turned around to look at his friends, but he also saw the entire congregation. It washed over him as a sea of black, brown, and beige colors, a wall of suits and ties and dresses, as if uniforms were given out at the door. The church was almost completely full and immediately, he recognized that they were the only people there under the age of thirty. Well, Wilma might be thirty-one, but none of the others knew that yet.

"Did your mom know all these people?" Harrison asked Ruth.

"Yea, she's been going here for a really long time. I think she started when I was just a baby, after my dad – left." She wondered if she would ever tell Harrison that her mom had murdered her father. Looking into his face, she didn't think so. She looked up at Hobart, who was sitting perfectly still, as if listening to the organ drone on and one, but she knew he wasn't listening because he called the organ "the monster box" and wished the church would let it go. She studied his soft face and in a flash, was both stabbed and warmed by the knowledge that her mother had trusted him with the secret of her life. She felt a voracious bond tethering her to that man sitting up there in a white dress and suddenly felt the urge to jump up, bound over the railing, and leap into his arms. She chuckled at the image, even as tears rolled down her cheeks. Harrison turned his head and saw her crying. He put his arm around her, resting it on the top of the pew, and they sat there like two teenagers at the movies.

The organ flared with a dramatic flurry of notes and ended with a big warble of sound. The Rev. Miller rose and walked to the lectern. He looked solemn.

"I am the resurrection and the Life, says the Lord," he began with studied formality. Then, he went on with a canticle that seemed to last forever. Harrison listened halfheartedly as Rev. Miller spoke, as well as when some people came up from the congregation and read passages from the Bible. Harrison was not totally unfamiliar with the verses, but it struck him as utterly alien and having nothing to do with life as any of them knew it. He heard Google whisper loudly to Enid, asking if she had ever been to a funeral before. Neither of them had, and Hopi said his grandfather had died once, and that made them all snigger. Harrison chuckled, too, at the raucous group behind him who had no clue about how to act in church.

Then, Hobart stood up. The first two pews suddenly saw something they understood and were riveted on him.

"Can we clap?" Google leaned over and asked Wilma, who was now the authority on all things church.

"No!" she whispered with some urgency.

Harrison watched Hobart walk to the pulpit and realized what it was he had been admiring about his minister friend intuitively all these months and now, suddenly, acutely. He was always just Hobart. Even there, in front of all those people and wearing that silly dress, he was just Hobart. He had been just Hobart at Hospice when Mimi was dying and they were crying. He was just Hobart at *the spot*, whether sitting in his 'office' at Table 86 or on the black couches. Hobart didn't change depending on who he was with or where he was, he was always just Hobart, and being just Hobart was pretty cool, Harrison thought to himself.

"HO-man's gonna lay it on us," Google whispered loudly.

"Shhh!" Enid replied.

Hobart climbed the three steps up into the huge, wooden pulpit directly in front of and above the pews where his friends were sitting. He looked down at them and smiled, his gaze resting on Ruth ever so slightly. They were close enough that they could see the light glistening off two tracks of tears, one on each of Hobart's cheeks, and that brought tears to everyone sitting in the first two pews.

"This is not a eulogy," Hobart said with a deep breath. He paused and gripped the lectern panel that held his iPad from which he read, swiped, and read from again.

"I am going to tell you something about Mimi Fruith that is also true about you and me. There is no way we can sum up her life or say anything that will come close to quantifying or measuring her life. Let me explain."

"I met a little girl at Hospice who asked me if 'that lady in there is dying?'" Hobart glanced at Ruth, who tilted her head, curious to hear a story about her mom she hadn't heard before.

"'Why do you ask?' I wanted to know. It turns out the little girl was at Hospice almost every day with her family who was there visiting her aunt, who was dying. The little girl was afraid to visit the aunt, so she watched the fish in the massive tank in the lobby. One day, from what I was told, Mimi got out of bed and walked down to the lobby. It was one of those moments that sometimes happens when people are dying, when they get a rush of energy and strength, or even lucidity when there had only been dementia. It's not unusual, even though it is mysterious."

"Anyway, Mimi met the little girl and invited her to visit her whenever she wanted. The little girl did, every day. Instead of going to her aunt's room, she would visit with Mimi. I got to meet the little girl several times on my visits to Mrs. Fruith."

Ruth was stunned to think about all the times that Hobart had been to visit her mom that she knew nothing about, and the depth of the relationship the two of them had that was totally independent of his relationship to her.

"You all knew Mimi, and you know the way she had about her, the deep and pervasive kindness that wrapped any and all into her arms. Well, the little girl was taken in completely, and couldn't wait to go visit 'the lady down the middle hallway' at Hospice. Visiting with me in the hallway one day, she was shocked to learn that Mimi was dying, too. She couldn't understand it. A dying person was too horrid to imagine for the little girl, which is why she hadn't gone into her aunt's room. The little girl suddenly turned around and ran down the hall back toward the fish tank. I learned later from the Hospice staff that she had gone in to visit her aunt."

"Now, that's just a simple thing, a little girl who Mimi helped to bridge her fear. It took no special effort or magic from Mimi, it's just Mimi being Mimi. But imagine thirty or forty years from now, that little girl grown into a woman, perhaps with her own children. We don't know what that little girl will do when she grows up, maybe be a CEO or a governor, heck, she might grow up to be President. Or maybe she'll be a poet or screenwriter or musician. Whatever, she will influence people whatever she does. Mimi touched her, gave her a way to cross the threshold of her fears, and we have no idea what possibilities that unleashes for her. If you have an imagination, the possibilities are limitless. That is just one little girl that Mimi touched in the very last days of her life. Just one little girl who will wander out into the universe and touch others."

Hobart stopped. He looked around the congregation, as if sizing them up for the first time. He looked back down at the first two pews as if to draw strength.

"This is what I want you to know. Mimi touched hundreds, if not thousands, of people in the course of her all-too-short life. We have no idea who or how. If everyone here were to stand up and tell all the Mimi stories they could remember, and even if we could realize all the ways that Mimi touched us and changed us, even all of that would only be a pale measurement of the fullness of Mimi's life. All the people influenced by Mimi, moving out into their own lives, and influencing others because of how Mimi touched them. You see?"

"Each of us is a star in a constellation of stars, a veritable galaxy of lives we do not even recognize that we have touched and influenced. It is beyond even our grandest imagination, how far our lives ripple out into the universe. You and me, no less than Mimi, every one of us does that for good and for ill. We cannot begin to know or measure the amazing brilliance and reach of even one life, let alone a life like Mimi Fruith's, whose loving kindness is legendary."

"So, what I want us to feel, even right now in the midst of the horrendous grief that is tearing us up inside, is awe." Hobart stopped and took a slow, deep breath, as if he had run low and suddenly realized it. He also looked directly at Ruth for several seconds of silence. "'Awe is not a word or emotion we talk about much. Awe, as in awestruck. Standing here, at the edge of Mimi Fruith's life, we should be awestruck, struck dumb by the sheer size of her life – and our own. If we can feel that awe, tiptoe up and touch it, we will be filled with gratitude for the amazing abundance each one of us holds with our own little lives. And that - gratitude - is what will get us through."

Hobart paused again and this time looked at Ruth only, as if what he was about to say were words only she could hear.

"Gratitude heals grief- it is the only thing that does. Not right away, but over time. Gratitude for Mimi's wonderful, amazing, impossible-to-measure, life. And even some gratitude for our own lives."

"So, in the moments that follow, even at the graveside, in the midst of our sorrow and grief," now he looked around at the congregation and back toward the first two pews, "I invite us to touch our gratitude for Mimi." Then, he paused and said more slowly, "And to God, gratitude to God, for giving us this incredible, amazing life that has left us."

Hobart bowed his head slightly, as if the effort had drained him, even as he pulled some string inside that called up a secret source of gratitude. That was what it looked like as he stepped out of the pulpit. No one could see he was shaking inside his robes, or tell that all he really wanted to do was go sit quietly next to Ruth.

Chapter Twenty-Two

"Scaling a Thoughtwall"

Google and Enid stood near the food table without moving. He was chowing down on the deviled eggs the church ladies had made for Mimi's funeral reception.

There seemed to be two very different reactions to the large, bespectacled man in the untucked, wrinkled, white button-down shirt and dirty cargo shorts undergirded by deck shoes without socks, and eating with abandon from the doily-festooned table. Two hunched-over elderly ladies smiled and actually pointed to additional items Google might find delectable as a gaggle of other, younger ladies behind the kitchen counter whispered about the rude and gluttonous man. While Google seemed to be in an eating contest for most eggs eaten, Enid was sampling the trimmed tea sandwiches.

"Try this," Enid said with a faint smile as she handed him an egg salad sandwich on white bread with the crust cut off.

"Yeah, good." He mumbled with a full mouth.

Meanwhile, Hopi and Raoul had captivated an audience of suburban looking middle-aged women by regaling them with stories of nightlife on Adam's Street, the notorious row of LGBT bars and clubs. Hopi and Raoul were dressed almost identically in sleek, gray skinny dress pants, starched white shirts with French cuffs, and matching gray, fully buttoned vests. It was a study in contrast with the women adorned in hot pinks, lime greens, and canary yellows, each one a blonde of a different color. They giggled at the animated stories Hopi and Raoul shared as all of them sipped coffee from ancient, flea-market-looking china cups and saucers.

Harrison, Wilma, Ms. Landrace and Bobby stood within reach of Cressida, who stood all by herself, receiving the long line of people waiting to offer their condolences. Most of them did not actually know Mimi's grown daughter, and she recognized few of them, but they all seemed to need someone connected to Mimi with whom to share their sorrow.

Harrison and Wilma each made sure Cressida had something to drink, refreshing it regularly, and Ms. Landrace finally convinced her to sit down as Bobby brought over an antique- looking church chair that hardly appeared more comfortable than standing. For her part, Ruth felt awkward and miserable, as if this was an ignominy she shouldn't have to go through. Mostly, what she felt was intense loneliness. The repetition of telling people how she had died peacefully, and then hearing about how kind her mom was, acted as a palliative. Grief was numbed, the pain staunched temporarily. But there was an icy aloneness taking hold, and she suddenly realized that even her feet felt frigid. She wiggled her toes to get some circulation, and even loosened the laces on her boots. She looked for Hobart, trying not to appear rude to whoever was standing in front of her at the moment, looking down as she sat there looking up.

Hobart was nowhere to be seen. He was in the private clergy bathroom, sitting on the stool, frozen with a kind of panic. He knew that Ruth would want him by her side, yet their intensely intimate *non-relationship* was a secret. He was afraid the church people would start to talk about it, and wonder in hushed voices whether he had abused a boundary by dating Mimi's daughter when he was the pastor. *I am not Ruth's pastor*! He assured himself of his innocence.

This is bullshit, I should be out there with Ruth. He was trying to convince himself to stop hiding on the toilet and have the courage of his convictions. Finally, he stood up, buckled his belt, and washed his hands. It was not courage he felt, but rather, he acted in spite of his fears.

Hobart entered the parish hall from a door behind where Ruth was sitting and receiving her mother's friends and acquaintances. He walked up behind the high backed wooden chair on which she was sitting and placed a hand lightly on her shoulder as he stood next to her. Ruth looked up with obvious relief and put her hand on his. Her smile was one of relief more than joy, and in her eyes, he saw tears pooling. He smiled gently down at her, leaned over, and whispered into her ear, "I'm here for as long as you need me."

"That could be a very long time," she whispered back.

"Dude, have you tried the eggs?" Google said with an "outside voice" to Harrison.

"No, but I can see from the yellow debris on your lips and shirt that you have," Harrison smirked.

"Do you think that the HO-man and Cressa-queen want some of that glutton-acious potluck over there? I could make a plate for each of them."

"You know, Google, honey," Ms. Landrace assured, "those ladies will be wrapping up *all* the leftovers for Cressida to take home with her. I think they are okay for now."

"Whoa, all of it? Party at Cressida's tonight!"

"Uh, maybe not," Enid said as she walked up and took her place next to Google. "She's going to need some space after this. She'll be exhausted, won't be able to sleep, really, and feel miserable."

"Have you lost someone?" Wilma asked.

"My mom died when I was thirteen, and I remember that feeling like it was yesterday."

"Ugh, grief. It's exhausting...and weird. You know?"

"Yea, after a while, when the really intense part is over, the grief comes and goes in waves, and you never know when a wave is going to hit."

"I know, right?" Wilma said with exuberance. "You'll be doing something ordinary, like opening a can of refried beans or something, and wham, it just clobbers you and you start crying. If anyone else is there, they wonder what's wrong, or worry that they did something to make you cry. It's so weird."

"Yea, she's got a long road ahead," Enid said motioning to Cressida. "My dad wasn't a whole lot of help, but I had brothers and sisters, aunts and uncles. Cressida, poor thing, has got no family. She's an uno."

The small knot of friends looked at one another in silence, each taking hold of an image of Ruth alone in the world. If they could have seen and heard the thoughts of the others like a YouTube video, they would have been startlingly similar. Harrison, Wilma, Google, and Enid were each thinking about how to be a friend to Cressida in the days ahead, while Ms. Landrace said a small prayer for the girl she had once taught.

The crowd began to thin, and the ladies in the kitchen were bantering about how to wrap each item for transport to Mimi's house, which ones would freeze well and which ones wouldn't. They wrote careful notes on each well-wrapped tray and platter. There was enough that it would fill the trunk of Wilma's car, and the back seat as well. Harrison made an arrangement with Hopi and Google to meet later on, thinking that he and Wilma would go back to Mimi's with Cressida and get her situated.

Hobart was still standing dutifully with Ruth, but his mind was fixated on what to do next. Normally, after a funeral or wedding, he would help Rev. Miller clean up and get things ready for Sunday morning. But he could not imagine leaving Ruth alone. Still, he did not know what to tell his boss.

Just as the images of this conflict were looping through his thoughts without a satisfactory conclusion, Rev. Miller stepped up from behind him and put a hand on his shoulder. Hobart jumped.

"Oh, sorry Hobart, I didn't mean to startle you."

"Uh, it's all right, I was just wondering –"

"What you were going to do about helping me? I think you need to go with Ruth, don't you?"

Hobart was startled again, only inside his head this time. What did he mean? Why would he say that?

"Clearly," Rev. Miller leaned into him and said quietly, "you and Ruth are more than friends, and she needs you to be with her, don't you think?"

Hobart shook his head without saying anything. Rev. Miller smiled and patted him on the shoulder. "You did a very nice job today. I know it was hard."

Hobart stood motionless as his employer walked away. The secret world of Hobart Wilson was being released to the public, whether he wanted it to be or not. He felt intense relief along with a twinge of anxiety; discordant notes plucked on the violin of his heart.

Ruth stood up as the last person in line walked away, a woman who said she had taught her mom in school, but didn't look old enough. She fleetingly tried to calculate how old the woman was if she taught her mom in high school, but no thought could be held for very long in the din of her crowded and aching mind. She turned and looked at Hobart. Hobart knew she wanted him to hold her, and though he wanted to, wearing his clerical collar and standing in the parish hall with all those church ladies in the kitchen, he hesitated. He looked at her streaked and flushed face, no less beautiful than when fully made up for a night out. Her crystal eyes looked into his, pulling him out of himself by some mysterious force. Involuntarily, his arms reached around her waist, pulling her in. She responded with abandon, nearly hanging on him as if his strength alone had to hold them both up.

710 N. Dill Street – *motherless home.*

Wilma was fussing in the kitchen, combining and organizing the food so it fit in the refrigerator and freezer.

Ruth had gone upstairs to change and collapsed on the bed, falling asleep with her face in the pillow. Harrison and Hobart sat in the living room, Harrison in Mimi's red chair and Hobart on the couch.

"It's not just my thoughtwall, you know. It's everywhere." Harrison said it in a tone as if he were being helpful, even while challenging the minister. "How can you still believe in God when so much shit happens? I don't just mean Mimi dying," he suddenly lowered his voice and looked to the ceiling as if Cressida above them could hear, "but, you know, all the shit. Global warming, earthquakes, and tsunamis, African warlords kidnapping villages of young girls, ISIS beheading journalists, Syrians gassing Syrians...Where's God?"

Hobart looked intently at Harrison and felt slightly defensive, yet also passionate about getting his answer right. "It's a thoughtwall alright, a wellhead, too. But it is the wrong question."

Harrison waited, slightly curious and also ready to pounce on vulnerable reasoning or poor logic.

"'Is God present with us in our suffering?' That is the question. The answer, of course, is experiential – whether we can experience God in our suffering. Some can and, apparently, some cannot."

"But what good is it if God is with us in our suffering, when God *could*, and if God is so wonderful, *should* protect us from harm? I mean, really, what good is it to have a god that is just there and not doing anything?"

"Well, maybe God can't do anything. Maybe if God did do something, it would muck everything else up. I don't know the answer to that, nor will we ever. It's like short-sighted and arrogant scientists who presume they know enough to be sure of the consequences of their every experiment and discovery when, in fact, the universe, and even every small ecosystem, are so complex that we cannot estimate every consequence. For God to intervene in one theater of life would be to violate another. So, maybe God can only be present, and with that presence, help to make our experience tolerable and even hopeful."

Harrison started to respond, but Hobart interrupted. "Like with Ruth, what are we going to do to make her feel better? Nothing. There is no way to feel better about Mimi dying. It sucks, and there's no getting around it. But what is the difference between us just going out tonight and leaving her alone and being here in the house with her? Is it no different?"

"Okay, so God helps us feel better about shit? That's it?"

"That's not what I'm saying. You are not fully grasping *this*, what *this* is. Being here, being here with Ruth is something, it is not just a token. It makes a difference. It makes a total difference."

"He's right, you know."

The voice was Wilma's, from where she stood in the kitchen doorway.

"I don't know how I would have gotten through the night I found Bernie if you hadn't been with me. You don't know because you were the one being there, but I know. If I had been alone, I don't know what I would have done. And it wasn't just that night. Getting through that night, because you were there, allowed me to get through the next days, too. Even when I pushed you away, I knew you were there, waiting. It wasn't just a *feeling,* it was a *knowing*. The knowing made everything different than it would have been if I had been alone."

Harrison and Hobart stared at Wilma with the light behind her darkening her silhouette. Silence followed.

"How do you know this God of yours is present?"

"That's the hundred-thousand-dollar question. I don't know if it is an experience you can give someone else. It might be like childbirth for men, an experiential leap you can't make. I really don't know, but I know there are things we can do to open the door to it."

"Like what?" Harrison said it to Hobart, but he was still looking at Wilma with both curiosity and admiration.

"Well, you know, meditation, yoga or tai chi, physical exercises that also have breathing and stretching components that marry the inside and outside, and stuff you already do, like reading and thinking about it. I like journaling because I think better when I write, but other people need to talk out loud about it. Most of the mystics, from all of the major religions, wrote about their dreams, encounters with God in nature, and with an almost sexual sense of passion."

"Sex! We can have sex with God? Talk about presence!" Harrison's face lit up.

"Funny. What I mean is they wrote love poetry as if God were some nearly physical presence that thrilled them, speaking in nearly orgasmic terms. I've never experienced God like that, mind you, but I have had the sense of God being present. Still, I don't know how to give that sensation to anyone else."

Wilma walked into the room and sat on the ottoman, near the red chair in which Harrison was reclining. She leaned over with her arms on her legs and in the dim light, it was impossible to see her face.

"I know what you mean," she said quietly and with a thin voice in a distinctly un-Wilma demeanor. "Do you remember," she said, looking over at Harry, "when I was wondering what I should do after Bernie killed himself?"

Harrison shook his head in assent.

"I didn't know where to go or what to do. I didn't think I could face people in the department and felt like I couldn't focus on classes and research well enough to get through it. But I didn't want to go back to my parents and there was nothing else I wanted to do. I didn't want to be away from you either, Harry, but I also didn't know how to feel okay about being with you. And Hobart, I'm not sure you're right about not being able to give someone that feeling. I think you did with me."

Hobart was startled. He had only had two private conversations with Wilma in the aftermath of Bernie's suicide and he had absolutely no sense that they had done any good for her. Harrison looked at Hobart, too, because he never knew that Wilma sought him out.

"It wasn't so much what you said, Hobart, but just the quality of your presence with me. Something about how you are allowed me to open up to everything that I was feeling and thinking, and not be afraid. And when I did, there was this...I dunno, knowing, I guess. I knew I was not alone, and I knew it would be okay, whatever happened, and that I was okay. It sounds odd, I know, but deep under all of what I was feeling I felt...well, loved. And I also knew, in those moments, that that was the thing Bernie never knew."

A calm lay over the room. All three of them felt as if they could breathe again, and the air they breathed was clear and clean, like walking on the beach embraced by the sound of eternal waves and held by the salt air. The three of them were hugged in the quiet stillness of a single moment. It was broken by Ruth calling weakly for Hobart. He nodded at them as he headed upstairs.

"Will you lie with me?"

In that instant, Hobart never wanted anything so much in his life. He gently knelt on the queen-sized mattress and scooted up next to Ruth. She immediately turned into him and, reaching her arms around his neck, pulled herself toward him. Separated by wrinkled and bunched up clothes and comforter, they held each other and fell asleep.

Chapter Twenty-Four

Squirrel's Delight

They stood at the grave.

It looked as if no human being had ever been to this spot before, but Mimi had, and so had Ruth – twenty-six years earlier. Her mother had dragged and rolled the dead weight of a human carcass into the gully while she slept in a car seat. The bloodied remains buried there were that of her father, the genes of her making. Ruth and Hobart stood silently, surveying the scene.

The ground was even now, covered by a combination of grass, ferns, and adolescent beech and poplars. Leaves rustled in the breeze, and a young June sun warmed them in morning light. The two twenty-somethings stood motionless, holding hands, each one resisting as much as they could the graphic images of what had happened here.

"Hobart, if I go to Michigan, will you come with me?"

"Michigan?"

"Yea, that's where my dad's family lived, remember? I don't know if they care, but I want to meet them and tell them what happened to their son or brother."

"You want me to go with you?"

"Is that so surprising?"

"Are we, well, uh, a couple?"

Ruth looked down at their intertwined hands and back up at Hobart. "Is that a real question?"

Hobart suddenly felt stupid because it was a real question, even though half of him knew the real answer. It was the other half of him that needed convincing.

He changed the subject.

"Aren't you afraid that if you tell them what happened, they will contact the police?"

"I think I'm going to tell the police."

Hobart was stunned and turned to face Ruth. "But it's your mother."

"I think that's what Mom wanted me to do. She wanted closure, right, and you knew my mom, that would have meant real closure. And really, what are they going to do to her now? She wasn't one to care about what people say, and anyway, it was self-defense. I think everyone has a right to know everything about the situation. So, no, I'm not worried about what his family might do. Of course, it won't be the first thing I tell them."

Hobart mulled it over. She was right, of course. Mimi was a straight arrow and probably expected Ruth to make the whole thing known so the book could finally be closed on it. In so many ways, Ruth was her mother's daughter.

"Hobart, will you say a prayer here?"

"Whoa, how did you know that?"

"Know what?" Ruth looked up at him in surprise.

"That's why your mom gave me directions to this place, so we could consecrate your

father's grave after all these years. I guess it was another part of the closure. She told me she wanted someone to pray over his grave instead of cursing it. Your mom told me that even after all she had been through, she always regretted cursing his grave."

"Okay, go ahead, you're the pro."

Hobart felt completely inadequate. What was he to say about a man neither of them knew much about, except that he bloodied a woman they both loved? Still, that man was her father, the man from whom a random egg had been serendipitously fertilized, making her life possible. There was something to be grateful for.

"Let us pray then." Hobart nearly mumbled it.

"Beloved, you are a lover of souls, even those whom we do not love. Bless the memory of the man whose bones lie here, and forgive him for his crimes and sins. Having received him already into the arms of Your mercy, bring us there also, as we seek to forgive him and to find in the memory of him, something to love. I give thanks this day, that in the union of Mimi and," he paused to ask her father's name, "and Derik you gave us their daughter, Ruth. Thank you. Amen."

Ruth looked up at Hobart, stroked his cheek with her fingers, and cooed, "We are a couple, you know."

Table 27 – *high back patio chairs with woven plastic webbing tightly bound to metallic frames matching the patio table, and a faded blue canvas table umbrella, placed in the center hole and fully raised.*

Google and Enid were hosting a late-night party at their table at *the spot*. Harrison and Wilma, Hopi and Raoul, Ruth and Hobart were spread around the table with the relics of desserts and coffees littering it.

"I can't stand the anticipation any more, McGoogle, what is it all about?"

Uproarious laughter exploded at the new moniker for Google, made even more humorous coming from Hobart.

"McGoogle! Priceless," Hopi sang in his high alto voice. As the laughter mellowed into titters, Google gestured calmly for the crowd to quiet down for an announcement.

"Okay, okay. Very good, Reverend. Okay, attention please, attention." He cleared his voice with high drama. "I have called you all here to make an announcement and invite your celebratory vibe."

All around the table, there was rapt, if slightly feigned, attention, demonstrated by people leaning in to hear Google share his news.

"Your old school chum, my inestimable Broheim, Sahib Jordan, the Effendi known to all as Harrison, except perhaps to Wilma, whose names of dark bewitchment and aphrodisiatic delight shall never be known to those of us around this table, has just proffered a column of dead presidents in exchange for a place at the table of Masters. We are here to toast him, and wish him well on this new adventure."

Silence and furrowed brows greeted Google's speech, which Google seemed not to notice. Instead, he sat back into his chair with obvious delight, one arm extended with a tiny espresso cup pinched between two massive fingers, pinky up, and grinning ear to ear at the pleasure he took in himself.

"He means," Enid inserted with perfunctory charm, "that Harrison Jordan has enrolled in the Master of Fine Arts program for Creative Writing."

A cheer went up and glasses clinked as smiles and congratulatory expressions were traded.

"When?" Ruth wanted to know with urgent exuberance.

"Not 'til September, and I'll still work at the bookstore. But, you know, I'm paying no rent – just utilities – and I thought, 'When is this ever going to happen again?' So, like, why not do it now? Besides, Wilma is always working at night so I might as well," he said with a mock grimace toward Wilma.

"Tell them the truth," she inserted, "you write all the time now."

"It's true, I can't stop. I love it. And," he turned toward Hobart, "you have inspired me more than once to figure out how to get these thoughtwalls into print. So, I raise my cup to you, Reverend Father!"

Another round of cheers and guffaws went up in Hobart's direction as Ruth leaned in to put an arm around his shoulder and squeeze. Hobart blushed and looked down.

After a pause and a quieter din resumed between them, Ruth clinked her half-empty, large, white ceramic mug with a spoon tinged by chocolate. All heads turned toward

Cressida as they always did whenever she had something to say.

"I have an announcement too, since we're making grand pronouncements this evening. You may have figured it out already because of Hobart, 'cause he always says it, but I am officially, as of tonight, changing my name back to Ruth. Going forward, if you would be so kind, I would like to be known as my mother's daughter, Ruth."

"Here! Here!" More glasses clinked with gestures and words of affirmation and celebration.

"The Ruth-ster is back!" Hopi cheered.

"To our Bra-hemite, Ruth Fruith!" Google smiled as he raised his tiny cup again.

Hobart reached under the table and squeezed her thigh.

Table 86 – *"At the risk of seeming ridiculous, let me say that the true revolutionary is guided by a great feeling of love." Che quote etched with a jackknife, now colored in with shiny red nail polish at the center of the table.*

Everyone else had gone, and Hobart sat with Ruth in the nearly deserted café fifteen minutes before closing.

"How do you know we're a couple?" Hobart asked. "I mean, when you think about it, what makes two people a couple and what doesn't? If we were –"

"Really? Really, Hobart Wilson?"

She interrupted and looked at him through her fiercely blue eyes lined in thin, dark pencil, tongue-wet, garnet red painted lips, and cheeks flushed with warmth. Her lithe hands, fingers made even longer by graceful nails painted the same garnet red as her lips, reached out and embraced both of Hobart's cheeks. Pulling without resistance, Hobart's face met hers. She opened her mouth and pulled him in, their tongues touching for the first time, dancing furiously unseen within the single chamber of their two mouths.

The squirrel in Hobart's stomach danced with delight.

About the Author

Writing about encountering the sacred without all the religion is what Cameron Miller does with fiction, poetry, newspaper columns, and preaching. Secularization and the achievements of science and technology have not repressed spiritual hunger nor obscured the ordinary presence of the holy. But organized religion has done a good job of covering both under a pall of moldering doctrine, jealous infighting, and resistance to change. Miller invites you to join the conversation and share any thoughts and ideas *Thoughtwall* Café may have evoked for you at subversivepreacher.org, from which I can also be reached via Facebook and Twitter.

In addition to writing novels, poetry, and newspaper thought pieces, Miller has had a long career as preacher, teacher, and conference leader. During that career it has been his privilege to teach comparative religion at the college level, serve as a university chaplain, and lead congregations in four states across settings from urban to rural. There is a deep and vast community of seekers and spiritual explorers out there, and he invites you to connect with them.

Miller's poems appear in print anthologies in "Poetry Quarterly," (Summer 2015) Prolific Press; "The Poet's Quest for God," (2016) Eyewear Press (UK); and "Crossroads," (2016) Inwood Indiana Press, as well as online at Silver Birch Press. A first novel in the genre of *God noir*, "The Steam Room Diaries," was published by DAOwen (CA, 2015). His second novel, *Thoughtwall Café, Espresso in the Third Season of Life* (Unsolicited Press) is due for publication in July 2018. Compelling him to frequently sharpen his pencil, Miller write a weekly column on contemporary issues published in The Finger Lakes Times (NY).

Acknowledgements

Local, independent cafés may have taken the place of churches and synagogues in American life, at least for the majority of those under forty-five. I am grateful to the ones I have known and to the sense of community experienced in them over time. To name only a few of my favorites: Sweetness 7 and Spot Coffee in Buffalo, New York, Newport Natural in Newport, Vermont, and Opus and Monaco's in Geneva, New York. Even when visiting places I have never been before, if I find a good local café it feels like going home. So, to all those who work behind the counter and the ones who count the slim profits from selling coffee one cup at a time, thank you for what you do.

While the second coming of age in the twenties is something most people navigate, my appreciation for how current generations are doing it – known by marketing monikers such as GenX and Millennials – has been nurtured by very special people: Clare McKenna, Harrison Warren, Jordan Luchey, Evan Lewis, Dan Miller-Uueda, Carl Crow, and Connie Estevez. Add to them the Buffalo Seminary swim team circa 2006, multiple City Honors (Buffalo) basketball and cross-country teams circa 2004-2011, and the Geneseo Blue Knights men's basketball team circa 2010. Finally, there were hundreds of students that opened their minds to me during the five years I taught "Abraham's Children" at Canisius College. While the motherload of data I garnered from all these folks over time has been filtered through my imagination instead of some exacting criteria of scientific inquiry, perhaps this experiential knowledge holds up to what you have encountered along the way. I hope so, and either way, thank you to all of them.

CPSIA information can be obtained
at www.ICGtesting.com
Printed in the USA
FFHW010747130319
50942067-56364FF